THE
LAST CHANCE
COWBOY

Books by Jody Hedlund

5

THE
Last Chance Cowboy

Jody Hedlund

BETHANYHOUSE
a division of Baker Publishing Group
Minneapolis, Minnesota

© 2023 by Jody Hedlund

Published by Bethany House Publishers
Minneapolis, Minnesota
www.bethanyhouse.com

Bethany House Publishers is a division of
Baker Publishing Group, Grand Rapids, Michigan

Printed in the United States of America

Library of Congress Cataloging-in-Publication Data
Names: Hedlund, Jody, author.
Title: The last chance cowboy / Jody Hedlund.
Description: Minneapolis, Minnesota : Bethany House Publishers, a division of
    Baker Publishing Group, [2023] | Series: Colorado cowboys ; 5
Identifiers: LCCN 2022034217 | ISBN 9780764236433 (paperback) | ISBN
    9780764241277 (casebound) | ISBN 9781493440573 (ebook)
Subjects: LCGFT: Novels.
Classification: LCC PS3608.E333 L37 2023 | DDC 813/.6—dc23/eng/20220721
LC record available at https://lccn.loc.gov/2022034217

Scripture quotations are from the King James Version of the Bible.

Cover design by Kirk DouPonce, DogEared Design

The author is represented by Natasha Kern Literary Agency.

Baker Publishing Group publications use paper produced from sustainable forestry practices and post-consumer waste whenever possible.

23   24   25   26   27   28   29   7   6   5   4   3   2   1

I will praise thee; for I am fearfully and
wonderfully made: marvellous are thy works;
and that my soul knoweth right well.

Psalm 139:14

CHAPTER

1

CHICAGO, ILLINOIS
MARCH 1871

"It's a boy." Catherine Remington held the squalling infant upside down by his ankles, making sure he didn't inhale mucus.

The new mother managed a nod, her face pale, her eyes closed, her pretty features etched with pain.

Catherine clamped the baby's cord in two places and then cut between. Everything about him was absolutely perfect. With each lusty intake of oxygen, his skin was turning pink. His pulse thudded steadily, and he flailed his limbs energetically.

If only the mother were faring as well, but blood continued to saturate the newsprint Catherine had spread over the dirty mattress.

"You did wonderfully, Kit." Catherine forced cheer into her voice. She started wrapping the baby in a soft cotton blanket, wiping the remaining blood and mucus from his nose and mouth. "He's a handsome fellow."

If only she could transfer even just a smidgen of cheer to the mother . . .

Kit rolled to her side and faced the wall. The outline of her body was visible under the threadbare blanket, and she was thin, almost emaciated, as though she'd been wasting away long before today. She'd spoken little during the long night of labor, and Catherine knew almost nothing about her— only her name, mentioned by one of the other prostitutes.

She shot a glance at the closed door. Where was the other woman? Attired in a fancy gown with rouge on her cheeks and lips, the woman had been in and out all night, checking on the progress but obviously working—if selling one's body could be called that. Why did she have to disappear now, when Catherine needed assistance to deliver the afterbirth and staunch the hemorrhaging?

The music and bawdy laughter emanating from the saloon next door had been jarring and ongoing for hours. Now, by the light of dawn, a stale silence had fallen over the place, which meant the cavorting had finally come to an end. That also meant everyone was sleeping, and Catherine would have no one to aid her.

"I'd like you to begin nursing." She finished swaddling the infant, his wails turning to whimpers now that he was snug and warm. She shifted Kit to her back and extended the baby, praying the nursing would contract the uterus and help stop the flow of blood.

But Kit didn't move, not even to open her eyes.

The lethargy wasn't a good sign.

Fresh urgency prodded Catherine, and she glanced around

for a place to lay the infant so she could tend to Kit. Other than the bed and a wobbly bedside table, the room had no furniture. A battered carpetbag was shoved underneath the bed, likely containing Kit's belongings.

Catherine slid it out to find a tangle of clothing and an extra pair of shoes inside. Quickly she arranged the garments to make a nest of sorts, then laid the baby there. He gave a few grunts of protest but settled to sleep.

Without wasting another moment, Catherine finished delivering the afterbirth. From what she could see, the membranes were intact without pieces left behind to cause additional problems. Even so, Kit was still hemorrhaging. Badly.

Catherine dug through her leather birth satchel and located a brown bottle with a tincture containing blue cohosh, shepherd's purse, and other herbs that might help.

As she attempted to get Kit to sit up, the new mother resisted with surprising strength.

"Please, Kit. You need to drink this bleeding medicine."

Kit pressed her lips together, then rolled to face the wall again.

Catherine set the bottle aside. If Kit wouldn't cooperate with taking the tincture, then Catherine was left with no choice but to manually compress the uterus.

She ripped a few clean rags and doused them with vinegar to use with the interior pressure. If the vinegar didn't help with clotting, then maybe she could find ice to get the blood vessels to contract. She'd watched her mother attempt the technique once, but it was risky, and ice wasn't readily available.

She shifted the blanket over Kit's legs. "You'll need to hold still while I insert the linen and put pressure on your uterus."

"Leave me be."

Catherine tugged at the woman's leg. "If I don't do this, you'll bleed to death."

"I'll die no matter what you do." Bitterness filled the new mothers's voice.

For several heartbeats, Catherine didn't know how to respond. She didn't want to admit Kit was right, but with the amount of blood she'd already lost and was continuing to lose, her blood pressure was dropping, and her body would soon go into shock.

At twenty-two years of age, Catherine was young for a midwife, but after assisting her grandmother and mother for so many years, she was more experienced than some midwives twice her age. She'd seen her fair share of childbed deaths, especially with hemorrhaging. In fact, very few survived the problem, although she'd heard of some doctors who had transfused blood and gotten good results. But she didn't have the equipment—or the extra blood—to attempt such a feat. She had to utilize the methods she'd already learned.

She hefted the woman onto her back again. Kit was light and easy to move, too weak to resist. "Your baby needs you, so we'll do everything we possibly can to make sure you're alive for the little fellow."

Kit shook her head frantically. "I can't give him the life he needs. Not here."

Catherine paused. She'd helped enough prostitutes deliver babies over the past few years, and she agreed that a brothel was no place for a child. "Do you have family who can help?"

"No, my papa disowned me when he discovered I was with child. He told me he never wanted to see me again."

"What about siblings?"

"My older sister helps me when she can, but she's afraid of Papa firing her from his store if he catches her doing anything for me."

Catherine heard what the woman left unsaid—that she didn't want her sister to end up at the brothel like her. "What about the baby's father? Maybe he can help." Most of the prostitutes took precautions not to get pregnant. But no method was foolproof. And Catherine had witnessed the births of far too many unwanted babies with no way to prove who the father was.

Kit stared up at the ceiling, her expression turning despondent. "He abandoned me."

"Then you know who he is?"

"Yes."

"You're sure?"

"I'm positive." Her voice dropped to a near whisper. "He proposed to me. I thought I'd be safe. That even if I did get pregnant, we were getting married, so it wouldn't matter."

Irritation quickly pricked at Catherine, as it did whenever she thought of the immense suffering she'd witnessed from unmarried women having to shoulder the responsibility of an unexpected pregnancy. It wasn't fair. Where were the men? Why weren't they being held accountable for their immorality? Especially when the vice from such men only seemed to be getting worse every day.

She agreed with her father's position as alderman of the Thirty-Third Precinct, that Chicago's red-light districts needed to be shut down permanently. But instead of politicians making changes for the better, more and more corrupt aldermen were gaining office. The good men, like her father, were finding themselves in the minority.

"If you're certain of the baby's paternity"—Catherine tried again to move the young mother's legs so that she could begin the manual compression, but Kit clamped them tightly together—"I suggest you contact the father, ask for his assistance, and hold him accountable for his actions."

"I can't. He's no longer living in Chicago. He returned to Colorado Territory."

"Write to him and request his help, at least monetarily. Many men are willing to give some assistance in order to keep the matter quiet." It was unfortunate but true. Some men could be coerced into doing their duty.

"I've written to him already, but he hasn't responded."

Catherine bit back a retort, wishing the man was present and that she could give him the lecture he deserved, but at the moment, she was wasting precious time discussing him. Dark crimson was still pooling against the newsprint, and it was becoming all too clear she needed an extra pair of hands to hold Kit in place if she had any hope of succeeding in the manual compression.

The prostitute who'd sent the errand boy to fetch her roomed across the hallway. Catherine had no choice now but to seek her out and wake her up.

"I'll be right back." Catherine crossed to the door and exited before Kit could object. As she stepped into the dank hallway, the light from the window at the far end spilled inside and illuminated a scene that made her blood run cold.

A well-dressed, bald-headed man with a paunch held a gun to another man's chest, a half-naked man who looked as though he'd just been dragged from the bed in the room behind him.

She didn't have to see the bald-headed man's face to know

who he was. She'd been at enough political events and parties to recognize him. Rocky Rogers Kenna, alderman of the Nineteenth Precinct in the First Ward.

She also recognized the half-naked man. His long neck and equally long arms had earned him the nickname Stretch in political circles, as had his penchant for stretching the truth. He led the charge of sullying the reputations of the aldermen who refused to join in corrupt policies, including her own father's, fabricating lies upon lies. Of course, most God-fearing people disregarded everything Stretch said. But still, he was a dangerous man to oppose.

Before she could make sense of what was going on, a gunshot echoed in the hallway, and Stretch stumbled against the wall. As he slid down, blood smeared a trail, the red a stark contrast to the light floral wallpaper. When he landed on the floor, he collapsed into an unmoving heap.

Rocky kicked Stretch, sending him sprawling into the open doorway, revealing a bullet hole directly at his heart. His body flopped, his arms and legs at odd angles.

He was dead. Rocky had killed Stretch.

Catherine sucked in a sharp breath.

Rocky pivoted and in the next instant was pointing his gun at her.

Too late, she cupped a hand over her mouth, her attention riveted to the barrel aimed at her. For long, tense moments, she cringed and waited for another blast and the pain of a bullet hitting her, perhaps ending her life.

As he lowered his gun, she still didn't allow herself to breathe. She wanted to escape back into the room behind her, but she was too paralyzed to move. She'd just witnessed a murder. Heaven help her. While she'd encountered a great deal of immorality and wickedness when answering God's call to aid the less fortunate, she'd never observed one man taking another's life.

Surely this didn't bode well for her. . . .

Maybe Rocky wouldn't care that she was there. Maybe he was corrupt enough he'd let her go on her way. Maybe he would assume she was one of the women who lived in the brothel and not bother with her.

One of the women? Catherine almost laughed at the outlandish supposition. Her evening dress wasn't anything like the revealing attire of the prostitutes. Hers was fashionable, with a long basque bodice that combined with her overskirt to create a layered look. She rarely used hoops since they were too cumbersome, and she hadn't yet taken to the large bustles at the back of the waist that were becoming fashionable. Her dark hair wasn't lavishly styled but instead pulled up into a simple knot. She wore no makeup. In fact, she guessed she appeared rumpled and harried, hardly a seductress.

"You're Paul Remington's daughter." Rocky's words echoed in the hallway, more of an accusation than a question.

No, apparently she wouldn't be able to slink away in oblivion. Even as she fought to find an excuse or ruse, she inwardly chastised herself for being a coward and considering running away from the scene of a crime. She couldn't, not when a murder had occurred, and the man who committed it needed to be brought to justice.

She straightened her shoulders. At five foot four, she needed every inch her petite frame could give her. "Yes, I'm Catherine Remington."

"What's a fine lady like you doing in this establishment at this time of day?" His words were hard and biting, almost as if she'd imposed upon him with her presence.

"As a matter of fact, I've been here all night assisting one of the young women during her time of travail."

He cocked his head, his brows lifting.

"I'm a midwife. I've been here delivering a baby."

"Well, it's a good thing you stepped into the hallway when you did, isn't it, boys?" Rocky directed his question toward two men standing just inside the open doorway above the dead body. They stepped over Stretch until they were both positioned behind Rocky, arms crossed and staring at her.

She'd noticed the men with Rocky on occasion. Perhaps they served as his guards or his servants. Either way, she wouldn't let them intimidate her.

"Young lady," Rocky said, "I'll need you to testify to the police and the judge on my behalf, let them know Stretch came after me and that I was left with no choice but to shoot him or lose my life."

Had Stretch provoked him? She glanced at Stretch's crumpled body. There wasn't a weapon in sight. Blood poured out of the open wound in his bare chest, forming a dark puddle on the floor. "I'm sorry, Mr. Kenna, but I can't testify to that end—"

"Sure you can. You were right here." He straightened his suit coat as though his business was finished. "You saw everything just the way I said."

He wanted her to lie for him? So he could get away with murder? Well, if he didn't already know, he was about to learn that she was a woman with as much integrity as her

15

father. "No, actually, I didn't see Stretch do anything to harm you."

Rocky started down the hallway toward her, and his men followed on his heels. Their footsteps tapped a dangerous rhythm. If he could kill Stretch, what would stop him from killing her?

Chapter 2

Catherine wove her fingers together to keep them from trembling. And she lifted her chin, as if that could somehow ward off any threat Rocky Rogers Kenna might pose. But the fact was, she was completely at his mercy with no means to defend herself.

He didn't halt until he was inches away. His eyes had grown darker at his approach, as though they were bottomless holes that led to his black soul.

If she were a betting woman, she'd guess he wouldn't actually end her life. Not after already having the hassle of one murder to explain away. Even so, she had to find a way to escape.

"Miss Remington." He sugarcoated her name. "I have no doubt you're an upstanding young woman. Everyone will believe you when you testify to my innocence in this unfortunate matter."

"I'll testify to the truth, Mr. Kenna."

"And the truth is that Stretch provoked me." His glare dared her to defy him, and he leaned closer, the sour waft of his breath hitting her in the face. It nearly rivaled the stench of sin that permeated every inch of the brothel. She knew of no other way to describe the mix of cigar smoke, rum, and perfume.

A door several rooms down opened a crack. A woman peeked out then retreated, rapidly closing the door. The walls were thin, and no doubt anyone who was awake was listening to every word of her conversation with Rocky. They'd also surely heard the gun blast.

Catherine swallowed the fear pushing up into her throat. "I'm sorry, but I can't—"

"I'll be sorry if I have to involve your father." His voice remained much too sweet. "It's no secret your father hated Stretch, especially after the accusations he made about your father's evasion of federal taxes."

"None of the accusations are true."

"But I'd hate for word to get out that Alderman Remington was involved in silencing Stretch."

Catherine's heartbeat pattered to a halt. Was Rocky insinuating he'd blame her father for murdering Stretch? He wouldn't be able to do so. He'd never find enough evidence to prove her father was involved. Yet lobbing such a serious allegation had the potential to hurt her father's political aspirations, especially since he intended to run for state representative in the next election.

She couldn't allow Rocky to ruin her father. The country needed more men like him, men who took a stand for truth and were above political games. Now that he and Mother were busy with campaigning, they didn't need her causing another scandal. She'd already disgraced and disappointed them. She couldn't do that again.

Rocky rolled onto his heels, his shoulders relaxing. "So what do you say, Miss Remington? Are you willing to testify to my innocence?"

What choice did she have? Besides, what if Stretch had provoked Rocky the way he'd claimed? Just because she hadn't noticed Stretch holding a weapon didn't mean he hadn't assaulted Rocky with the intention of harming him.

Rocky's lips twitched with the beginning of a grin, almost as if he knew he'd won.

"Very well, Mr. Kenna. I guess I must participate in your scheming."

"Good girl." He spun and shouldered past his men, heading back toward Stretch. "I'm glad I can count on you."

She pressed her lips together to keep from giving the crooked alderman a piece of her mind. At the same time, she reached for the door handle of Kit's room, needing to get away and come up with a solution to this new dilemma.

"I'll have the police collect a statement from you later today," Rocky called as she slipped into the closet-like room. "Don't let me down, Miss Remington."

She didn't answer—couldn't answer. Instead, she closed the door and leaned against it. What in heaven's name had she gotten herself into?

No matter how much she might try to convince herself, she knew as well as Rocky that he was guilty of cold-blooded murder. How could she say anything but the truth?

At a groan from the bed, Catherine jumped. Kit was lying listlessly, her legs coated in blood, her long, dark hair tangled around her.

Death was lurking nearby and ready to claim this woman.

Packing the uterus would be excruciating for Kit and probably wouldn't help at this point. Should she let Kit rest peacefully in her final moments?

Catherine's chest twisted with the familiar battle—doing as much as she could until the last moment versus allowing a patient to die with dignity.

She approached the young woman and brushed her hair away from her face.

Kit's eyes fluttered open. "Do you want to help me?"

"Of course I do." She'd failed in her mission to gain an assistant and didn't dare go back into the hallway. "I can still try to stop the bleeding—"

"No. Not that." Kit held out her hand. It shook with the effort.

Catherine took it gently. "Then what?"

"Take the baby to his father. He has family who will help him raise the child." The plea was strong and certain. And Kit's eyes filled with such hope that Catherine was tempted to tell her yes simply to keep the hope alive.

But honesty won. "That's not possible."

Kit's grip grew stronger. "You're a gentlewoman. You can. I know you'll take good care of Austin."

"Austin?"

"I'm naming the baby after his father's father."

"How about if I send the baby's—Austin's—father a telegram letting him know to retrieve the baby for himself?"

"No. He won't respond."

Catherine couldn't argue. If the baby's father hadn't replied to any letters, why would he have a change of heart with a telegram?

"Please? Take him?" Kit's whisper dropped, her breathing shallow. With so much blood loss, her organs were shutting down. It wouldn't be long before death claimed her. And now in her dying moments, she was valiantly trying to make sure her baby was taken care of.

Kit glanced at Austin still nestled in the carpetbag. "He looks just like his father."

With dark brown hair and a handsome face, the baby had strong, distinct features. Catherine didn't see much of Kit in the child and suspected he would indeed grow up to resemble his father.

"He'll take one look at Austin and realize the baby's his." Kit closed her eyes, weariness again creasing her face.

Catherine sat on the edge of the bed and stroked the woman's forehead. Her skin was cold, no longer getting the heat it needed.

"Please. I beg this of you."

Catherine brushed her fingers through Kit's hair, fighting back the despair that crept in whenever she lost one of her patients. Even though her mother and grandmother had both admonished her to accept loss as part of the cycle of life, Catherine still hadn't learned to accept death as easily as they did. They'd taught her that she wasn't the one to light the flame, and she couldn't blame herself when a fragile flame flickered out. Ultimately, God determined the brightness and length of each light.

"There's a brooch in the bag," Kit whispered. "It was from the baby's father to me when we got engaged."

"I'll fetch it for you—"

"Also, there's a journal, and it contains pertinent information about Austin's father."

21

"I'll make sure both items stay with Austin."

Kit's eyes opened. "I don't want him to go to an orphanage. He needs his father. He's a good man."

A good man? Catherine held back a snort, not wanting to cause Kit any grief in her last moments. The truth was, a good man wouldn't abandon a woman this way, allowing her to sink into such deprivation.

"Please?" Kit peered up at her with such desperation Catherine couldn't make herself say no. But she couldn't agree to travel to Colorado and deliver the child, could she?

Catherine tried for a smile. "I'll do my best." She wouldn't promise anything more than that.

The words must have satisfied Kit, because she closed her eyes, sank into the mattress, and released a deep breath. When she didn't draw in more air, Catherine breathed out a sigh of her own.

The woman's hand slipped from Catherine's and fell to the mattress. Kit was gone.

Catherine reclined in the wingback chair in her bedroom and finished feeding Austin the last of the bottle. A dribble of the warm milk slipped from his puckered lips. With his eyes closed, his dark lashes rested against ruddy cheeks. His little nose twitched. And his dimpled chin wobbled as though he were still sucking.

She touched his tiny fingers grasping hers. He was adorable. But she couldn't keep him much longer, at least not without telling her family about him. So far, in the hour since she'd returned home, he'd kept fairly quiet. But it wouldn't be long before he cried, and then her mother and father and all the servants would know what she'd done—that she'd broken one of the cardinal midwife rules—no bringing babies home.

Her mother and grandmother had always warned against it, especially when their work took them to the less fortunate populace, where disease, deprivation, and death were rampant.

"We can't possibly care for orphaned babies, Catherine," her mother had told her the first time she'd held a newborn after the mother's passing.

"Please, Mother. He needs us."

"God's gifted us with bringing life into the world," her mother replied while briskly repacking her satchel with her birthing supplies. "He's gifted others with sustaining that life."

At eight, Catherine had started accompanying her mother and grandmother on their midwife calls, assisting in small ways, such as warming blankets, boiling water, washing and holding the baby after the delivery, dressing the infant's cord, and massaging the mother's uterus.

As she'd gotten older, they'd allowed her more responsibilities. But the task of holding a motherless baby had never gotten easier.

Most of the time when the mother died during or after childbirth, the infant went to stay with relatives. In rare cases, Mother took the orphan to Grace House, a small privately run orphanage with loving workers who almost always found a family eager to adopt the newborn.

The babies were well taken care of. This little one would be too. A loving and eager childless couple would no doubt scoop him right up and give him a better life than he could ever imagine.

"Is it time to take you to Grace House, little one?" Catherine whispered as she stroked the baby's cheek.

After she'd made arrangements for Kit's body with the madam of the brothel, no one had objected when Catherine offered to take the infant away. Before leaving, she'd asked around for information about Kit's family, learning that her father ran a store on Harrison Street and a sister lived on Clark. Catherine had sought them out, but in spite of her pleas, none of the family wanted the baby and had slammed their doors in her face. She'd even gone to a grandmother's home but had been told in vulgar terms to go away.

Finally, exhausted, Catherine had Slim drive her home. She was fairly certain the old groomsman knew she had the newborn concealed in the carpetbag, but he'd wisely said nothing as he assisted her down in front of her family's brownstone town house, especially because she said she would require transportation again shortly.

The ticking of the mantel clock reminded her it was past time to call for Slim to bring the carriage around.

She placed the bottle on the pedestal table beside the chair and propped the baby against her shoulder, firmly patting his back.

How could she take Austin to the orphanage after she'd promised Kit she would do her best to hand him over to his father's care? Could she keep the infant here at the house for a little while, just until she contacted the father and informed him of his child? She certainly couldn't travel across the country and deliver the child, not when she didn't know if the man would even want the baby. What if he wasn't suitable?

"He's a good man." Kit's words echoed through Catherine's

mind. She sensed the sincerity of Kit's declaration, that even though the man had run off, she'd seen qualities in him that were worthwhile, qualities that would make him a decent father.

Catherine continued a steady thumping against Austin's back, until he released a slight burp. Not only did she have the question of the baby's care and future riddling her, but she also was perplexed about how to handle Rocky's threats. The vision of Stretch's body sliding down the wall and blood pooling on the ground had stayed with her all throughout the morning.

Even now, the trail of smeared blood on the wall haunted her, sending a shiver up her spine. She was an eyewitness to a murder, one that had the potential to lock the crooked Rocky Rogers Kenna away in prison. Yet how could she stand up against him when he was paying policemen, lawyers, and judges to work for him? No one would listen to her lone testimony.

However, if she went to court and lied for Rocky, she'd betray her conscience. How could she announce to the world that he was innocent when he was guilty of not only Stretch's murder but likely others? If she let him get away with his crime, she'd be as guilty as he was.

"Oh, Lord God, what should I do?" The uncertainty weighed heavier with every passing moment, until at last she had to stand or be crushed.

She situated the baby in the crook of her arms, then paced toward the long window that overlooked the street and then back to the chair. The hearth fire was cold since she'd informed her servant not to bother her, and the chill of the March day followed her.

She paused next to her double bed, unwrinkled and undisturbed after she'd been away all night. Fancy pillows of various shapes and sizes decorated the gold damask coverlet. Should she try to get some sleep? Maybe after resting she'd be able to think more clearly. She could use the pillows to box Austin in next to her.

Or should she seek out her mother and solicit her advice on the matter of the newborn as well as the crime she'd witnessed?

Mother had been in the drawing room having tea when Catherine had passed by. Yet even if Mother exuded wisdom and provided a godly example on how to show charity, Catherine already knew what the practical, no-nonsense woman would say—at least about the baby. She'd tell Catherine not to let her emotions stand in the way of doing the right thing.

But what was the right thing for this baby?

Catherine peered down at the infant, sleeping soundly now that his belly was full. Would living with the father be for the best?

Before she could convince herself not to pry, she bent and dug through Kit's carpetbag until her fingers connected with the hard cover of a journal. She tugged it out. The dark blue cover was soiled in places—with tears? The edges were tattered and the pages loose. Maybe she'd find answers to her questions within. At least she hoped so.

After retreating to the chair and positioning Austin more securely, she opened to the first page. On the inside cover, Kit had written in delicate cursive: *This journal belongs to Katherine Ann Olson.*

Of course Kit was a nickname for Katherine. Catherine had already guessed they shared the same name. What was surprising was the amount of detail in the entries. The date on the first one was from January of 1869, over two years ago. Scanning through the pages, Catherine could see that Kit had written something, even if small and inconsequential, almost every day. Most of it seemed to be about working in her father's store and the various people who came to it, particularly young men who paid her attention.

Catherine turned to the end, noting the last entry was over a week ago: *The baby is due any day. I pray to God this child will have a better life than I did. If only the baby could be with his or her father, Dylan McQuaid, in Fairplay, Colorado. While I didn't know the baby's father long, I am certain he will love and raise this child.*

The despair lingered in each letter and reached out to tug on Catherine's heart. Poor Kit.

Catherine paged backward until she found a record mentioning Dylan McQuaid. It was dated last June of 1870. She skimmed the paragraphs describing him—how charming and handsome he was, how he worked as a police officer, how he came into the store and talked to her.

Not many entries later, Kit described how Dylan had proposed marriage and how she'd given in and slept with him, telling herself everything would be okay because they were getting married. The next few accounts dripped with anger after Kit discovered Dylan had left Chicago for Colorado and hadn't bothered to say good-bye.

Catherine could feel the heartache as Kit penned her loss, especially as she came to terms with the fact that Dylan's proposal had been made while he'd been drunk and probably hadn't meant anything to him.

Then came the pages filled with bitterness at the realization of her pregnancy. Kit had attempted to hide it for some time, but eventually her father discovered her condition and threw her out of the house. Without anyplace else to go, she sought out a former friend who lived at the brothel.

Kit hadn't actually resorted to prostitution. The friend had provided for her. Even so, the nature of Kit's entries made it clear that once the baby was born, she didn't know what other options she would have to provide for herself and the child. She'd sent two letters to Dylan, asking for his help. Even though she'd been angry at the man for deserting her, she'd still believed he was a kind man, that if he only knew about the baby, he'd help.

At a shout from the street outside the house, Catherine snapped the journal closed. She rose and crossed to the window. At the sight of several police officers dismounting from horses, she jumped back, her pulse spurting.

They were here for her. Rocky had indicated he'd send them. They would want to question her about the murder. She'd either have to implicate Rocky and harm her father's career or lie about Rocky and add to his corruptness.

Unless . . .

She glanced from the journal to the carpetbag and then to Austin still sleeping contentedly in her arms. She could leave today, now, and avoid the confrontation with the police altogether. If she removed herself from Chicago for a while, then she'd entirely bypass the whole messy scenario. Doing so would force Rocky to face the consequences of his actions.

Perhaps she could also spare her parents more embarrassment. After the recent announcement in the *Chicago Tribune* regarding Chester Jones's engagement to another woman, Catherine had once again become the topic of gossip among her social circles. It was already common knowledge that Chester had put an end to their relationship because he didn't like how seriously she took her midwifery. But the announcement had mentioned that he'd moved on from the "tedious Miss Remington" to a more suitable and refreshing woman.

The article had called her tedious. As in dull, unpretentious, and bland. She'd already been rejected by three other suitors over the past two years, which made Chester's description sting horribly. But at last she understood why no one wanted her. Not only were her midwifery aspirations unbecoming to most men of her social standing, but she couldn't compare to the more exciting, vivacious, and entertaining women of marriageable age.

Recently, the whisper of anxiety had begun to clamor louder, taunting her that she'd never be able to find anyone and would end up a spinster. Was getting married and having babies of her own simply unattainable?

As much as she cared for her parents, she shuddered at the prospect of living out a lonely existence in their home, and her discontentment had only grown over the months since parting ways with Chester.

Though her parents were always busy with campaigning—so busy that Mother had given up her midwifery—Catherine had sensed their consternation with her inability to secure an advantageous match. She'd failed to uphold the Remington reputation the way her older brother had by marrying into wealth and preparing for a career in politics.

Yes, she'd go. Rather than casting more dark clouds over her family, leaving was the best option. She'd use the excuse of taking Austin to his father in Fairplay, Colorado. Perhaps she'd stay for the summer and make sure this Dylan

McQuaid was truly capable of raising the child. Then, by autumn, hopefully, Rocky would be in prison where he belonged, and she would be able to return without worrying that he'd bring harm to her family. Maybe also by that point, everyone would forget about Chester's unflattering description of her, and suitors would call again.

Without sparing another moment, she wedged Austin between pillows, emptied Kit's garments from the carpetbag, then hastily filled it with her own clothing and toiletries. She stuffed in as much as she could fit and then did the same to her midwife satchel. Thankfully, Father had ensured her purse had been well endowed before she'd answered the call last night. And she had saved some from her midwife services—from patrons who could afford to pay. She tucked both into the bag.

Donning her coat, she peeked out the window. The police had finished hitching their mounts and were ascending the stairs. What would they tell Mother for wanting to speak with her?

As they knocked, she waited. When the door opened a moment later, the voice of one of the men ascended to her window. "We've come to arrest Catherine Remington."

Arrest? That was ludicrous. She'd done nothing wrong.

"She killed a young woman and her companion, Alderman Stretch Watson." The officer's voice floated up again, likely in response to her mother's questioning. They were accusing her of killing Kit and Stretch?

The blood rushed from her head, leaving her dizzy and weak. She should have known Rocky would figure out a way to shift the blame entirely so he would come across looking innocent. He'd likely pay the prostitutes and the brothel madam to lie on his behalf regarding Kit's relationship with Stretch. And he'd find a way to make all the evidence point to Catherine.

Yes, she had to leave. She had no other recourse.

She crossed swiftly to the bed, swiped up Austin and the bags, then sprinted out of her room to a back servant staircase.

Even if her father hired the best lawyers to defend her, Rocky had powerful connections and was proving to be more cunning than she'd anticipated. She couldn't fight Rocky, not when he was determined to make her his scapegoat.

She raced down to the lower level, burst through the door into the kitchen hallway, and almost bumped into Slim sipping from a cup of tea. The older man's eyes widened at the sight of her in the servants' quarters.

She straightened her hat and readjusted the baby, no longer worried about anyone seeing her with the infant. "I'm ready to depart."

"Now, miss?"

"Immediately."

He bobbed his graying head. "I'll bring the carriage around front."

"No need. We'll leave via the alley route."

He set his cup of tea onto a sideboard filled with dishes and reached for his coat on a peg near the door. "Grace House, miss?"

With the cook peeling potatoes in front of the worktable and watching her with as much surprise as Slim, Catherine had to be careful what she said. She couldn't leave a trail for Rocky to follow.

"Yes, of course." She handed the carpetbag to Slim. "I'm

delivering the baby to Grace House." Now when her mother came looking for her, the servants could give an answer to take back to the police. The men would likely wait for her return. Or maybe they'd ride to to Grace House hoping to intercept her there.

Whatever the case, she'd have a substantial head start in getting to the train station. The Pacific Railroad had been completed almost two years ago, a transcontinental track that connected the eastern states to the West. She intended to be on that train and well on her way before anyone was the wiser.

CHAPTER
3

FAIRPLAY, COLORADO
MAY 1871

Dylan McQuaid sighted down his rifle, following a horse and rider on the opposite ridge. His finger twitched with the urge to shoot the feather off the fella's hat. He could easily make the shot.

Doing so would sure as stars send a message to J. D. Otto, that he knew about the rustling.

Except it wouldn't do any good. The fella wasn't technically doing anything wrong today. Wasn't stealing cattle. Wasn't even trespassing.

Didn't matter that Dylan had trailed J. D.'s cowhands off and on for days, watched them for hours, and tried to figure out who they were aiming to steal from next. Problem was, they were sneaky little buggers and had perfected their ability to siphon off cattle from the other ranchers without anyone being able to stop them.

Nope. Dylan lowered his gun and swallowed his disappointment. "Shucks."

Under the canopy of pinyon pine, juniper, and white fir, he waited with his horse in the late-afternoon shadows. Even though the higher altitude contained a chilly bite in May, he didn't mind. Kept him from getting overheated as he patrolled the grasslands and foothills.

He inhaled a deep breath. He not only loved the brisk air, but he loved the earthy scent of melting snow mingled with rocky soil, the waft of new pine needles, the crisp cleanness of each lungful.

Boy howdy, was he glad to be back in Colorado. "Have I said it enough, Lord? If I haven't, I'll say it again. Thank you."

He peered out over the sprawling hills studded with boulders and pine. Dandelions were growing in clusters, some next to the remaining piles of snow. Grass was starting to turn green. And he'd even seen a butterfly earlier. Spring was coming to the high country, later than most other places. But it was a sight to behold.

"Thank you for lettin' me come back here. For giving me a second chance." His whispered prayer settled in the silence around him, broken only by the nearby trickling of a creek filled with melting runoff.

At times like this, all he could do was bask in wonder that he was home, that he was a free man, and that the county had chosen him to be sheriff.

Harlan Hatfield up in Como had been spitting mad that the special election had been conducted while he was back east over the winter, especially since Hatfield was the one who'd suggested the county needed to have their own sheriff—him.

But Mayor Landry Steele and the ranchers of Park County were fed up with the rustling and didn't want to wait to take care of the problem until August when the county planned to hold a regular election. With Dylan's experience on the police force in Chicago, as well as his sharpshooting skills, they'd all but handed him the job on a temporary basis.

The sight of the badge on his coat had sure made his brothers proud. Now that he'd been in the position for the past few months, he could see himself doing it long-term— wanted to do it long-term so he could keep on making his brothers proud. But also so he could reclaim a measure of his own pride.

From what Dylan could tell, Hatfield was a trustworthy and upright fella. A middle-aged man with a head for business, he wanted what was best for Park County and all of South Park. Dylan could respect that. And he could respect that Hatfield was campaigning all over Park County.

He just didn't like that Hatfield wasn't willing to give him a fair shot and was instead chawing on about how no one with a tarnished reputation should be sheriff, especially someone who had a wagonload of problems in his past.

Dylan was doing his best to prove he was a changed man. But he still had a ways to go. If he could take care of the rustling problem, maybe he'd have a better chance at winning the election.

With his gloved hand, he polished the silver star affixed to his vest with the word *Sheriff* etched across the center. Two years ago, even a year ago, he never would have believed he'd be standing in the rugged wilderness a new man, walking an upright life, steering clear of all the snares that had once held him captive.

But since the day he'd left Chicago, he'd run away from his vices and hadn't looked back. Like the prodigal son, he'd repented of his waywardness. He'd taken to heart the words of Psalm 1 and vowed not to walk in the counsel of the ungodly, not to stand in the way of sinners, not to sit in the seat of the scornful.

He could admit, at times his old cravings reared up mighty hard. But he purposefully hiked a mile around any place selling liquor and women. He never went inside a saloon, not unless he absolutely had to, only when his deputy couldn't handle drinking disturbances on his own. Even then, he never stayed inside long, always settled business outside.

Every time he turned away from temptation, he felt himself growing stronger. Maybe one day he'd be as solid, strong, and steady as his older brothers. Maybe he'd even eventually be like his pa.

With a final scan of the area, he holstered his rifle in the scabbard on his saddle, reached for the lead line, and began to guide his gelding out from the cover. After spending most of the day on the range assessing the rustling situation, he was past due back in town. Even if Stu could manage without him, Dylan hated being gone for too long.

As he mounted and began the ride back to Fairplay, he whistled one of the hymns they'd sung yesterday in church, and he tried to guess what Trudy would have for supper. His deputy's wife had become like a ma to him, a better ma than his had ever been. Trudy didn't take no for an answer when it came to joining Stu and her for supper most evenings.

Truth was, he didn't want to say no. Trudy Gunderson was the best cook this side of the Divide. Just the thought of her flaky biscuits with thick sausage gravy sent his stomach rumbling like he had the appetite of a grizzly coming out of hibernation.

As he neared the north end of Fairplay, he slowed his mount to a respectable trot. The street was busy with the end of the workday, men and womenfolk alike milling about. Mayor Steele had done a swell job over the past ten years of turning Fairplay from a ramshackle miners' camp to a respectable family town with new businesses and residences going up every day.

Even during the few years Dylan had been gone, Fairplay had expanded so that it resembled eastern towns with neatly laid-out streets and well-plotted lots. It boasted a couple of churches, a brand-new schoolhouse, and even a bank. While not as rowdy as some of the other mining towns, Fairplay still had its share of saloons and places of ill repute. Dylan ought to know. He'd frequented them all during his drinking days.

He tipped his hat to several men in passing. When they touched the brims of their hats in return, a sense of deep satisfaction stole over him again. Doing what was right had brought him a whole heap more contentment than wild living.

The squat log building in the center of Main Street doubled as the sheriff's office and courthouse now that Fairplay had become the county seat instead of Buckskin Joe. The place wasn't anything like the police station where he'd worked in Chicago. But at least he had a building to make things official-like.

The mayor had given him the one-room cabin behind the courthouse as his residence so he could move off his brother's ranch and live in town. The logs had been cut flat to form corner joints, and the structure was sturdy enough.

His brothers had helped him caulk between the logs and patch the leaky roof. Once they'd finished, the place had kept him nice and warm.

As he reined in front of the sheriff's office, Stu stepped out the door, letting it slam shut behind him. With a scraggly brown mustache, long sideburns, and an overgrown beard, the man had enough facial hair to rival a moose. Truth was, not only did Stu look like a moose, but he was as cantankerous as one. When God created Stu, He'd missed out giving the man even an ounce of humor. The deputy was incapable of laughing or smiling—wouldn't be able to do either even if someone paid him in gold to try.

Stu stepped away from the door. "Got some trouble."

"Nothin' new there." Dylan tossed the man a smile. "Reckon you and trouble are best friends."

"Reckon this time trouble's here to make friends with you." Stu ambled toward him, his brows clouding together.

With one foot on the ground and the other still in the stirrup, Dylan paused in his descent. Something in Stu's expression went beyond the usual crankiness to exude genuine concern.

What was going on? Apprehension shimmied up Dylan's spine. It was the same feeling he'd always gotten when he'd indulged in a vice he knew he shouldn't have. Except that he'd been sober and celibate since his last night in Chicago almost a year ago, before he'd walked to the police station and found Bliss's letter there, informing him that his gambling debt and the death threat against him were both gone and he was free to return to Colorado.

"Someone's come from Chicago to see you." Stu reached for the horse's bridle.

"Chicago?" Why on earth would anyone from Chicago want to see him? He hadn't had any friends there except Jericho Bliss. Everyone else had been attracted to him for what they could gain, primarily for the fun he brought to a gathering. None had been loyal or faithful. And none of them had cared when he left. So who would visit now? All these months later?

Was one of the chiefs seeking him out, hoping to gain more evidence about the corruption within the police department? He'd been working to help uncover those taking bribes and had shared as much inside information as he could before leaving town.

He hopped to the ground and stared at the door. He wasn't keen on stirring up the past, had wanted to keep it buried in the boneyard where it belonged. On the other hand, he had a duty before God and man to do the best he could to reveal crime, and if he could still be of assistance, then so be it.

He grabbed his revolver handle, as if that could somehow give him the nerve he needed to walk into the courthouse and face the ghost from his previous life. He'd make this quick, give his visitor information, and then send the fella on his way.

He stalked toward the door, his spurs jangling.

"She's making a mighty big claim, dontcha know."

"She?" Dylan halted and spun, searching Stu's face more closely.

"Yup. She." Again, the man's eyes contained a concern that set Dylan on edge.

"Did she mention her name?"

"Nope. And didn't ask. Figured yous the one she's here to see, not me."

What was a woman from Chicago doing all the way in the

West, looking for him? Dylan stuck his other hand on his second revolver. A fella visiting him was one thing. But he was gonna need more than a little nerve to face a woman. He was gonna need a whole heap of it. When a woman sought him out, it was usually because he'd done something lousy and she was in the mood to dress him down for it.

What had he done this time? He didn't even want to imagine, knew it wouldn't be pretty.

"Yous best get on in there. She's been waiting awhile."

Dylan gripped the revolver handles, steeling himself. Not only was she gonna be madder than a cornered skunk for whatever offense he'd caused, but she'd be miffed at having to wait. He started toward the door again, but this time slower, his spurs hardly making a sound, as if they were following along reluctantly.

When he reached the door, he hesitated. He was a new man. God had forgiven him for his past sins. Now all he had to do was apologize to this woman, tell her he'd been an idiot, and ask how he could make amends.

He could do that. No problem.

But even as he opened the door, his guilt opened wide right along with it. He'd never been with a woman who hadn't wanted to be with him. He'd always made sure of that. Even so, he'd still been wrong to give in to fleshly pleasures outside the bounds of marriage. He regretted his immorality and wished he could go back and stay chaste.

The interior of the office was lit by late-afternoon sunshine spilling through the front windows. The place was crowded with bookshelves, a couple of desks, an assortment of equipment and weapons hanging from the wall, and a drawer containing county records.

The woman was sitting in the chair beside his desk, her back facing him. "Thank you, Deputy Gunderson. Just set the warm water on the desk please."

Dylan closed the door quietly behind him.

The woman was wearing a fancy hat that prevented him from seeing her face. But he could see that she was attired in finely tailored garments that were just as fashionable as her hat—dark green with a velvet trim. Elegant and refined. Too elegant and refined to belong to any of the women he'd known.

He released a taut breath. Maybe he'd jumped to conclusions about the nature of this woman's visit. Maybe she wasn't an angry lover seeking revenge for something he'd done.

He shook his fingers, releasing the tension.

"Any sign yet of the sheriff?" she asked as she bent over a bundle on her lap.

"Reckon I've seen him a time or two." He couldn't keep the teasing from his voice.

She hopped in her chair, clearly not anticipating anyone but Stu. She twisted her head, giving him a view of her pretty face with well-rounded chin and cheeks, pert nose, and full lips. Her eyes were the loveliest of her features, a hazy green that gave off a keen, intelligent aura. They were wide and fringed with dark lashes and filled with surprise.

"You're not Deputy Gunderson."

Dylan offered his most charming smile. "Thank goodness for that."

Instead of the return smile he'd hoped for, she scanned him from his battered hat down to his scuffed boots. "Dylan McQuaid?"

Her tone changed, sounding like a judge about to deliver a pronouncement. Something told him this was gonna be worse than he'd thought. And he had the sudden urge to deny he was Dylan McQuaid, fling open the door, and head right back outside.

But that was something the old Dylan might have done, not the upstanding man of God he was trying to be. "Yep. Dylan McQuaid. At your service."

She rose then, gathering up something in her arms. As she turned, he realized that something was a babe. She tucked a blanket around the child tenderly, her gaze softening with the love only a mother could have.

As she finished, she turned her attention upon him again, almost disdainfully, lifting her chin and looking as regal as a queen—not that he'd ever seen a queen. She held the infant up at an angle that allowed him to get a view. "Mr. McQuaid, I'd like you to meet your son."

Chapter 4

Son?

Dylan was rarely speechless, but his tongue was stuck in his mouth as securely as a possum in a trap.

The petite woman dug a hand into her pocket, retrieved an item, and then held it out to him. "If the baby's family resemblance to you isn't proof enough, then perhaps you'll recognize this item."

Before he could closely examine the babe, his attention dropped to her outstretched palm and a silver brooch made of silver, rose gold, and onyx, with a cameo at the center. It was his. The one Bethina Eggleston had given him, her promise that she loved him and would wait for him. Except that it hadn't been a promise, and she hadn't loved or waited for him. She'd left for California with her family and hadn't even said good-bye.

He took it from the woman and turned it over, examining it. He'd hung on to it over the years, at first because he'd pined after Bethina, but then as a reminder of how easily people could love and leave.

In his haste moving back to Colorado, he'd assumed he'd lost the brooch. How had this woman ended up with it?

As if seeing the question in his expression, she answered. "It was part of your proposal of marriage."

Proposal of marriage?

"On the night before you left Chicago."

His thoughts returned to that night. He didn't remember much, but he did recall waking up in bed next to a woman who had told him he'd proposed marriage. She asked him to come to her home for dinner that night, said her dad wanted to meet him. He was ashamed to admit it now, but leaving Chicago had given him the excuse he'd needed to avoid seeing her again.

What had her name been? Her father had owned Olson Grocery Store on Harrison. She'd been pretty with long, dark hair—just like this woman.

He studied her face again. Was this the same person? She didn't look familiar. Then again, there were plenty of other women he didn't recollect.

Olson Grocery Store. Catherine. Yep. That was it. Catherine Olson. She'd had a nickname, though. Hadn't she?

"The baby is yours." This time when she spoke, her voice wavered. She dropped her attention to the child but not before he saw tears glistening in her eyes. She bent and pressed a kiss to the babe's cheek, hiding her emotion.

The infant's eyes were wide open and watching her, as though he sensed her agitation.

The child had brown hair and green-blue eyes just like

his. And she was right. The babe had the strong McQuaid features he'd seen in his brothers' kids.

Even so, he had to ask a few more questions, didn't he? "When was he born?"

"March twelfth."

That seemed about right for conception to birthing, which meant the babe was over two months old. Dylan wasn't knowledgeable about babies, but two months of age seemed to fit the little fella.

"I regret to say, the labor didn't go well." Her expression turned grave.

"I'm sorry." His own ma had suffered terribly during the birthing process. The last stillbirth had killed her. Although his older brother Flynn had kept him and his other siblings away whenever Ma had gone into labor, her screams of agony had reached him anyway and still haunted him.

"I truly am sorry," he said again. He should have been there to support and comfort her afterward.

"Thankfully, the baby was—is—just fine." She nuzzled her nose against the babe's cheek. "He shares the same birthday as your father and the same name. Austin."

Dylan stood straighter. She was right. His pa's birthday had been March twelfth. He must have told her at some point in their short-lived relationship. How had she remembered so much about him, when he couldn't even remember what she looked like?

The answer to that smacked him with another round of guilt. All the drinking and carousing had turned his life into a blurry whirlwind where he'd just moved from one woman to the next.

She hugged the infant tightly for a long moment, then

thrust him out. "I've come to the end of my journey with the baby. Now it's your turn to take care of him."

"Whoa now, darlin'." Taking a rapid step back, Dylan held up his hands as if she were pointing a pistol at him. "I can't take care of the little tyke."

"I'm here to deliver him to you so you can raise him."

Understanding began to carve its way through Dylan's thick head. She was giving him the infant and wasn't intending on staying.

Her hazy green eyes pleaded with him to accept the child but at the same time were filled with a sadness as deep as a mountain valley. She obviously loved the infant. So why did she want him to raise the babe?

"Please." She stretched the babe out farther. "Just take him."

He crossed his arms. "I don't know anything about babies."

"You'll learn. He's a sweet boy and an easy baby."

"Then why aren't you keeping him?"

Her eyes widened as though he'd suggested something indecent—like hopping up on a saloon stage and dancing in her undergarments.

The very thought sent chagrin through him, and he lifted his hat and palmed the back of his neck. This whole exchange was going to pieces faster than a flaming haymow.

"As much as I love Austin, I can't keep him," she finally replied, her voice low and raw. "I'm a single woman. I don't have the means or a place to go . . . and it wouldn't be right."

He kneaded the back of his neck. She was single. Unmarried. And had a child. How would she support herself and the babe? No doubt she'd been shunned by her family and friends for having the child out of wedlock. She'd probably become an outcast in her community. Without a husband, how would she provide for herself and the infant?

There weren't many opportunities for a woman, especially one with a tainted reputation. In fact, during his time in Chicago, he'd seen too many women in the same situation turn to whoring to survive. Their lives had been ruined as they'd sold their souls to provide for a child.

At the prospect of that happening to this woman, his stomach turned as rancid as cheap whiskey.

He closed his eyes and sucked in several breaths. This was all his fault. He was to blame for her predicament. And he couldn't allow her to go off on her own with the babe—his child—and fend for herself. He didn't know how she'd made it as long as she had.

Now she obviously had no choice but to hand the child over to him. No doubt she was doing so to give the boy a better life than she could provide on her own.

The infant, still in her outstretched arms, released a wail, as though protesting having to leave his mother.

Tears glistened in her eyes, tears she couldn't blink back fast enough. One spilled over and ran down her cheek.

"Please, Dylan." Gone was the formality. Only desperation remained in her tone and in her expression. "Please, just take him."

Him. Austin. His son.

Dylan's gaze locked on the tiny babe bundled tightly in a blanket. His face scrunched up and turning red, Austin gave another wail, this one louder than the last.

If he didn't raise this child, what kind of life would Austin have? Would he grow up in a brothel? Maybe end up in an orphanage? Or worse, homeless on the streets?

His stomach roiled again. How could he let something like that happen to his own flesh and blood?

He turned his attention back to Catherine. He was ashamed to admit how little he knew about her—the mother of his child. But with the tears streaking her cheeks and the anguish in her eyes, he couldn't doubt her sincerity in wanting to do the right thing for this babe, even though giving him up was tearing her apart. From what he could tell, she was kindhearted and loving.

Even so, once more he had the urge to run outside, mount his horse, ride away, and pretend this wasn't happening.

This woman, this child—they were gonna ruin the good name he was building. People would talk when they learned he had an illegitimate son. Hatfield would have one more thing to use against him in his efforts to convince folks not to vote for him in the August election.

Hold on. What if he could rectify the situation? What if the child wasn't illegitimate? And what if he had a wife?

Instead of proving Hatfield right, that he was nothing more than a scalawag, he could show everyone that he was responsible and willing to rectify his mistakes. Sure, there would be some high-and-mighty folks who would still look down on him, but they would anyway regardless of how righteously he lived.

He oughta just give this woman some money and send her and the babe away. After all, how could he ever be one hundred percent certain the child was his?

Even as his thoughts clamored within him to find a way to rid himself of this new problem, a nudge within his spirit told him he couldn't. He knew the truth. She wouldn't have come this far and gone to this much trouble if he wasn't the father.

The old Dylan would have made excuses. But the new man he was striving to become was done thinking only about himself. Instead, he had to face the consequences of his past sins head-on.

"Here's what we're gonna do, darlin'." He raised his voice above the infant's increased squalling. "We're gonna get married."

"Married?" The word squeaked out between Catherine's trembling lips. Had she heard Dylan correctly? "You can't be serious."

"I'm dead serious." His green-blue eyes had lost the mirthfulness and reflected a solemnity that gave her pause. How could he suggest getting married when they'd only just met?

As Austin's cries escalated, she drew the baby back, cradling him and rocking him. It had taken every ounce of inner strength to hold Austin out to Dylan. Now that he was back in her arms, she wasn't sure she'd be able to let him go ever again.

She leaned in and kissed his head, breathing in his sweet, clean scent. Over the past two months of traveling, she'd tried to prepare for today, had warned herself repeatedly not to get attached to the baby. But after being with him night and day, she'd fallen helplessly in love with him. And Austin was just as attached to her. After all, she was the only mother—the only adult, for that matter—the child had known.

Parting ways was even more difficult because it was abundantly clear Dylan didn't want the baby. She didn't want to admit that she'd been abrupt with the news about his paternity because she'd hoped to catch him off guard and shock him so he'd insist on her keeping the baby.

But as with every other time she'd considered traveling all the way to California with Austin, she reminded herself this was what Kit had wanted. For her to deliver Austin to his father so he could raise the child. The baby wasn't hers to keep . . . even though her heart was tearing out of her chest at the prospect of walking away and leaving him with this man.

Now Dylan was suggesting they get married. "I don't understand. Why would you want to get married? You don't know me."

"It's clear the little fella loves you and needs a mother." He nodded at Austin snuggling against her and burying his face in her jacket.

"Isn't your family here? Surely your brothers would be willing to help." She'd read through Kit's journal from start to finish several times, and she'd studied every detail about Dylan, including the mention of his family living here in Colorado.

Dylan's brows arched above his expressive eyes. He seemed to make that particular expression whenever she surprised him, and apparently he hadn't expected her to know about his family living in the area.

Should she show him Kit's journal?

A strange possessiveness wove through Catherine. The journal felt too private to give to a man who'd all but abandoned Kit to face pregnancy and childbirth alone.

"My family's real helpful, but my brothers have their own

families to worry about. They don't need me dumping my mistake on them."

"Mistake?" Her spine stiffened. "Austin isn't a mistake. His life is a precious gift."

"Aw, shucks." Dylan situated his hat back on his wavy brown hair and crossed his arms again. "I didn't mean it that way. 'Course his life is a gift. I just mean, that the"—he cleared his throat—"the way his life came about was the mistake."

At the realization of what Dylan was insinuating, a flush swept into Catherine's cheeks. She didn't get embarrassed often. But when she did, her face turned into a shining red beacon that let the world know just how mortified she was.

Thankfully, Dylan was staring at the floor, twisting the tip of his boot and not paying attention to the color of her face. "Listen, Catherine . . ."

She startled. How did he know her name? Maybe she'd spoken it to Deputy Gunderson when she arrived, and perhaps he'd relayed it to Dylan.

"It is Catherine, isn't it?" He shot a glance at her.

"Yes."

He nodded, then shifted his attention back to the floor. "I want you to know that I'm not the same man I was in Chicago. The day I rode away, I left my old ways behind. I repented of my wild living, and now I'm doing my best to please the Lord and walk in the ways of righteousness."

As she'd thought about Dylan and the stinging lecture she'd wanted to give him for how he'd abandoned Kit, she'd rehearsed many different scenarios and come up with various rebukes in response to his excuses. This heartfelt profession of faith had never been in the mix.

"I apologize for everything that happened," he continued, "and for running off."

At the sincerity of his tone, she had the strange need to say something soothing to him. But just as quickly as the urge came, she squelched it. This man had acted despicably and deserved to feel uncomfortable. Especially after all that had happened to Kit as a result of his negligence. "Thank you for apologizing, but that doesn't change how difficult everything was."

"I know." His shoulders drooped—very broad, muscular shoulders. He was a powerfully built man and exuded an aura of strength and purpose. She'd noticed that from the moment she laid eyes on him. As she studied him more closely now, she had no trouble seeing he was an incredibly handsome man.

Long lashes and dark brows framed his deep-set eyes. His nose had a slight quirk, likely once broken. But his cheeks and jaw and chin were flawlessly chiseled, as if God had perfected the masculine mold with this man. He had crinkle lines at the corners of his eyes and mouth, clearly accustomed to smiling often.

Kit hadn't been exaggerating when she'd described Dylan's good looks. Even so, the young woman had been foolish to give herself to him outside the bounds of marriage. As much as Catherine wanted to lay the blame for all that had happened at Dylan's feet, that wasn't fair. Kit bore responsibility too.

"I can't change the past," Dylan said slowly, as if he were weighing out his words to make each one count. "But I can try my best to be an honorable man moving forward."

She nodded, and she respected him for that. If he'd known

Kit was pregnant, would he have stayed? Or made sure she was taken care of properly? At least he'd apologized and seemed genuinely distressed at the news that the labor hadn't gone well.

Dylan chanced another glance at the baby, as if to validate the child was really his.

"He has your chin. And the same-shaped face."

"Yep. I ain't arguing with you. I can see he's mine."

"Then you'll take him in?"

"As long as you'll stay and be his ma." This time Dylan met her gaze. The sincerity there was difficult to resist. Regardless, she had to protest. She most certainly couldn't marry a complete stranger. Why would he want to? He knew nothing about her.

He held up a hand as though to block her from speaking. "Don't say no. I realize this isn't the order it's supposed to happen. But let me correct my mistake by doing the responsible thing and give you and the boy a good home."

He didn't owe her anything. "I can't—"

"Do you have someplace else to go?"

After two months, she was tired of traveling, of watching over her shoulder and wondering if Rocky was chasing her. She'd taken precautions everywhere she went, especially after she'd caught someone following her during her time in St. Louis. She'd had to sneak away in the middle of the night and had been praying ever since that she'd make it undetected to Denver and now Fairplay.

One thing was certain—she couldn't return to Chicago anytime soon, at least not until she was certain the whole affair had been forgotten and that any harm she'd caused her father's political aspirations had vanished.

She couldn't keep back a weary sigh. "No, I don't have any place to go." And she was running low on funds. The cost of the train and stagecoach tickets, as well as lodging, food, and supplies for Austin, had drained her more rapidly than she'd anticipated.

Almost broke with nowhere left to run, she wanted to stay. Why not remain here in Fairplay and be close to Austin? She could change her identity. Already a few times she'd taken Kit's name and gone by Catherine Olson. Was that too similar? Should she find another name altogether?

"I don't have much," Dylan said. "But I have a little cabin just out back. Reckon we could get by until I have the chance to build us a real house."

Then he was serious about marrying a stranger? She shook her head. The idea was preposterous. Wasn't it?

She supposed it wasn't all that different from the single men and women who advertised in newspaper circulars like *The Matrimonial News* to find a spouse. Such couples often married shortly after meeting for the first time. She had to admit, she'd considered placing an advertisement for herself, wondering if that was the only way she'd find a husband.

He paused, clearly seeing her resistance. "What? You don't want to live in a log cabin?"

"No, that's not it at all." A log cabin would be unusual, but after living in hotel rooms for the past two months, any secure place to call home would suffice. "Getting married to you wasn't part of my plans. What if I served as your housekeeper instead?"

He opened his mouth, then stalled. The office was growing dark with the lengthening shadows. But the surprise in his handsome features was evident enough. "I can understand that you're upset at me. But don't you think it'd be in Austin's best interest if he had both a ma and a pa?"

"I'm sure you'll find someone to settle down with eventually." But did she want some other woman raising Austin in her stead? "You probably already have a woman here."

He closed his mouth. A second later, his lips twitched up, and his eyes crinkled at the corners. "You fishing around to see if I'm single and eligible?"

"No, of course not."

His smile inched up. "Well, you ain't got nothin' to worry about, darlin'. I'm free for the taking."

CHAPTER

5

With him standing there larger than life, all rugged and handsome and charming, flames spread into Catherine's cheeks again. It was becoming clearer with each passing moment why Kit had fallen for this man. Even so, he was a scoundrel for using the young woman, and Catherine couldn't forget it.

"I'm not interested in marrying a womanizer, Mr. Mc-Quaid." She didn't care that her tone was sharp. Surely he couldn't believe himself to be a great catch, not after his indecencies with Kit.

His grin slipped away, replaced by a sudden rigidness to his expression and stance. He dropped his gaze, but not before she witnessed the shame in his eyes.

Oh heavens. What right did she have to condemn and belittle him, especially after he'd apologized and told her he was trying to live rightly now?

Heavy silence settled over the room. Now it was her turn to apologize for being so quick to judge. If God could forgive him for his past mistakes, she needed to as well. It's just that she'd been the one to witness Kit's downfall and death. If Dylan had behaved more responsibly, maybe she'd yet be alive. Before Catherine could formulate the words, a knock sounded against the door and pulsed through the room.

"Widow Fletcher is here." Deputy Gunderson's voice came through the crack in the door. "Tried to send her on her way, but she's having nothing to do with me. Says she has to talk with yous."

Dylan didn't look up. "Tell her I'll swing by her place later, that I have something real special for her."

"Already told her that. But she's insisting on waiting."

Dylan scrubbed a hand over his face. "Alright. Tell her I'll be there in a second."

"Already told her that too."

Dylan lifted his hat, combed his fingers through his hair, and replaced the hat. He straightened his neckerchief, then rested his hands on the handles of both revolvers. "I've gotta go take care of an important matter. Will you promise to wait here for me so we can finish talking?"

As he raised his green-blue eyes, the plea in them was so sincere and his long lashes so beautiful, she wouldn't have been able to resist even if she'd wanted to. "Alright."

He nodded at the chair she'd vacated. "Have a seat, and I'll be back before you can blink."

"I'll wait, Dylan. I want to work this out just as much as you do."

He expelled a long, tense breath, then turned, opened the door, and stepped out. He neglected to close the door all the way, and Catherine crossed to it and peeked outside after him.

The gruff-looking Deputy Gunderson stood next to a

diminutive woman in a red calico skirt and matching bodice, the color so bright she could have been plucked right off a cherry tree. Without a hat, her hair was in disarray, gray curls springing out in all directions.

"There you are, young man." Her voice wobbled and her hands shook as she held them out toward Dylan.

He clasped them, lifted one to his lips, and kissed it. "Now, Mrs. Fletcher, what are you worrying your pretty head about?" Although Catherine couldn't see his expression, she could easily picture the charming smile he'd donned for the older woman.

"I've found evidence of another mouse, Sheriff." The older woman's delicate face creased with anxiety. "It's gotten into my drawers and nibbled on some of my garments. I'll have you know, it's eating my unmentionables."

Deputy Gunderson took a step back and wiped a hand across his mouth as if trying to smother a laugh. Catherine waited for Dylan to chuckle or make light of her problem, certainly not an issue to bring to the attention of the sheriff.

But he didn't laugh. Instead, his tone was serious as he replied, "That's terrible, Mrs. Fletcher. Tell me all about it."

She talked on about the mice droppings and the holes chewed right through her clothing and how she was afraid to sleep at night as a result. All the while, Dylan held her hand and gave her his full attention.

"I tell you what," Dylan said when she finished. "I heard Flynn's got some kittens out at his place that are almost weaned. I'll go on out there this week and bring you back a mouser."

"Would you do that?" Mrs. Fletcher's question held a note of relief.

"'Course I would, darlin'. Anything for you."

The older woman's smile broke free, and she beamed up at Dylan. "Sheriff, you're such a sweetheart. I just don't know what I'd do without you."

"I'm sure you'd get along fine." He stepped over to a horse and flipped open the saddlebag. "I was gonna stop by and give you these. But since you're here now, you may as well get them in water before they wilt."

Catherine's fascination with Dylan was growing by the moment. As he removed a slightly crushed bouquet of colorful wildflowers from the bag and held them out, Mrs. Fletcher's smile broadened, and Catherine's heart melted just a little.

"For me?" The older woman took the array of spring blooms.

"Yep. Just for you."

"They're like the ones Mr. Fletcher used to bring me."

Dylan didn't respond, just hooked his fingers in his belt.

"That Dylan McQuaid is such a peach, isn't he?" came a woman's whisper near Catherine's ear that made her jump. She shifted and found a middle-aged woman peering out the crack in the door beside her.

"Never met a kinder man in all my days." The woman smiled at the unfolding scene and dabbed at the corners of her eyes with a handkerchief.

Catherine took a step back. Who was this newcomer, and where had she come from? With a bun knotted high on her head in the shape of a beehive, the woman wore a simple brown skirt and bodice along with a well-worn grayish apron tied around her thick waist.

"Dylan brings her flowers at least every other day"—the

59

woman continued staring out the door—"just the way Arnie used to before he passed away."

"Why does he do it?" Catherine's attention returned to Dylan, who was walking with Mrs. Fletcher down the street, matching his long stride with her shorter one.

"That's just the way Dylan is. Trying to bring comfort and joy wherever he can."

Catherine couldn't think of another man alive who would pick flowers for an old widow simply to make her happy. Certainly not her father. Whatever he did was calculated to help him in his next political aspiration. Every handshake, every smile, every kind word. Not that he wasn't a kind man. He was. It was just that he rarely did anything without an ulterior motive, including how he interacted with her.

"He's worth more than a million gold nuggets," the woman continued. "Not to mention, he's such a cutie-patootie."

Cutie-patootie? What did that mean?

The woman backed away from the door, braced her hands on her hips, and took in Catherine and Austin, who was sucking at his fist and starting to make more noise, the sure sign he was hungry. She would need the warm water she'd requested from the deputy soon so that she could mix it with the last of the packaged milk she'd purchased in Denver.

"I'm Trudy Gunderson." The woman smiled and held out a hand.

Was this Deputy Gunderson's wife? At the sight of a rear door open a crack, Catherine guessed Trudy had sneaked in that way and caught her spying on Dylan.

"I'm Catherine." She reached for the hand.

Before she could shake it, Trudy gathered her in a big hug. "Welcome to Fairplay." She squeezed and rocked for several seconds too long, then finally let go when Austin let out a cry of protest.

Trudy tickled Austin under the chin. "Now who's the cutie-patootie here?" Her smile was so wide and her presence so full of sunshine that he abruptly stopped his fussing and stared at Trudy's animated face.

"This is Austin."

"He's just as fine looking as his daddy." Trudy spoke with high-pitched baby talk. "Aren't you, you sweet little plum pudding?"

And how did Trudy know this was Dylan's son? When Catherine had walked over to the courthouse after arriving on the stage, Deputy Gunderson had been adamant that she couldn't see Dylan—until she'd gotten peeved enough and spilled the nature of her visit. He'd likely already guessed it by the family resemblance, since he hadn't shown any surprise at her news. Now, it appeared he'd already shared it with his wife. How long before the whole town knew?

Trudy babbled some baby talk for several more seconds before she halted abruptly and homed in on her. "Stu said you're here to make a man of Dylan?"

"A man of Dylan?" Catherine stumbled over the words.

"Yes, I admire you for coming all this way and asking Dylan to take care of you and the baby."

"Oh, I wasn't intending—"

"Knowing Dylan as I do, he'll learn to be a good daddy. You just need to give him the chance."

"I will. But—"

"And he'll be such a good husband. The best a girl could ask for."

"I'm not so sure about that. Dylan is quite the rogue."

Catherine blurted the words in her rush to say a full sentence without Trudy cutting her off. Somehow the declaration came out louder than Catherine had intended.

Trudy's smile faded, and her mouth and eyes rounded.

Apparently Dylan had already won the heart of every woman in the West, and saying anything negative about him was liable to get her hanged on the nearest tree.

"What I meant to say is that I don't understand why he never wrote back when he learned about the pregnancy."

"Dylan hasn't gotten any letters. And let me tell you something, dear. If he had, I would have known, because Trudy Gunderson makes it her business to know everything about everyone here in Fairplay." The middle-aged woman patted Catherine's cheek as if the news that she was the town meddler was supposed to be comforting. "Now, you listen here, and you listen good. Dylan McQuaid cares. That man cares more than anyone else I know. And if you give him a chance to prove it, he will."

What could Catherine possibly say to that?

Austin's fussing started up again. Thankfully, Trudy set aside the matter about her marrying Dylan and assisted her in finding warm water and making Austin's bottle. By the time Catherine was sitting in the desk chair feeding the baby, Dylan stepped back inside.

Trudy was hovering over her, and at the sight of Dylan she straightened and beamed at him. "Dylan McQuaid. You sure do know how to make a handsome son."

Dylan halted in the doorway, reaching a hand backward and gripping the door handle as though he wanted to retreat as fast as he could. He took a deep breath and then seemed to force himself to look at the baby.

Trudy poked Catherine's shoulder. "Catherine, why don't you let Dylan take a turn feeding his son?"

She held the infant a little tighter. "Oh, I don't know. Austin might get frightened."

"He's doing fine without me," Dylan said at the same time.

Trudy glanced between them, her brow furrowing. "Oh no. The two of you need to learn to work together. Now, Catherine, stand up. Let's go." The woman prodded again, giving Catherine little choice but stand up.

Once the chair was vacant, Trudy looked at Dylan and pointed to it. "Sit."

He didn't have enough backbone to resist Trudy's antics either, and a few moments later he was seated in the chair and holding the baby awkwardly while feeding him the bottle.

Austin's eyes widened at the sight of the strange man, and his bottom lip wobbled.

"You best talk to the baby before he cries." Trudy stood over Dylan's shoulder, every bit like a mother hen, clucking and bossing and making things happen the way she thought they needed to be done.

Dylan swallowed, his eyes as round as Austin's. "Hi there, little fella."

Austin paused in sucking, taking in the greeting from his father.

"He likes the sound of your voice." Trudy tried for a whisper, but her voice was filled with too much excitement. "Keep talking to him."

Dylan nodded, as though Trudy's advice was the lifeline keeping him from drowning. "How are you, little fella? Looks like you're mighty hungry."

By the time Austin finished the bottle, he didn't seem to

mind Dylan holding him. In fact, he almost seemed to be enjoying Dylan's ongoing dialogue, prompted by Trudy. And Dylan had begun to lose the cornered-rabbit look, was relaxing, and even offered the baby a smile.

Standing awkwardly beside the desk, Catherine wanted to be happy, knew she should be happy. But the interaction only filled her with dread. Kit had been right. And so had Trudy. Dylan would make a good father.

Had she secretly hoped he'd be degenerate, despicable, and disgusting so she'd have no choice but to take Austin away from him and make the child hers? Had she wanted him to cast Austin and her out, giving her the liberty she needed to make a life of her own without him in it?

But Dylan hadn't done any of those things. In fact, with each passing moment, she admired him even more. And she knew she couldn't run off with Austin. Was her best option to accept the proposal of marriage and stay?

What would her parents say? She'd sent a note home with her driver, Slim, before she'd boarded her train, not wanting them to worry overly much. Of course she hadn't told them where she was going just in case Rocky decided to search for her. She'd written to them again from Missouri. But she hadn't since then, and she wasn't sure when it would be safe to pen another letter.

Would they be relieved someone finally wanted to marry her? Or would this kind of marriage of convenience only cause her father more scandal?

"Now, lift him up against your shoulder." Trudy hefted the baby for Dylan, positioning him against Dylan's shoulder. "You need to pat his little back just right and get the bubbles out."

"Bubbles?" Dylan held Austin gingerly.

"Yes." Trudy repositioned the baby at his shoulder. "Dontcha know babies have bubbles in their tummies? And if you don't take good care of getting those bubbles out, you'll have all sorts of fussiness. Isn't that right, you cutie-patootie?"

Dylan's handsome face was as serious as if Trudy had told him Austin was liable to catch measles if he didn't get burped correctly. As Dylan gave a thump that was so soft it wouldn't have made a dent in a pillow, Catherine couldn't keep from smiling.

Trudy zeroed in on the smile, as though she'd been waiting for it. "Aren't they precious?" She beamed at Catherine like a proud grandmother.

"Yes." Catherine couldn't deny the beauty of seeing Austin with his father, even if the sight made her heart ache.

At her one-word admission, Dylan glanced at her, guarded, as if prepared for more bitter accusations and reminders of his mistakes.

She still needed to apologize for her unkind words from earlier. The least she could do now was offer him some encouragement. "I'm sure it won't take long for Austin to learn to like his daddy. He's already off to a good start."

Dylan's shoulders seemed to relax a little. "You don't think he's scared of me?"

"Not anymore." Austin was definitely comfortable, apparently sensing a connection with Dylan.

"Okey dokey." Trudy's smile widened, and she started toward the door. "I guess that means it's time to move things along."

Out the window, Fairplay's main thoroughfare was growing busier. The waft of roasting meat of some kind indicated the supper hour was fast approaching. Catherine needed to get a room in a hotel for the night before darkness fell.

Trudy threw open the door. "Stu?" she shouted outside.

A terse "What?" came from nearby.

"Go track down Father Zieber. Tell him to meet us at the church in an hour for a wedding."

"In an hour?" Stu's call back echoed Catherine's response.

"Yes, an hour."

"Oh criminy. My stomach's rumbling. We can have the wedding after supper."

"You get on out of here." Trudy planted her hands on her hips, and her expression said she wasn't about to take any nonsense from the grouchy old deputy. "Your stomach can just hush up and wait until after the wedding."

"What if it doesn't want to wait?"

"Stuart Gunderson." Her tone turned ominous. "You get on to finding the reverend. We're having the wedding first, and that's all I have to say about it." With that, Trudy spun and scanned Dylan from head to toe. "You got a clean suit?"

"Yes, ma'am."

"Then go wash up and put it on."

Trudy then turned toward Catherine and smiled. "Now you and Austin come along with me to our house. I've always wanted a daughter I could help get ready for her wedding. And today, God's giving me my chance."

Catherine took a rapid step back, bumping into a bookcase and knocking over a bottle of ink and a pen. She grabbed the items and tried to right them only to tip them over again. "I beg your pardon, but this is moving much too fast."

"Nonsense. This wedding is long overdue." Trudy looked

at the baby as if to make her point. "Besides, the quicker you two get married, the less gossip and damage this will do to Dylan's position as sheriff and his chances at getting reelected come August."

Catherine wanted to blurt out that she didn't care what damage came to Dylan's position as sheriff, that he should have thought of the repercussions before he'd slept with Kit. But she pressed her lips together before she said something else she'd need to apologize for later.

Dylan shoved back from his chair and stood, fumbling with Austin. Catherine quickly rescued the baby, gathering Austin close.

"Trudy, darlin'." Dylan tipped up his hat and gave her a slow grin, one that could charm the rattle out of a rattlesnake. "I think me and Catherine need a few minutes to talk."

The older woman crossed her arms. "Go ahead."

His smile only grew wider and more irresistible. "Privately."

Under the warmth of his eyes, Trudy started toward the door, the stubborn set of her mouth melting away. "Okey dokey. But I'm only giving you five minutes. Then I'm taking Catherine, and we're going to get ready for the wedding."

After Trudy stepped outside and closed the door behind her, Catherine released a tense breath.

Dylan stared at the door like a man who'd just been condemned to jail.

"I'm sorry for what I said earlier." She blurted the words before she lost the courage. "I shouldn't have thrown your past mistakes at you. You're not entirely to blame for what happened—"

"I was living a reckless and foolish life. And I am to

blame." Dylan's expression turned serious, his eyes just as handsome now as they were when he was charming. "The right thing to do all around is for me to marry you."

She liked that he was willing to take the blame for all that had happened, but still, marrying her just so he could have a mother for his son was a big step. "But I don't know much about you, and you know absolutely nothing about me."

"I know you love Austin. That's enough."

Was it enough?

"Plenty of folks get married for the sake of giving their children both a ma and a pa," he continued. "We won't be the first."

"You're right." How could she turn down this opportunity to become Austin's mother? It's what she wanted more than anything. She wouldn't have to leave him. And she wouldn't have to worry about where to go next.

This remote town up in the mountains of Colorado was as good a place to hide as any. She'd be far away from the murder accusations. No one would ever have to know about it.

"And in case you're worried"—Dylan scratched at the layer of stubble on his jaw—"I won't pressure you . . . for, well, you know."

For a heartbeat, she could only stare at him, trying to make sense of his cryptic comment. When he glanced at her with a look that lingered on her mouth, mortification flooded her. Oh, heaven help her. He was talking about the physical aspect of their relationship. She hadn't considered that far ahead.

He cleared his throat. "Ever since leaving Chicago, I've been celibate. I vowed I'd never again use a woman for selfish reasons, and I intend to keep that vow even in a marriage."

She had to say something. But what was appropriate for this extremely awkward conversation? "That's very noble of you." Once the words were out, she wanted to slap her forehead.

He was quiet for a moment, which only seemed to magnify the noise from the street outside—the rattle of a passing wagon and the plodding of horse hooves. "Well, that's all. I just wanted to assure you that after we're married, I won't be trying to get you into bed."

She pressed her face into Austin, hoping to hide the heat radiating there. She'd met other women, particularly widows with children, who remarried for practical purposes. Even in partnerships without love, those women didn't shirk their marital duty. Catherine had been told by more than one such woman that the blessing of childbearing made the discomfort of the marriage bed worthwhile.

She understood their comments much better after having Austin in her care these past two months. She'd loved finally getting to enjoy the baby and not just the birthing. And now, she wanted to have more. In fact, she wanted a houseful of children, Lord willing. If she had any hope of that dream coming true, she would have to sleep with her husband at some point. But if Dylan was on a mission to prove himself a changed man and would give her some time, then she wouldn't object.

He cleared his throat again. "I hope you understand that after doing things all wrong in the past, I want to refrain and show you respect."

"Yes, of course." Had he read her mind? She hadn't displayed any hesitation, had she? After all, she didn't want to send him the wrong message that she was interested in sleeping with him.

"Good." The relief in his voice should have assured her, but it set her on edge. What if he didn't want to have additional children? Should they talk about that before getting married?

The very thought of having such a discussion with him mortified her, but she pushed forward as delicately as possible. "It's only natural that we take time to get to know each other before we pursue—having more children."

His gaze jerked up to hers. "More children?"

"Yes. Not right away. But at some point." She lifted her chin even though she was sure her face was brighter than Mrs. Fletcher's cherry-red garments.

He seemed to contemplate her words, almost as if debating within himself. "Alright. I'm sure we can manage that."

Austin wiggled in her arms, releasing an unhappy wail. But it was a welcome distraction from the conversation. "His diaper cloth is due for a change."

The door swung wide to reveal Trudy. "You can change the baby when we get to my house." The woman's rounded eyes bounced back and forth between the two of them. No doubt she'd heard every word of their conversation.

Catherine wished the floor could open up and swallow her. But from the way Trudy latched on to her arm, she doubted the woman would let her disappear even if the floor did open.

"Come on with you." Trudy tugged her toward the door. "It's time to get ready for your wedding."

CHAPTER

6

Dylan stood at the front of the chapel and tugged at the top button of his shirt and then at the bow tie. If the shirt didn't strangle him first, the tie would.

"Oh, for crying out loud." Standing beside him, Stu shoved his arm. "Stop your fidgeting, or I'll drag yous out to the nearest watering trough and give yous a dunking."

Dylan dropped his hands to his sides. "I'm just hot. That's all."

Five glowing candles in the candelabra next to the pulpit illuminated the church, including the dust and spiderwebs Father Zieber was busily wiping away from a corner in the ceiling. The elegant silver candlestand was a fairly new addition to the church decor that the Ladies Guild, headed by Mrs. Fletcher, had donated just for weddings and holidays. At least that's what Father Zieber had declared as he'd lit the candles.

"You sure you're ready to take this step, Dylan?" The minister paused in collecting cobwebs. "Marriage is a covenant, and not to be entered into lightly."

"I should have married her before I slept with her and had a child with her. And since I didn't, I'm rectifying that now." Dylan glanced again to the door and then to the darkness out the windows. Trudy had said an hour. And it had been longer than that. Where were they? Had Catherine changed her mind?

He could admit the news of a son had thrown him off guard. He was still uncomfortable with the prospect of having a family. But now that he knew he was a father, he wasn't gonna shrug off his duty. The sooner he married Catherine, the sooner he could assume responsibility.

"Maybe we should consult Flynn or Wyatt?" The reverend was tall and burly with graying hair. He'd been the traveling preacher in the South Park area for as long as Dylan could remember. "In fact, if we wait for the wedding until tomorrow, we can invite them to attend."

"No, Father. I'm getting married tonight. And that's all there is to it."

As much as Dylan respected the kindly man, he didn't want his brothers—or anyone else in the community—involved yet. Truth was, he'd be able to face everyone better if he was already well on his way to cleaning up the mess he'd made.

"I've joked with your brothers and Ivy about their hasty marriages." Father Zieber eyed the opposite corner of the one-room church building. More spiderwebs dangled there. "Even if they've had wonderful success and wedded bliss, I still don't recommend rushing into marriage."

"I'm not rushing." Dylan arched his neck and plucked at his tie again, earning another jab from Stu. "As I said before. This is long overdue."

"So you know her well?"

"Well enough." Dylan tried to recall any conversations he'd had with Catherine when he'd been living in Chicago. But honestly, his mind was as blank as a six-shooter without bullets. He could've passed her on the street and wouldn't have recognized her. But it didn't matter. She was the mother of his son. And he was marrying her.

Father Zieber made his way to the next offending cobweb. With only six pews on either side of the center aisle, the church was usually full to overflowing each Sunday. "It might be a good idea to learn a little bit about her past. And her faith."

"She's a fine woman, from a fine family." From the little he remembered, her father had been an upstanding citizen. "It's not like she's a criminal running from the law."

"Very well." The minister swiped the last of the sagging webs, shook out his handkerchief, and then stuffed it back into his pocket. "I trust that you'll make it your mission to love your wife the way Christ instructed?"

"Didn't realize Christ had instructions for me." Dylan wanted to tug at his shirt again, but at Stu's glare, he stuffed his hands into his pockets.

"Yes." Father Zieber reached for the broom beside the door and began to sweep the floor. "The Bible most certainly has advice for how husbands are to love their wives."

Dylan had watched his brothers with their wives. They'd all set good examples for loving and respecting women. Even so, he reckoned he still had a heap to learn. "Maybe we can sit down soon and you can fill me in on the advice."

"I'd love to." Father Zieber had made time for him often over the past months, stopping whatever he was doing every occasion Dylan showed up at his home with one question or another about how to live for the Lord.

"Yous want advice?" Stu smoothed down his mustache then ran his fingers through his scraggly beard. "I got one thing to say."

Dylan snorted. "Sure. Let me have it. Your best piece of advice."

"Keep your woman happy."

"That's it?"

It was Stu's turn to snort. "It's a lot harder than it sounds. I'll have you know, some days it's near impossible."

Dylan fought back a grin. Before he could formulate a response, the door opened and Trudy breezed through.

Stu scowled. "It's about time, woman!"

"Now, Stu Gunderson"—Trudy patted her towering bun—"don't you go getting your trousers in a tizzy."

He grumbled under his breath.

"You'll be happy to know I've got a big wedding feast cooking on the stove, and you'll get to eat just as soon as we're done here."

Just as Trudy finished speaking, Catherine stepped hesitantly inside carrying Austin. She wore an elegant light blue gown that seemed to shimmer in the candlelight. The scooped bodice dipped low, revealing her slender neck and an expanse of creamy skin. The gown fit snugly, outlining an ample womanly form that tapered into a slender waist. Her dark hair was pulled up into curls that only added to her charm. She was as lovely a bride as he'd ever seen. In fact, she was a lovely lady in every sense of the word.

Dylan had the urge to whistle his appreciation of the fine picture she made. But he clamped his jaw tight and fought against lusting after her. He knew his weaknesses, and one of his biggest was the desire of his flesh. He'd always given in to his need to chase after women. Even when he'd been just a youth traveling west by wagon with his family, he'd relished every opportunity to get alone with a pretty girl so he could steal kisses.

In the years after arriving in South Park and living on Wyatt's ranch as a cowhand, his chasing after women had only increased, and he hadn't been satisfied with just kissing. When he'd fallen in love with Bethina, he'd thought maybe he'd be able to settle down with her. He tried to respect her, had wanted to keep the physical aspect of their relationship pure until he married her. But it had been a real struggle. He'd messed up and kissed another girl at a dance. And that's all it had taken for Bethina to leave him behind. After she moved, he'd had no trouble giving up the rest of his morals—what remained of them.

Trudy bustled forward, hurrying Catherine down the aisle. "Why, Dylan McQuaid, dontcha make a fine sight, all spiffy in your suit."

He straightened his shoulders and puffed out his chest. "Of course I do. That's the only thing this suit is good for. Making a man look handsome."

Trudy positioned Catherine beside him in front of the podium and took the babe from her, insisting that Austin wanted Gramma Trudy—which apparently was the new nickname she'd given herself.

At the wide, happy smile on Trudy's face, Dylan bit back a teasing comment. Trudy and Stu didn't have any children or grandchildren of their own. And Trudy wasn't shy about sharing how difficult her barrenness had been. Now that she was past her childbearing years, she seemed to have made peace with not being able to have children. But watching her with the infant, he could tell she missed having little ones in her life.

"Father Zieber," Dylan said, "this is Catherine."

"Welcome, my dear." The minister shook hands with her.

She smiled politely—if not a little stiffly. Was she having second thoughts about going through with this?

Dylan cocked his head at the babe. "And that little fella is my son, Austin."

Father Zieber peered down at the child and smiled. "He looks just like you, Dylan."

The infant made a noise, almost as if he were agreeing.

"How has motherhood treated you thus far?" Father Zieber turned his attention back to Catherine.

"Austin is a very sweet baby."

Stu rocked back on his heels. "Guess he takes after yous and not his father."

"Hey now." Dylan grinned at his deputy. "I'm a whole heap sweeter than you."

"I'd be a lot sweeter if my wife let me eat once in a while."

"Now, Stu." Trudy leveled a withering glare at the man. "I told you already. I've got a feast waiting at home, including your favorite—plum pudding."

Stu nodded at Father Zieber. "What are we waiting for? Let's get this wedding over with."

Father Zieber hesitated, as though he aimed to talk with Catherine longer. But Dylan was relieved when he started the ceremony. He didn't need the minister prying, discovering concerns, and convincing them to postpone the wedding. And he didn't want to risk Catherine changing her mind.

He just wanted to be done with the whole thing almost as much as Stu did.

Thankfully, Father Zieber kept the wedding to the basics, and within minutes they were stating their vows and Dylan was slipping on a ring, the one that had been Ma's when Pa had been alive.

He'd never told any of his family that he'd taken it from Ma's drawer after her death. No one else had seemed to care what became of Ma's few possessions. Maybe they'd been too busy or too preoccupied. But Dylan had cared that it had been the ring Pa had given to Ma when they'd said their vows.

Dylan had always loved watching Pa and Ma interact, especially just how tender his pa had treated her, like he was living out his vows every single day. That made the ring something special. And Dylan had kept it all through the years, intending to give it to his bride on his wedding day.

'Course, after getting his life turned back around, he'd sworn off women, at least for quite a while. But now that he was doing the responsible thing for once in his life, he saw no reason not to give Catherine the ring.

As she lifted her hand to examine the silver band, it slid around, a mite big on her finger. "The seed pearl daisy at the center is beautiful."

"Daisies were my ma's favorite flower."

"Then this was your ma's wedding ring?"

He nodded. "Yep. And now it's yours."

She examined it a moment longer before she lifted her gaze. For the first time since she'd arrived, the coldness was gone, and warmth turned her eyes a light woodsy green. "Thank you. But I don't feel as though I deserve it."

Was she embarrassed by her mistakes too? "None of us are deserving. Right, Father?"

"Right. But fortunately for us, we have a God whose love is so great that nothing we do could ever separate us from Him."

Regardless of so great a promise, Dylan still never felt worthy of God's forgiveness and love. With all that he'd done wrong and the way he'd lived, he couldn't imagine ever feeling free of the guilt and shame. It was his cross to bear, a heavy reminder not to wander again.

"Now," Father Zieber continued, "for as much as Dylan and Catherine have consented together in holy wedlock and have witnessed the same before God and this company, and thereto have given and pledged their troth either to other, and have declared the same by giving and receiving of a ring and by joining of hands, I pronounce that they be man and wife together. In the name of the Father, of the Son, and of the Holy Ghost. Amen."

"Amen." Dylan bowed his head. He prayed God would help him be a good husband and pa, even if he was only half the man his own pa had been.

Father Zieber closed his prayer book. "That's it."

"Lovely." Trudy's eyes filled with tears. "The two of you are just lovely."

Catherine stared at the ring again as though trying to grasp the fact that she was married.

Dylan tried for a smile. But suddenly he couldn't keep from feeling like he was on a bucking bronc and trying to hang on. He wasn't worthy of marrying anyone. He didn't have what it took to be a father. What if he made more mistakes? Big ones? He'd not only hurt himself, but he'd hurt his family.

As the doubts crowded in, he scrambled to thrust them from his mind. After all, what was done was done. Now there was no way to get out of the predicament—another reason he'd needed to get married tonight, so he wouldn't tuck tail and run.

Stu grunted and started to head away. "Let's go eat."

"Now hold on right there, mister," Trudy called. "This wedding isn't over yet."

Stu paused and rolled his eyes. "What now?"

"Dylan needs to kiss his bride."

Catherine took a rapid step back, only to have Trudy give her a gentle push that sent her stumbling against Dylan. He had little choice but to catch her, settling his hands on her hips. Even so, her chest bumped against his. The softness of her womanly form pressed up against him and sent a jolt of heat right through him.

He needed to release her. Fast.

Her cheeks reddened. Regardless of her embarrassment, she rested her hands on his arms and made no move to free herself.

His pulse gave a dangerous stutter. Did she want a kiss?

"Don't you agree, Father?" Trudy said. "A wedding isn't a wedding without a kiss."

"I heartily agree." Father Zieber clamped Dylan on the shoulder. "May as well do this right."

Catherine looked straight ahead at the button below his bow tie and nibbled at her bottom lip. Her very full, rounded, pink, kissable lip.

The heat swirled through him faster. Boy howdy. His desires had lain dormant these many months. And he was afraid if he awakened them, he wouldn't be able to hold himself at bay. He had to remain celibate for the time being and prove to them both that he was a changed man and wasn't using her for his own needs anymore. She deserved that.

When she chanced a glance up to his face, he cocked his brow, giving her the opportunity to object, to step away, even to slap his face if she wanted to.

But she simply dropped her attention back to his button and caught her lower lip between her teeth again.

He swallowed hard. He'd let himself kiss her. Just one kiss to seal their vows. Then he'd go right back to being chaste. That's what he'd do.

She'd been the last woman he held and kissed before leaving Chicago. Maybe it was fitting she was the last one he'd ever hold and kiss again.

With a final squeeze on his shoulder from Father Zieber, Dylan took that as his cue to finish up. He angled toward her lips.

She parted them slightly, as though readying herself. And as he drew near, she sucked in a breath and held herself motionless, acting as if she'd never before kissed a man and had no idea what to do.

That wasn't the case. The babe she'd birthed was proof she wasn't innocent anymore . . . of course, because of him. Guilt threatened to rise, but he pushed it down for now. They were man and wife, and he had the reverend's, Trudy's, even God's permission to kiss Catherine.

He bent the remaining distance, hovered above her for an instant, then gently captured her mouth. Just a quick kiss. That's all he needed to give her.

As he closed his eyes and let his lips move, she didn't respond. Once more, he had the feeling she didn't know anything about kissing. After a moment of letting him explore, she pressed back—moving against him so softly and earnestly that it sent a strange, new energy into his blood, an energy he'd never experienced before and one he didn't understand. All he knew was that kissing this woman was exquisitely delicious and perfect.

"Oh, criminy. Save it for later." Stu's caustic comment cut into Dylan's haze. "I don't have all night to watch you going at it with your wife."

Catherine quickly broke away, her lips and the soft pressure of her body falling away from his. She turned toward Trudy, but not before he caught sight of her flustered hands and flushed cheeks.

His fingers lingered on her hips, relishing the curves. He wanted to draw her back, not nearly sated or satisfied. His blood pumped swiftly, heat pulsing throughout his body. The heat of need. Selfish need.

Shucks.

He let go of her and stuffed his hands into his trouser pockets. Here he was, only one tiny kiss into his marriage, and already he was acting like his old promiscuous self.

"It was a very nice kiss, if I do say so myself." Trudy patted Catherine's cheek, and the young woman—his wife—ducked her head and then pressed her fingers to her lips, as if attempting to make sense of the kiss.

The sight of her fingertips brushing her lips only sent a stab of desire into him. Desire to feel those lips against his again, to test another kiss, to discover if the next one would be as delicious as the first.

Nope. He wasn't gonna dwell on it, had to think of something else. Quick-like. "Thank you, Father." He reached for

Father Zieber's hand and shook it. "Thanks for being willing to come out tonight and perform the ceremony."

"You're welcome, Dylan." The reverend clasped Dylan's hand firmly. "I have every confidence you'll be a godly husband and father."

Good thing Father Zieber believed in him because Dylan didn't have much confidence in himself.

"You're coming to the wedding feast, Father Zieber." Trudy repositioned the sleeping babe in her arms. "I won't take no for an answer."

"I wish I could." Father Zieber stepped over to the candelabra and began to blow out the candles. "I do love your plum pudding. But I have a previous commitment, a baptism."

Dylan tried to focus on Father Zieber and Trudy's conversation, but his attention shifted to Catherine as she tucked in a loose edge of Austin's blanket. As if sensing his perusal, she slanted a look at him, her gaze landing square upon his lips. It wasn't the bold gaze of a practiced woman. Instead it was shy and curious . . . and interested?

Oh, blast it all.

He tore his sights away. He'd gone so long without a woman that now he was just imagining things. Wasn't he?

With a shake of his head, he started after Stu. Either way, he had to squelch his desires before they could grow.

CHAPTER

7

Catherine stood aside while Dylan carried her carpetbag and leather satchel into the cabin. The dwelling wasn't far from the main street, and the night noises of the town wafted their way—the lively piano music from a saloon, laughter, and loud voices arguing good-naturedly.

"Sorry it's so messy," Dylan called from inside as a chair clattered to the floor. "But I didn't expect to have visitors tonight."

Visitors? She wasn't a visitor. She was his wife.

A shiver wound up her backbone as it had every time she considered what she'd done. She'd married a stranger. She'd forever linked her life to that of Dylan McQuaid. And now, nothing or no one could sever that tie. For better or worse, they were married.

All throughout the wedding supper at the Gundersons', she'd wavered between disbelief and dismay at her impulsiveness. Normally she planned everything carefully. But ever since the accusation of murder and making the rash decision to run away from Chicago, she'd jumped from one hasty choice to the next.

From now on, she had to settle down and regain a sense of order to her life.

"Come on in," Dylan called as a light sprang to life inside the cabin.

She stared through the open doorway, a lantern revealing the clothing and shoes strewn over the floor, along with newspapers, coffee mugs and plates, keys, ropes, and who knew what else.

Dylan was in the process of standing the chair upright in front of a table—the only chair from the looks of things. A stove took up one corner with the table positioned close to it. On the opposite side was an unmade bed with her bags deposited on the end. A simple—but small—chest of drawers formed a bedside table.

She'd never been in a log cabin before. The dark wood combined with just one window added to the shadows. Several rafter beams crossed above the room, and the gabled roof rose to a low ceiling.

Grabbing a handful of kindling from a woodbox, Dylan crouched in front of the stove and opened it. "Make yourself at home. I don't have much, but I'm sure I can scrounge up anything you need for yourself or Austin."

"Yes, I can let you know." She'd likely need quite a bit. More diaper cloths, milk, new clothing to replace what he'd outgrown. Eventually he'd require a crib. For now, he'd have to continue sleeping with her. "Or perhaps I can do a little shopping of my own. If there's a general store in town?"

"Yep. Simpkins General Store. Across the street and about halfway down." Dylan's suit coat stretched tight, outlining his broad back and shoulders. He was incredibly handsome in the suit, so much so that Catherine could finally empathize with the few pages in Kit's journal where she'd gushed over Dylan's good looks and how swoon-worthy he was.

Catherine had tried not to glance at Dylan during the meal, but her mind kept going back to their wedding kiss, no matter how hard she attempted to stay on the topic at hand. It had been her first kiss. And it had been soft and sweet and everything she'd ever dreamed a kiss would be.

Although his kiss had sent tingles all throughout her body and made her want to continue kissing him, she couldn't keep from thinking that he was an expert kisser because he'd been with other women. She wasn't his first the same way he was hers. And that thought was unsettling, although she didn't know why it should be.

Thankfully, amidst the awkwardness, Trudy had no trouble carrying on a steady stream of conversation—most of it revolving around local matters. She'd seemed all too eager to discuss the personal history of every resident of the town, including hers and Stu's.

Catherine had learned that the Gundersons had moved to Fairplay last autumn from Denver after discovering that the town had need of a morgue. Before coming to Colorado during the gold rush, they'd lived in Minnesota, where they'd both grown up and gotten married.

Apparently Stu's work as a mortician wasn't entirely demanding since people weren't dying every day. So when the position of a part-time deputy had opened up, he'd taken it.

The couple of times the conversation had turned to her, Catherine had steered it away. She couldn't tell everyone that her father was Paul Remington, a prominent alderman in

Chicago, especially with the accusations of murder hanging over her head. Maybe at some point she could be more honest about her background and what had happened. But for now, she needed to be vague.

When she'd stated that things had ended rather abruptly with her family and that they wouldn't be involved in her life anymore, Trudy had patted her hand and said, "It's okay, honey. Dontcha worry your little head. We'll be your new family now."

The wedding feast had been surprisingly delicious, even though Catherine hadn't been familiar with some of Trudy's "hot dishes" as she called them. Of course, Stu had hardly spoken a word, too focused on consuming his meal to engage in small talk.

Now, as she took in Dylan's long, lean outline in his suit again, her stomach gave an anxious flutter. How was she, simple and plain Catherine Remington, married to such a good-looking man? He was the type who could have any woman he wanted—beautiful, ravishing, and exciting women. He'd get tired of pragmatic, boring old her. Eventually he'd realize she was tedious the same way Chester Jones and the three suitors before him had.

She should have insisted on remaining Dylan's housekeeper. Why had she agreed to this marriage scheme? There was a reason she was still single at age twenty-two.

As Austin lifted a hand out of his blanket and reached for her face, she dropped her attention to him. His beautiful eyes, surrounded by long lashes, peered up at her. Love flooded her heart, and she kissed his balled fist.

This was why she'd married Dylan. So she could stay with Austin and be his mother. She couldn't forget it. The marriage had nothing to do with how handsome and charming Dylan was, and she couldn't let herself worry about what he thought of her in return.

Flames crackled to life in the stove, and Dylan added a log. "You're gonna be surprised at how much regular stuff we have up here in Fairplay. It might be a ways up here in the mountains, but the teamsters haul everything up the passes from Denver on a regular basis."

"That's good to know." She tiptoed farther into the room, careful not to step on something, which was difficult since his belongings were strewn everywhere. "Austin's in need of additional supplies."

"Anything, darlin'. You name it. I'll get it for him. And I'll get anything for you too."

He was a genuinely kind man, and that quality was almost as attractive as his physical appearance. "Thank you, Dylan. I wasn't expecting you to be so kind." The second she spoke, she wanted to retract her statement, since it was another reminder of his abandonment of Kit and Austin.

Dylan poked at the fire, the flames casting a golden hue over him. He stared ahead, his expression turning somber.

"I'm sorry. I shouldn't have said that." She wished she had better control over her tongue. On occasion, she was too forthright and let her emotions show too easily. She supposed it was a natural influence from outspoken parents. "I'm just learning so much about you today that I didn't know."

"You got every right to be mad—"

"No, I don't."

"It's understandable."

"Let's just put the past behind us and move forward, shall we?"

He stood and faced her, brushing kindling from his hands. "It's what I've been trying to do since coming back here. But I guess sometimes the past needs to catch up so we can take responsibility for it."

Once again, she appreciated his humility and willingness to accept his mistakes and make amends. "Not every man would so readily do what you've done today. In fact, I never anticipated your proposal, thought I would have to figure out where to go next."

"I admit, this is gonna take some adjusting to." He glanced out the still-open door to the courthouse across the yard. "Once word gets around town that I had a child out of wedlock, people'll question whether I'm fit to be sheriff."

"Do you think your position is in jeopardy?"

"My competitor in the upcoming election, a fella by the name of Harlan Hatfield, is sure gonna use this to show that I ain't respectable enough for sheriff." He hooked his fingers around his revolvers, something he seemed to do when he felt threatened. "He's already doing his best to drag up my past. And some folks hereabouts hold it against me and are just waiting for me to fail."

She was half-guilty of expecting the same from him. Chagrined, she focused on Austin. "How will your family take the news?"

"Reckon they won't be all that surprised." His tone dropped with discouragement. "But I'm hoping they'll understand that in spite of my mistakes, I'm doing my best to make up for them."

He didn't say so, but she suspected his plea was directed toward her as much as his family. "If I can see your efforts, I'm sure they will too."

He nodded, stared outside a moment longer, and then returned his attention to Austin with a sigh. "I need to make the rounds, show my presence around town. Will you be alright?"

"Oh, yes." She glanced at the mess.

He followed her gaze. "Again, sorry it's not in better shape. I'll pick up later when I get back."

"We'll be just fine." She'd get Austin settled, then she'd tidy the place. In the process, she'd take stock of the supplies she needed to turn this hovel into a home.

Several hours later, she plopped into a chair with an unladylike *oomph*. Exhaustion burned along her nerve endings, the same kind of exhaustion she often felt after overseeing a birthing—a good feeling tinged with the satisfaction of the accomplishment.

She'd managed to clean and organize everything with the supplies she'd located in the shed behind the cabin. Not only had she scrubbed the place from floor to ceiling, but she'd attacked the stove until it sparkled, cleaned the window, polished the furniture, and washed every last dish and cup. She'd neatly tucked any of Dylan's clothing that looked clean into the bedside drawers and hung coats on the pegs behind the door.

The only thing she hadn't accomplished was laundry, which she'd decided to do in the morning. She'd paid to have her garments laundered in Denver during her brief stay. But now she'd gathered a sizable stack needing to be washed, including the bedsheets, towels, and a number of Dylan's garments, in addition to Austin's diapers and clothing. Although she'd never done laundry before, she'd noticed the washboard and tub in the shed and wanted to learn how to use them.

The shed also contained an assortment of furniture she guessed belonged to the cabin and courthouse. She'd dragged in a chair identical to the one already there, along with another set of drawers, where she unpacked Austin's and her meager clothing items.

She'd wanted to haul in a kitchen cabinet that contained an odd assortment of cookware and baking supplies. But the piece was too heavy, and she would need Dylan's assistance with it. She was tempted to ask him to help her when he got home, but the hour was getting late.

She glanced to the window covered with a simple piece of cheerful yellow calico she'd found in the drawer. A matching yellow tablecloth was now spread over the table with an empty jar in the center awaiting a pretty arrangement of flowers of some kind.

The circular braided rug she'd positioned in front of the stove was a mixture of blue, green, and yellow. And the rectangular rug she'd laid down beside the bed was a matching version.

The darkness of the Colorado night didn't give her any indication of what time it was. But she guessed it was well past midnight. She was used to staying up all night for deliveries. More times than not, babies decided to begin their entries into the world at nighttime rather than during the day.

She always seemed to gain a burst of energy when darkness fell, a burst she rarely felt in the morning, which had made the early hours of Austin's waking and bottle feeding challenging. She'd often needed to nap when he did to catch up on sleep.

As it was, she hadn't expected Dylan to remain out so long. And with each passing hour, her worry mounted. Where was he? And what was he doing?

She didn't want to be the kind of wife who had to keep tabs on her husband's whereabouts and doings every second of the day and night. But with Dylan's history of drinking and carousing, should she be concerned? What if he hadn't changed as much as he claimed?

A yawn pressed for release, and she captured it behind her hand. The day had been especially stressful. In fact, the entire stagecoach ride up into the mountains had filled her with dread so that by the time she'd arrived in Fairplay late in the afternoon, she'd been tempted to turn around and head back to Denver on the first stage out.

She was thankful now that she hadn't given in to the impulse and had forced her feet in the direction of the courthouse—although when she'd stepped inside, she'd never dreamed she'd end the day as a married woman.

Even with the unexpected turn of events, she could admit she was relieved to have a permanent residence. While this little cabin couldn't begin to compare to her family's luxurious townhome in Chicago, it was a fresh start in a place where no one had to know about the accusations of murder.

The door handle rattled, and the door inched open.

She jumped up from her chair and grabbed the broom positioned near the stove. She hoped it was only Dylan, but just in case, she lifted the broom above her head. She wasn't afraid of fending off unwanted advances, had needed to do so from time to time during her midwifery visits to women in seedy neighborhoods.

As Dylan stepped inside and caught sight of her with the

broom in the air, he retreated against the closing door and held out both hands. "Whoa, now. Not sure what I've done. But it can't be that bad, can it?"

She lowered her makeshift weapon. "I was just being safe."

He latched the door and then lowered a bolt. "Safe? Wish I could say I was safe, but my son's existence is proof I'm not." Although he finished with a teasing grin, his words made her insides flip with strange nervousness.

This was her wedding night after all. What if he'd changed his mind about sharing the bed with her? She glanced at the now neatly made bed with Austin sleeping soundly in the middle, wedged there with pillows.

Dylan released a low whistle, his eyes widening as he took in the interior. "Looks like you've been mighty busy."

She trailed his gaze, suddenly hoping she hadn't overstepped by making so many changes. Although her family had always had servants to maintain the house and perform menial tasks, she'd learned how to work hard during her long hours accompanying her mother on deliveries.

"It gave me something to do to pass the time." She replaced the broom. "I hope you don't mind."

"Mind?" He gave another whistle. "Darlin', I don't expect you to clean up after me. But I sure ain't gonna complain about having the place livable."

"I found some of the furniture and other items in the shed."

He nodded. "Yep, should have mentioned that it's full of stuff and that you can use any of it you need."

Maybe if he hadn't run off the minute they'd walked in the door . . .

He removed his hat, started to toss it on the table, and halted, searching for a better place to put it.

"Here." She crossed to him, took the hat, and then hung it next to hers on a set of double pegs on the wall behind the door. "And your coat can hang on the peg here." She held out her hand, waiting to take the item from him.

He shrugged out of it. His bow tie was gone and his vest unbuttoned. But he still made a dashing picture. "Didn't think you'd be up this late."

"I'm used to staying up until all hours of the night."

"You are?" He handed her the coat, his brows lifting and concern crinkling the corners of his eyes. "You didn't have to—well, you know—join up with a house of ill repute to support yourself and the babe, did you?"

"What?" She almost slapped him for his vulgarity. But then she stopped herself. It was only natural that he was wondering how she'd managed thus far as a woman alone with a baby. "No, of course not. I had some money saved."

He immediately lowered himself into the chair and buried his face in his hands. "I'm a lowlife piece of scum for letting this happen to you."

"I made choices too."

"But I'm to blame. I'm sorry, Catherine. So sorry."

His slumped shoulders and the dejection in his voice tugged at her heart. "We're here now. That's all that matters."

He nodded but still held his head in his hands. "Just the thought that you might have had to resort to selling yourself to care for Austin rips me apart." His voice turned hoarse.

Kit had come close to that, probably would have had to if she'd survived the birthing. But he didn't need to hear that tonight, not with the weight of guilt upon him.

Catherine hesitated. Then she crossed to him and placed a hand on his shoulder. "As I said, let's put the past behind us. We're here now. God's given us a sweet baby to take care of. And we can focus on being good parents."

Before she could remove her hand, he reached up and laid his hand over hers. Though he still wore his gloves, the gesture was strong and sure and somehow reassuring. With all the doubts she'd had since running away from home, maybe this was a sign that she was doing the right thing for Austin.

As if she'd spoken the name aloud, the baby released a tiny wail. She released her hold on Dylan, crossed to the bed, and picked up Austin, quickly bringing his cries to a halt. "Are you hungry, my precious boy?"

He pressed his fist against his mouth and sucked at it noisily.

"Strange time for him to be eating." Dylan rose from his chair and watched the infant with wide eyes, as though he wanted to bolt but didn't know where to go.

"Babies eat smaller meals more frequently." She headed toward the wall shelf near the stove where she'd placed the bottles and supply of Ridge's Food for Infants she'd purchased in Denver. Although she and her mother had used the powdery substance in other situations when lactation problems arose for new mothers, Catherine preferred to make her own milk substitute with a mixture of cow's milk, water, cream, and honey. Perhaps tomorrow she'd be able to locate all that she needed to provide Austin with a healthy alternative to breast milk.

As she set supplies on the table and spooned powder into the bottle, Dylan watched her. "I can hold the babe while you get the bottle ready, make your job there easier."

"I'm used to doing this one-handed. I've actually become quite good at doing many things one-handed."

"Yep, I reckon so." Dylan stuffed his hands in his pockets and shifted. "From the looks of things, you could probably assemble the bottle one-handed with your eyes closed."

Austin made hungry grunts against his fist, but he hadn't wailed again.

She turned to the stove and picked up the kettle of water she'd warmed earlier. She removed the lid and tested the water with her finger. It wasn't too hot or too cool. With the kettle in hand, she pivoted back toward the table only to find herself bumping into Dylan, who had moved and was standing behind her.

Startled, she hopped back a step. "Oh heavens."

"Let me help." His voice was soft and sincere, and his green-blue eyes, framed by those long lashes, were fixed upon her, like a puppy dog's, warm, wide, and irresistible. How could she say no?

She glanced down at Austin. She wasn't sure she was ready to hand over the baby. She hadn't felt that way about letting Trudy hold him, although Trudy didn't have the power to take the baby from her. What if Dylan decided he didn't like her? What if he got tired of her, cast her aside, and kept Austin?

Until they consummated their marriage, he could always file for an annulment. Truthfully, even if they did have a true union, he could decide to end things—perhaps even give her a divorce—at any time. She'd witnessed such castaway women often enough to know that no marriage was ever truly secure.

"I promise I won't break him." Dylan's lips quirked up into a half grin, one that was just as irresistible as his voice and eyes.

"Very well." She released her grip on Austin and gently

transferred him to Dylan's outstretched arms. "You'll need to make sure his head is supported. He's getting stronger, but his neck is still wobbly."

Dylan gingerly positioned the baby, following her instructions for how to steady him in the crook of his arm, how to keep the blanket wrapped tightly, and how to bounce the baby if he started to fuss more loudly.

"I've wrangled ornery calves and wrestled angry pigs." Dylan stood stiffly, unmoving, while staring down at the baby. "Reckon I can handle this little fella too."

Again, she tried to squelch her misgivings. Was it too late to grab Austin and run far away? As soon as the thought came, she shook her head. "Apparently I must be the one to inform you that babies aren't like ornery calves or angry pigs."

His lips curled higher. "He squeals like one."

"No, he does not." She placed the kettle spout up to the bottle and poured in the water.

"And he smells like one. I caught a whiff of him earlier at the Gundersons', and he takes after a whole pen of smelly pigs. Don't you, little fella? You had enough stink to knock out a grown man."

At Dylan's gentle baby voice, Catherine couldn't contain a smile. He related well to the baby. In fact, she'd never seen a new father do so quite as proficiently.

As she finished making the bottle, he watched the process, asking questions about putting it all together, how much and how often Austin ate, how long it would be before he could eat regular food, and other pertinent questions.

She answered him as best she could and coached him through the feeding, changing, and interaction afterward.

When Austin finally tired again, Dylan laid the baby back

on the bed, tucked the pillows around him, then stood and peered down at his son with a curious yet awestruck expression. "He sure is a handsome fella."

She paused in rinsing out the bottle to study Dylan. Austin was just as handsome as his father, but she couldn't say something like that.

Before she could figure out what to say or do, Dylan surprised her by bending down and pressing a kiss against Austin's cheek. When he straightened, he glanced at her sideways as though gauging whether he'd been caught in the act. At seeing her staring, he untucked his shirt and then began to unbutton it.

Mortified, she spun so that her back was facing him. At the swish of his pants sliding down and hitting the floor, she stood motionless with the dish towel in one hand and bottle in the other.

He was undressing in her presence.

Of course he was. There was nothing indecent about it. He had every right to do so.

Nevertheless, flames shot into her face, but she still didn't dare move, not even to press her hands against her cheeks to cool them down.

After more swishing and thudding and the release of a long, tired breath, she peeked his direction to find that he'd sprawled out on the floor, covered with a blanket. With eyes closed, he rested against a pillow, his bare arms crossed behind his head. Those bare arms gleamed in the lamplight, showing off bulging biceps and other thickly corded muscles she couldn't begin to name. Only the top part of his chest showed above the blanket, but it was enough to know that his chest was just as muscular and magnificent.

"Good night, Catherine."

When she chanced a glance at his face, he had one eye half-open and was peeking at her. She jerked her attention back around. Heaven help her. She was making a fool of herself by ogling him. She needed to stay dignified and not turn into another Kit, too enamored with him. "Good night, Dylan."

He was silent for several heartbeats. "Thanks for being such a good ma to my son."

The words rushed in and warmed her heart, making her like him even more. "You're welcome."

She quickly finished wiping the dishes, found her night-gown, then extinguished the light. The darkness of the interior gave her all the privacy she needed as she changed. Even so, once she was in her nightgown, she dove under the covers and pulled them up to her chin.

For long minutes, she held herself stiffly, not sure whether to hope Dylan would join her or whether to pray he followed through on his decision not to share their marriage bed. When his breathing finally filled the air, it was even and deep with the rhythm of sleep. Only then did she close her eyes.

CHAPTER
8

Dylan tiptoed through the house, the babe snuggled against his chest. He paused at the window and lifted aside the curtain Catherine had tacked into place. The May morning was well underway, the sunlight bright and the traffic busy on the sliver of Main Street he glimpsed beyond the courthouse.

Stu could manage without him, was used to him coming in midmorning or later, especially since he stayed up late most nights patrolling the streets and keeping the peace.

He hadn't expected Catherine to be awake when he'd come home last night, had hoped she'd already be abed so he wouldn't have to face the temptation of watching a pretty woman walk around his home.

But even now as she slept, he was fighting his inner demons. Every time his glance strayed to the bed to her soft, pliable body, to her long, dark hair spread out all around her, to her sweetly rounded face so peaceful and innocent in slumber, his blood heated a degree warmer.

He couldn't let himself dwell on the fact that his wife was

in his bed. He had to think about everything but that, just like he'd done last night when she extinguished the lantern and started readying for bed. As soon as he heard the shifting and shuffling of clothes, he scrambled to find something else to fill his head in order to push out the image of her undressing just a few feet away from him.

He'd latched on to his guns and had mentally gone through the process of cleaning his revolver, focusing on the mundane task until she crawled into bed. Even then, his thoughts strayed to her lying close by, and he had to mentally clean his gun again.

Now he was trying his best not to picture her in any way except as the mother to his child. When Austin had started fussing a while ago, Dylan decided to tend to the babe and let Catherine sleep. As he lifted Austin away from the spot next to her, she hadn't stirred.

Eventually, Austin's grunts turned hungry, and Dylan had gone through the steps of making a bottle. He'd spilled the powdery formula and water at least half a dozen times, but eventually he managed to get everything put together. His admiration for Catherine's ability to hold the infant and get anything done one-handed had grown tenfold.

She'd made it all look so easy, including changing Austin's diaper. But Dylan had barely taken the soggy linen off when the boy let loose an arching stream that almost hit him and instead left a puddle on the floor.

Somehow, Dylan had folded another diaper back into place, but he hadn't been able to get it to stay together the right way, and he guessed he'd soon be wet with urine.

He'd also started a pot of coffee percolating, and now the rich roasted brew wafted in the chilly morning air. Austin babbled soft gibberish, which Dylan hoped meant the babe was content. "What do you think, little fella? You gonna like living with me? Maybe I'll make an alright pa."

Dylan peered down at the miniature version of himself. His son. He couldn't deny Austin was his, but the fact that he had a child was still surreal.

"Hopefully you don't make all the same mistakes I did," he whispered. "Reckon I'm glad God waited to give you to me until I had my life back on track I could be the kind of pa you need."

His pa had been honest and kind in all his doings. If only he hadn't been the first in a long string of people to leave him. After Pa's death, Wyatt had gone away to make his fortune, then Ma had died, and Brody had run off to the war. Every day during the trip to the West, Dylan had feared he'd lose someone else he loved next.

Maybe that loss and loneliness had pushed him to find security and companionship in the arms of women. Or maybe he'd hoped to dull the ache and fear of losing people he cared about. Whatever the case, he'd learned that chasing after women hadn't made him feel any better about his losses or his life. In fact, it had only made him feel worse.

Austin released a chirp.

"Does that mean you agree?"

His son's wide-eyed gaze never failed to make his whole insides turn softer than sweetgrass in sunshine.

At a yawn and the shuffle of blankets from the bed, Dylan allowed himself a glance in Catherine's direction to find her stretching like a cat waking from a sound nap. Her eyes were still closed, but Dylan guessed it wouldn't be long before she awoke altogether.

He let the curtain fall into place and made his way to the stove. As he placed a mug on the table and began to pour, she released a startled gasp. "Austin?" She sat up halfway and glided her fingers over the spot where the babe had slept.

"I've got him." Dylan hefted the boy higher as he finished filling the mug with coffee.

From the corner of his eyes, he could see that she was pushing herself up farther. "How long has he been awake?"

"Maybe an hour."

She rubbed her eyes and shoved the covers away with her feet. "He must be really hungry."

"Don't worry." Dylan started across the cabin toward her. "I fed and changed him."

She paused, her nightgown tangled in her legs. "You did?"

"Yep. Had the best teacher." As he reached the side of the bed, he held out the steaming mug, avoiding looking at her feet and the expanse of her legs. "For you."

She stared at it, her brows crinkling. "For me?"

"Yep. Thought I heard you tell Trudy after supper last night that you liked your coffee black."

"I do." Her response held a note of surprise, and yet she still didn't take the mug.

"Go on." He moved it closer. "Have a sip."

Tentatively she took it. "Thank you, Dylan. But I don't feel right about you bringing me coffee like this. I should have been the one awakening first and making it for you."

"Naw. You needed the sleep. And I didn't mind getting up and spending a little time with this fella." Dylan combed his fingers through Austin's fuzzy hair.

Her forehead furrowed with worried lines. She probably wasn't used to having men do nice things for her. No doubt he was high on her list of despicable men. He wanted to change that real fast.

Before she could find a way to hand him back the coffee and get out of bed, he returned to the stove. As he poured himself a cup of coffee, she finally settled against her pillows, lifted the coffee to her nose, then inhaled the steam. She closed her eyes, delight rippling over her features, before she took a slurp.

"What do you think?" He brought his own mug up and breathed in the rich, roasted aroma.

"It's perfect." She took another sip, then her lips curved into a shy smile. "Thank you."

As she sat in bed with her hair falling over her shoulders and her expression softened with contentment, he felt a strange pleasure he'd never known, the kind of pleasure that didn't stem from selfish fulfillment but from sacrificing himself to make someone else happy.

Even though she'd tugged the covers back to her waist, hiding her legs, she was still a sight to behold. "I could get mighty used to this pretty view every morning." The words came out before he could filter them.

As she comprehended that he was staring at her, she ducked her head. Most women he'd known would have said something back, likely something suggestive. But Catherine's innocence was refreshing, even enticing.

With as innocent as she was, how had they ended up together in Chicago? He'd only ever flirted with women who showed interest in him first. Catherine wouldn't have done that. So what exactly had brought them together?

The question pushed to the tip of his tongue, but before he could gather the courage to ask it, knocking sounded on the door. Placing his coffee mug on the table, Dylan resituated Austin in his arm. Then he walked to the door, getting more comfortable holding the infant with each passing minute.

He swung the door wide to the sight of his nephew and niece, Wyatt's two oldest, Ty and Ellie. Dylan had always thought his brothers' kids were as puny as peas in a pod. But now compared to Austin, Ty looked like a giant. He had Wyatt's rugged build and dark hair and eyes. Already at seven years old, he was a handsome fella and bore the McQuaid name well.

Ellie was a couple of years younger than Ty with fair hair, pale blue eyes, and dainty features. Where Ty was boisterous and outgoing and daring, Ellie was gentle, tenderhearted, and reserved.

Over the past months, Dylan had loved getting reacquainted with the two along with a passel of other nieces and nephews belonging to not only Wyatt but also Flynn and Brody. From the looks of Ivy, her babe was due any day now, and he'd soon have another little niece or nephew. Boy, was she gonna be surprised to discover he'd beat her to having a kid.

As Ty and Ellie peered at the infant, their mouths dropped open.

"Hey there, you scalawags." Dylan grinned at them, teasing them as he usually did.

"So the news around town is right." Ty peeked beyond Dylan, his eyes rounding even wider at the sight of Catherine in his bed.

Dylan could only imagine the rumors spreading through Fairplay this morning. In fact, he dreaded facing the gossip.

He supposed that was part of the reason he wasn't in a big hurry to make an appearance.

"Ma said to come on over and see if it was true." Ty's wide eyes fixed back on the babe.

"Yep." Dylan rubbed Austin's head. "You can tell your ma I'm married and have a babe."

"That sure did happen mighty fast, Uncle Dylan. Didn't realize babies could arrive so quick-like after having a weddin'."

Inwardly Dylan smacked himself upside the head. Here was just one more reason why he regretted all his mistakes. He was setting a poor—extremely poor—example for his nephews and nieces, who all looked up to him. "Listen, Ty. This ain't how things are supposed to happen. Someday, a long way down the road when you get to marrying and having babies, you follow your ma and pa's example, not mine."

"Don't worry. I ain't never gonna get married. All that kissin' and stuff is gross."

At the disgust in the boy's face, Dylan smothered a grin. He didn't have the heart to tell Ty that someday he'd be chasing after gals with the same fervor that he chased after bugs and fish.

"How are you this morning, princess?" Dylan tweaked Ellie's nose, earning one of her beautiful smiles.

"I'm fine. What's your baby's name?"

"Austin."

"He's sure cute."

"That's 'cause he takes after his pretty ma." Dylan tossed a glance toward Catherine, who had pulled her cover all the way to her chin and was observing the exchange with mortification in her eyes. No doubt her cheeks were red too.

The question flitted through him again. How had he ended up with someone so prim and proper?

Ellie and Ty tried to glimpse Catherine, but the shadows of the dark interior kept her mostly hidden.

"Ma told me to relay a message—that she'll plan to have a wedding celebration supper out at the ranch tonight, and she'll be inviting all the family."

Dylan's stomach cinched. Did he have to go? Standing in front of everyone with his wife and son by his side would be akin to confessing his sins publicly. Namely that he'd been a womanizer. 'Course they all knew that already, along with the many other mistakes that had gotten him into trouble and forced him to run away from Colorado.

Folks from here to Alaska knew he'd gotten into such bad gambling debt to Bat and his gang that they'd put a death warrant on his head. He was free from it now, thanks to Ivy and her husband, Jericho.

Even so, he wasn't ready to face his family with the living proof of all he'd done wrong.

As though sensing his hesitation, Ty's gaze narrowed on him. "Ma said she wouldn't take no for an answer."

Dylan should've known this would happen. Fact was, if he didn't go out to Wyatt and Greta's place and make the introductions, they'd come looking for him, probably show up at his house unannounced just like Ty and Ellie. He'd be a heap better off making introductions all at once instead of dragging things out. "You can tell your ma we'll be there, that I can't ever turn down the chance to eat her good home cooking."

After a few more instructions, Ty took Ellie's hand in his and led her back to the main thoroughfare, likely to one of the establishments where Greta sold her baked goods. Ty's gentleness and kindness to his sister was no doubt a product of watching how Wyatt treated Greta. Wyatt cared for his wife like the world revolved around her. In fact, all his brothers had fine wives they loved passionately. And they weren't afraid to show it.

Dylan closed the door and held in a sigh. Somehow he'd always been the odd one in his family, the one who never fit in, the one who struggled to live up to the McQuaid name. And now, in addition to all the other things, his marriage was different too.

CHAPTER
9

"He's adorable, Mr. and Mrs. McQuaid." Fairplay's school-teacher, a woman who'd introduced herself as Mrs. Phineas Hallock, beamed down at the swaddled bundle in Catherine's arms.

Catherine stood stiffly next to Dylan outside the mercantile as the stout woman in a flamboyant purple gown chucked the baby's chin. Catherine waited for a biting comment or underhanded put-down relaying disapproval for Dylan having a baby outside the bonds of holy matrimony.

Already, several prominent town matrons had stopped Dylan on Main Street to meet his new wife and to remark on his hasty marriage. While they'd retained a polite façade, Catherine was familiar enough with society manners to know when she was being snubbed. They clearly thought less of her because of her quick marriage to Dylan. She guessed most of them also assumed the baby was hers. And although she was tempted to refute that, she refrained.

She wasn't sure she wanted to reveal all that had happened in Chicago, not when Rocky might still be trying to pin the blame on her. The less she said, the safer she and Austin would be, especially if Rocky had men out hunting for her.

Now with her impulsive marriage, had she put Dylan in danger? Was it better if she stayed silent so she could protect him too?

She was ashamed to admit she hadn't told Dylan her real last name, since they hadn't yet signed a marriage certificate. It wasn't for lack of time or conversation that she'd refrained from mentioning it. After Dylan's nephew and niece had left earlier, she'd wrapped herself in a blanket and joined him at the table, where they finished off the pot of coffee and burned away most of the morning talking about the history behind Fairplay, how much the town was growing, his position as sheriff, and the upcoming election against Harlan Hatfield.

He'd asked her about her trip west and how she'd managed with Austin. She told him about her detour to St. Louis and her time there before she finally headed to Colorado. She'd decided on the circuitous route just in case anyone was following her. But she didn't mention that to Dylan.

He'd finally headed out to the office only to reappear a short while later, claiming that Stu wanted him to take the day off and spend it with her, show her around, and help her get acquainted with the town.

She hadn't objected. In fact, the prospect of getting to be with Dylan the rest of the day had made her giddy. And she'd had to chastise herself severely for how easily she was falling prey to his charm.

Even now, as he smiled broadly at Mrs. Hallock, he was winsome enough to cause the matron to faintly blush.

"He's very fine indeed." Mrs. Hallock pulled herself up and returned to the shade of her parasol.

The sunshine of the high altitude was brighter and more intense than that of Chicago. But Catherine rather liked the change from the dismal, overcast skies that covered the Midwest so often during the spring.

"And Catherine is a real fine ma too." Dylan slipped an arm around her waist as he'd done from time to time while they'd chatted with folks. She knew he didn't mean anything by it other than showing her support. But every time he touched her, she felt as though someone twisted a knob and lengthened a wick inside her, making her nerves flame with awareness of him.

Mrs. Hallock smiled at Catherine warmly. "Well, welcome to Fairplay, Mrs. McQuaid. I'm sure you'll love living here as much as I have."

"Hopefully I can make Catherine as happy as Phineas has made you." He winked at the woman.

Mrs. Hallock flushed again and fanned her face as she finally hurried away.

Catherine stepped out of Dylan's embrace, needing to fan herself too. Charming didn't do him justice. Somehow, he could win over everyone without even trying. He'd done so with Austin, with her. And with every other man, woman, and child in town. Even with his glaring mistake here for all the world to see, he was too likable for anyone to condemn for long.

She couldn't keep from comparing Dylan with her father. Alderman Remington could be a charmer too. But his efforts were always calculated to make himself look better in the public eye, including using her or anyone else around him to that end.

Dylan, however, had no ulterior motives. He seemed to care about people, not because he was campaigning for the election or what they could do for him or how they made him appear, but simply because he was genuine.

He stepped up and shook the hand of another passerby, asking the fellow about his sick wife. He exuded both strength and compassion, and she could watch him all day as he talked and walked and interacted.

But when he slanted a glance at her, she pretended to study the packages and parcels stacked on the boardwalk, all the purchases he'd made for Austin and her. He'd bought her everything she'd shown an interest in and then some, had told her she could have anything she set her heart on.

After having to be so thrifty over the past weeks to stretch her dollars, she'd used caution, not wanting to take advantage of Dylan's generosity.

"McQuaid." The tense call came from several businesses away. A burly man with a thick brown beard had stepped out of the dining room of Hotel Windsor. He looked out of place in the black suit he was wearing, almost as if he'd been stuffed inside it like sausage into casing.

Dylan stiffened but didn't turn his attention toward the newcomer, even though the man he'd been talking to had grown silent.

"This is exactly the kind of thing an upstanding sheriff wouldn't be doing." The burly man nodded at Catherine and Austin, his brows furrowed with censure and his eyes filled with condemnation.

Dylan released a nearly imperceptible sigh before straightening and facing the newcomer. "Mr. Hatfield, I'd like you to meet my wife, Catherine, and my son, Austin."

Mr. Hatfield? Dylan's competitor for the sheriff position?

Catherine sized the fellow up again, searching for clues that he wasn't worthy of the job. She'd been around enough crooked politicians to know what one looked like.

However, even though the hems of his sleeves were frayed, his boots scuffed, and his fedora dusty, his expression was earnest and his eyes honest. He was just the way Dylan had described—a concerned, well-meaning, upstanding man. There wasn't anything wrong with him, and he'd likely make a good sheriff.

Except that even in the short time she'd been in Fairplay, she could see that Dylan loved his position and didn't want to give it up. . . .

"Ma'am." Mr. Hatfield tipped his hat at her. As he took her in more carefully, his eyes narrowed as if he were attempting to figure out how he knew her.

Her pulse picked up speed, and she dropped her sights to Austin, pretending to straighten the knitted cap covering his head. Did Mr. Hatfield recognize her? If he'd ever visited Chicago, it was possible he'd seen her with her father during his campaigning.

She tensed and waited for him to say something, to accuse her of murder. If the allegations—even though false—came to light, she had no doubt she'd ruin Dylan's chances at being elected as the permanent sheriff.

"A sheriff needs to be above reproach, McQuaid." Mr. Hatfield rubbed at his long beard as a woman and several young children exited the dining room and came to stand beside him—likely his family. The woman wore a simple but clean gown and a scarf tied over her hair. Her plain features were unassuming but tired, as though she never quite got enough sleep.

"I'm doing my best, Hatfield." Every trace of charm had disappeared from Dylan's face. Instead, intensity and strength tightened his features, showing him to be a man not easily swayed.

"This—" Mr. Hatfield nodded at Catherine and Austin— "it's all the more reason for you to step aside and let me do the job."

"We'll let the people decide—"

"Unfortunately, the people can often be duped."

"I'm not aiming to dupe anyone."

The two men squared off in a staring contest.

"Pick your fight with me, Hatfield," Dylan finally said, his voice hard. "Leave my family out of it." With that, Dylan drew her toward him again, this time into the crook of his arm. "Come on, darlin'. Let's get you and Austin home."

Home. She let Dylan guide her along, the word ringing through her mind. Could this really be home? Or was showing up and inserting herself into Dylan's life a big mistake?

CHAPTER

10

"Almost there." Dylan refrained from leaning in and speaking near her ear. Even though he wanted to brush his lips over her skin and get the faintest feel of her, he couldn't. Not after succeeding at holding himself back for the past hour.

With Catherine sitting in the saddle in front of him and squeezed up against him, the five miles was the longest it had ever been.

Thankfully, Wyatt and Greta hadn't yet moved into their new house near the inn they'd built adjacent to the hot spring on their land, which would have prolonged the ride. They planned to make the switch over the summer before they officially opened Healing Springs Inn. But for now, they were still living in the original house Wyatt had built when he'd claimed the homestead over nine years ago in '62.

Dylan held himself as far from Catherine as he could, but the jarring gait of his gelding tossed her body against his way too often, making it nearly impossible for him to think on much of anything except how soft and pretty and sweet she was.

He was gonna need to invest in a wagon first chance he got. Not only did he want to avoid a repeat of having her pressing against him, but one horse was impractical for a family. Austin might be tiny enough now that Catherine could hold him in her arms. But he'd get big soon enough.

And Catherine wanted more children someday. Although he'd never thought much about having a family of his own, he supposed he could see himself with a few more young'uns.

Whatever the case, he was trying to keep his thoughts from veering toward his physical needs. He had a heap of work ahead of him in being a good husband and father first.

He'd tried to protect her today from the backlash he'd known they'd get, tried to ward off comments, tried to keep people focused on how cute Austin was. But deep inside, his shame and guilt tied tighter knots, especially at the realization that his past lustful living was the cause of people thinking less of Catherine.

After they'd returned to the cabin with their purchases, they gave Austin another bottle. While the baby napped, Dylan helped her bring in more furniture from the shed and arrange it just where she wanted it. By the time the baby awoke and had another bottle, it'd been time to leave for Wyatt's place.

"The view is simply breathtaking." Catherine stared ahead at the eastern landscape that made the ranch one of the prettiest places on earth. The foothills in the distance gave way to towering mountains. The thick evergreens formed cloaks, leading to rocky peaks capped white with snow.

The ranch sat against the majestic backdrop. The house,

barn, and outbuildings had turned a rugged gray with time. With some of the cattle feeding nearby, along with pronghorns grazing in the distance, Dylan couldn't keep from being amazed by the view the same as Catherine.

"Fell in love with this place the first day we rode up." He breathed in the crisp air—so clean and thin compared to the heavy polluted air in Chicago.

"I can see why." Her shoulders rose as she inhaled a breath too.

In spite of the temptation he was feeling from riding so close to her, he could admit he'd enjoyed her company and conversation. She'd asked him questions about his family, the ranch, raising cattle, and the rustling problem. She was a good listener and full of astute observations.

"I'd love to hear about your trip west." She resituated Austin, who had begun to fuss. "I'm sure it was much different than mine."

For the remaining distance, he shared the highlights of his journey over the Santa Fe Trail with Flynn and Ivy and Bliss, how they'd driven a herd of Shorthorns from Missouri up to Wyatt's ranch, the trip taking them approximately six months. During the trek, Flynn had met and fallen in love with Linnea, a botanist on the expedition with her grandfather. The couple had married shortly after arriving in South Park and had a little girl named Flora.

"So Flynn owns half the ranch?" Catherine asked as they neared the ranch yard.

"Yep. But his place is about a mile to the north."

"And Brody and Savannah live with Flynn whenever they come up to South Park?"

"They stay in the house Brody built a short distance from

Flynn's." Dylan had told her earlier about Brody's ability to tame the mustangs that ran wild in the mountains and about how, after gentling them, he drove the horses down to the Double L on the Front Range, where he and Savannah lived most of the year with their two little boys. Brody had developed quite the name for himself as a horse gentler, and people from all over the country paid a pretty penny to buy his horses. Savannah not only helped Brody with training his horses, but was also a skilled veterinarian.

"Will we get to see them today?"

"No, they won't come up until June. But you'll get to meet Ivy and Bliss." He'd informed Catherine about his younger sister's marriage to his best friend, who was a detective, bounty hunter, and security guard for the Pinkerton Agency. The two owned a parcel of land to the south of Fairplay and had invested in raising sheep. After the past year and a half, the herd was still small, but several ewes had just given birth.

As they drew nearer to the house, the children playing in the yard caught sight of them. "Uncle Dylan!" His nephews and nieces came running and skipping toward him.

Beyond them, his brothers and Bliss rose from the benches at the trestle table that had been brought out of the house and situated in the yard to make more room for the ever-expanding family. Judd, the white-haired cowhand who was an adopted father to all of them, stood a little more slowly.

No doubt the womenfolk were inside working on the last preparations for the meal, which meant he'd have to face Wyatt and Flynn and Bliss without their wives. Blast it. He'd rather wrestle with a pack of wolves in the wild than deal with his brothers alone.

Stiffening his shoulders, he reined in the horse. In front of him, Catherine sat up straighter and adjusted her hat. He hadn't expected a grocer's daughter to have such fine hats and garments. But he could admit he was relieved she would make a good impression not only with her appearance but also with her manners. Whatever circumstances had transpired to thrust them together in Chicago, she was obviously a woman with a good upbringing. Just because she'd had a lapse in her morals and made a mistake by sleeping with him didn't discount all her other fine attributes.

As she clutched Austin tighter, her hand trembled a bit. Even though her expression gave away none of her nervousness, was she worried about meeting his family?

Moving to dismount, he pressed into her just briefly. "You ain't got nothin' to worry about," he whispered near her ear. "They're gonna love you."

She shifted closer to him, as though drawing strength from him. "Are you sure?"

"You're beautiful, smart, and sweet. What's not to love?" Though he tried for flirtatious, somehow the words came out with a sincerity that surprised him. Her beauty wasn't jaw-dropping or eye-catching like some of the women he'd known. It was subtler and simpler, which he liked even better.

"Thank you, Dylan." She tilted her head to whisper to him, putting her lips within kissing distance.

He glanced away and swallowed the sudden intense desire. Nope. He couldn't go there and do that. No how, no way.

He dismounted and reached up for her. As he lifted her and the babe down, he could feel the men watching them even as his nephews and nieces clamored around him for attention. As he steadied her on the ground, he felt her tremble again.

He leaned in. "We can do this. I promise. Just stay close to me." The best thing he could do in this awkward meeting of his family was to stand by her side, protect her, and take the brunt of the disapproval, just like he'd done in town.

She smiled up at him, the first real smile directed his way since she'd arrived. Somehow, that smile sent a jolt of energy through him, like the energy he felt after accomplishing something big.

He took a few moments to interact with his nieces and nephews until Wyatt stepped up to them holding his youngest, a boy of about one who'd been born last summer shortly before Dylan had arrived.

Wyatt gently shooed the children away before giving Dylan his full attention. "Heard you went and got married yesterday." Questions lit up Wyatt's eyes, and his brows furrowed with concern.

Flynn limped toward him, his face radiating with tension—or disapproval?

That familiar sense of inadequacy roiled inside Dylan, the one that taunted him that he could never live up to Wyatt and Flynn or even Brody. "Yep. This here is my wife, Catherine, and our babe, Austin."

She nodded at Wyatt and then Flynn. "Pleased to meet you."

"Pleased to meet you too." Wyatt spoke kindly and reached out to touch Austin's hand. As his brother studied the infant's face, tenderness chased away the dark clouds. "He's the spittin' image of Dylan when he was a babe."

Wyatt was eight years older and had always been someone Dylan looked up to—still did.

Before Dylan could finish the introductions among the

men, thankfully the womenfolk began making their way out of the house, carrying platters laden with food. For a short while amidst the commotion, Dylan made the rounds with Catherine and Austin, accepting the well-wishes and hugs from Greta, Linnea, and Astrid. When he reached Ivy, she punched him in the arm.

"Ouch!" Dylan rubbed the sore spot. "What was that for?"

"For not letting me come to the wedding." She balled up her fist, and he stiffened, waiting for another hit. Instead, she pressed the small of her back, which accentuated her very pregnant belly.

"How far apart are your birthing pains?" Catherine studied Ivy's face.

"Birthing pains?" Bliss, standing next to Ivy, went pale.

Ivy waved a hand. "It ain't nothin' to worry about. I've been having contractions for weeks."

"Your baby has dropped." Catherine spoke matter-of-factly, glancing pointedly at Ivy's abdomen. "Your travail is soon, if you're not already in the throes of it."

"Ivy?" Bliss's voice rose with censure, and he wrapped an arm around Ivy's waist as though he intended to pick her up off her feet and carry her inside.

"I'm fine." Ivy stood on her toes and kissed Bliss's cheek. "Told you I still have at least a week or two before we need to be taking precautions."

Catherine shook her head and started to say more, but the others were already pushing them toward the table. Within minutes the adults were seated at the table and the children on blankets nearby. They quieted while Wyatt said grace, but just as soon as he finished, the hubbub rose again.

As the food was passed, Dylan felt himself begin to relax

as the conversation settled to the usual talk of family matters, the calves, and all the other everyday goings-on, including the progress on the new inn and the hope to open it by midsummer. His brothers both complained of losing additional cattle to rustlers. And Dylan questioned them more about J. D. Otto, his main suspect. They even talked for a bit about the most recent sighting of Two-Toed Joe, an enormous grizzly believed to weigh over a thousand pounds.

Ever since returning, Dylan had realized the clamor of his kinfolk all together like this was the sweetest sound. While he'd been in Chicago, he'd missed their chatter, laughter, even the arguing and grumbling. He wouldn't take family time for granted ever again.

With Catherine holding Austin beside him, Dylan could almost imagine that at long last he was respectable. Even if he'd come about his family in an unconventional way, there was something grown-up about being married and having a child. Maybe he could begin to shed his image as the unattached bachelor with the wild and sordid past. Maybe everyone would finally take him more seriously.

As Bliss leaned in and stole a kiss from Ivy, Dylan glanced down at the remains of gravy left on his plate. The two had been married for a year and a half and still acted like newlyweds.

The sight of his best friend doting on his sister never failed to make Dylan squirm. He'd tried to forgive Bliss for breaking his promise to keep his hands off Ivy. But he wasn't there yet. Still harbored resentment for the way Bliss had gone behind his back and fallen in love with her.

"C'mon, Dylan." Ivy's tone taunted him. "Now that you

got someone to kiss, maybe you can stop being jealous of me and Jericho."

"I ain't jealous." Dylan drummed his fingers on the table, working hard to harness his tongue and keep it from running away on him.

"You sure as the sun rises are."

"Nope, sure as the sun rises ain't."

"Prove it." Ivy's glare needled into him worse than a thorny cactus spine.

He hated when anyone told him to prove himself. He could hardly ever turn down the challenge, and Ivy knew it.

The table grew silent, and everyone stared at him expectantly, all except Catherine next to him, who was preoccupied with tucking Austin's blanket around his sleeping frame.

Dylan lifted his chin and glared back at Ivy. "I don't need to prove it."

Ivy's lips curled up with the beginning of a smile. "Fine. But that's only because you're scared worse than a skunk seein' his shadow."

She thought he was scared of kissing? He released a low, scoffing laugh. If she wanted him to prove he wasn't jealous or scared, then he'd show her.

Before Catherine could react, he reached for her, then swooped down and captured her lips.

CHAPTER
11

Catherine nearly jumped at the contact of Dylan's lips against hers. She'd tried to pretend she wasn't paying attention to his conversation with Ivy. But he was sitting so close, she couldn't keep from being aware of his every move and word. It was almost as if he were a magnet drawing shards of her thoughts and attention no matter how much she tried to resist.

Embarrassed heat skittered through her. From the silence, she gathered everyone was watching. She couldn't exactly pull away and tell Dylan no, not in front of his whole family. She'd have to play along with whatever he was doing. What *was* he doing? Trying to impress them? Giving way to his sister's teasing?

His lips plied hers gently, sweetly. And he cupped her cheeks and angled her head so his mouth could fuse with hers more fully. Heaven help her, the touch of his lips was just as amazing today as it had been last night after their wedding. She could admit she'd dreamed about his kiss, and she liked this one just as much, if not more.

She barely had time to respond to his delectable urging when the pressure of his kiss deepened and quickened. The powerful intensity of it sent a jolt of pure pleasure through her. She rose slightly to fuse herself more fully, opening up to him. She had the overwhelming need to lift her hands, toss off his hat, and bury her fingers in his overlong locks.

Somehow his kiss was like a key twisting within her, opening a part of her that she hadn't known existed. She'd hadn't realized a mere kiss could be so arousing, filling her with a sweet, keen need for more kissing and more of him.

Before she could do something mortifying—like release the moan forming in her throat—he broke away, dropping his hands from her and leaning back.

"There." He grinned at Ivy, his eyes glinting with challenge. "Beat that."

Catherine's lips tingled, and her body thrummed. She was undone, and she didn't know how Dylan could talk or move or think after such a kiss.

"Oh, I'll beat it. And raise you one." Ivy wound her arms around Jericho's neck and dragged him into a kiss. Taller than the McQuaid men by a couple of inches, Jericho was a fine-looking man with a slightly fairer complexion but no less rugged than Dylan. His arms went around his wife eagerly, and he responded with an ardor that brought a blush to Catherine's cheeks.

Wyatt and Flynn whistled at the increasingly passionate kiss between Ivy and Jericho. But Dylan scowled. Even so, he reached for Catherine again, as though he still had something to prove. She'd sensed his tension with Ivy and Jericho and knew she needed to put an end to the sibling rivalry or whatever it was.

Nevertheless, she was discovering that Dylan was nearly impossible to resist. And she had the sudden urge to pass Austin off to his nearest aunt so she could kiss Dylan without the baby between them.

As Dylan slipped a hand behind her neck and guided her mouth back to his, her body tightened with anticipation. His lips fused with hers again.

This time, she was ready. She needed no preamble. She met him swiftly and willingly, letting him take control once more, turning the key even deeper, unlocking and unleashing desire so that it spilled through her.

Heaven help her. She could very well go on kissing him forever.

He'd claimed that he wanted to give them plenty of time and space before getting physical. If this was time and space, then what would real intimacy look like? She couldn't even begin to fathom it.

But what did this kiss mean to him? Did it affect him the same way? Especially after having kissed so many other women. How many other women *had* he kissed?

As if hearing her unspoken question, he broke away and sat up, dropping his gaze to Austin, avoiding hers.

Her lips felt strangely swollen and her breath choppy. And she had the feeling everyone at the table could tell exactly how much his kisses had affected her.

She waited for Dylan to lift his eyes to hers and reassure her that everything would be okay, that he liked kissing her as much as she had him. But he bent and placed a kiss on Austin's cheek.

Her pulse slowed its runaway pace. After kissing other women, what if he didn't like kissing her? What if she didn't measure up?

"You did alright." Ivy snuggled into the crook of Jericho's arm while grinning at Dylan. "But I reckon you're gonna need a heap more practice if you ever wanna beat me and Jericho."

Dylan chanced a glance at his sister. Upon seeing the humor lighting her face, his lips twitched into a faint grin of his own. "This ain't a competition, Ivy."

"Sure it is." With her dark hair and dark eyes, Ivy was stunning. And from the way her husband watched her, it was clear he thought so as well.

Would Dylan ever look at her like that?

Catherine tucked the thought away. It was much too soon to be thinking about such affection. Besides, she couldn't forget how unappealing other men had found her. The fact that Dylan had kissed her a few times didn't change that.

Ivy grimaced and then squirmed, likely having another contraction. Catherine had been monitoring them, and she guessed they were less than ten minutes apart now. Whether Ivy believed so or not, she would likely have her baby today or tomorrow.

"From what I can tell so far, Catherine's nigh to a saint." Ivy studied Catherine carefully as she'd done several other times, her eyes brimming with mistrust. "How'd she end up with a rascal like you?"

"Now, come on, Ivy." Bliss gently squeezed her. "Give Dylan a break."

"Naw, it's alright." Dylan's shoulders slumped a notch. "I can admit I'm a rascal."

"No, you're not anymore." Catherine spoke the words softly, didn't mean to. But they slipped out anyway.

He lifted his gaze to hers as though searching for and desperately needing someone to believe in him and affirm the changes he was trying to make. Although she hadn't known the old Dylan, she'd seen enough of the man he'd become to recognize he was striving hard to live an upright life.

She offered him what she hoped was an encouraging smile.

He seemed to soak it in before facing Ivy and the rest of his family. "I met Catherine at her father's grocery store. She was real sweet, and I ended up talking with her."

What? Catherine froze.

"So your father owns a grocery?" someone asked.

No, her father was Alderman Paul Remington, a well-known activist for ending corruption within Chicago's political establishment. But she couldn't blurt that out here and now.

"Yep," Dylan continued, "it's a fine grocery, and Catherine worked there with her family. Well, until . . ." He glanced at Austin as if to make his point. "Now they don't want anything to do with her."

Why was Dylan saying this about her? Kit was the one from the grocery store, whose family had abandoned her. Why would he need to say all this to his family and make them believe she was Kit?

Unless he wasn't pretending . . .

Her heart jumped into her throat. Did Dylan think she was Kit? And that she'd birthed Austin?

He couldn't possibly. Surely, he'd taken one look at her and realized she was a stranger, that he'd never seen her before. How could he not? Even though she and Kit shared some similarities in appearance, they were different enough that the possibility of Dylan confusing them hadn't even crossed her mind.

If Dylan had mistaken her for Kit, then that would account for why he'd known her name and why he'd asked about having a nickname. And, of course, she hadn't mentioned her last name yet. He hadn't asked, and she'd just assumed it hadn't mattered to him.

Dread began a slow slither through her body.

"I admit," Dylan said, his voice dropping with chagrin, "I didn't really know Catherine all that well before—" He cast a glance in the direction of the children, who were occupied playing games and out of hearing range for the awkward confession.

Catherine opened her mouth, needing to clear up the confusion, wanting to set Dylan straight about her true identity. But what could she say here, now? In front of his family?

She clamped her lips together, trying to think of something—anything—that wouldn't give away the real reason she'd had to run away from home.

Dylan cleared his throat. "I honestly don't have much recollection of my time with Catherine. But I'm aiming to make up for my past mistakes by taking good care of her and Austin now."

He didn't have much recollection of his time with Kit? Was he insinuating that he'd been inebriated during his encounters with the young woman? That in his alcohol-induced condition, he hadn't taken the time to get to know her, not even enough to remember what she looked like?

Catherine's stomach churned. If that was the case, then it was no wonder when she arrived yesterday with Austin he'd assumed she was the baby's mother. What reason had she given him to believe otherwise?

She tried to ward off the rising panic. But it continued to swell, pushing and clawing at her throat, demanding that she speak up now and tell these good people the truth about the mix-up. They'd all understand she'd made an innocent mistake, hadn't meant to trick Dylan into marrying her, had merely been prey to miscommunication.

Around her, Dylan's family, especially his sisters-in-law, assured him he was being honorable. His brothers chimed in with affirmation, praising him for stepping up to take care of a family so readily. But as they conversed, guilt settled over Catherine in heavy layers until she felt as though she were suffocating.

"Are you alright?" From the bench beside her, Greta's kind question brought a halt to the chatter. Wyatt's wife wasn't as outgoing as the other women, but with her light brown hair and silvery blue eyes, she was every bit as pretty. "You look as though you might faint."

Dylan immediately reached out a steadying hand too. "I'll hold Austin if you'd like."

Now was her chance to set everyone straight. But as Dylan gently pried Austin from her, she had the premonition that she'd never get to hold the baby again if she revealed she wasn't Kit—Katherine Olson—and was instead Catherine Remington. They'd know she was an impostor and didn't really belong. Dylan might never let her near Austin again.

Tears sprang to Catherine's eyes. Already she'd made a mess of her life with everything that had happened in Chicago. Already she'd lost everything and everyone she'd known. Now the prospect of having Austin ripped from her too, after he'd filled the void left by losing her family, was almost too much to bear.

"It's okay." Greta rubbed her back.

"I'm sorry," Catherine whispered, blinking back tears. "The whole situation has been so difficult."

"It's not your fault." Dylan's tone was laced with anguish.

She closed her eyes, finally comprehending that Dylan had married her because he'd wanted to do the right thing by Kit, and he was nobly taking the blame of their infidelity upon himself. He was truly a good man in spite of his past indiscretions. And because he was a good man, he deserved the truth from her about who she was.

Swallowing hard, she breathed in and opened her eyes, meeting Dylan's furrowed gaze. He needed to know he'd married the wrong woman, even if he gave her an annulment and ordered her out of his house and demanded that she stay away from Austin forever. No matter the result, she had to tell him.

But not here. She searched the perimeter of the yard for a place they could go to talk. Maybe she ought to wait until later when they were back in town. At least then if he kicked her out of the cabin, she could get a room in a nearby hotel.

Yes, she'd tell him later. In private. She'd face the consequences then.

"You're a McQuaid now." Greta hovered near her. "And McQuaids are faithful and forgiving. You'll find that out soon enough."

Would they accept her as one of their own once they knew the truth? Catherine suppressed the doubts. For now, she had to pull her emotions together and act like everything was fine.

"Should we head on back home?" Dylan glanced at the

evening sky, now turning a shade of lavender with the sun beginning its descent behind the western range.

The sooner they left, the sooner she'd have to make her admission. "I'm not in a rush."

"You sure?" Dylan studied her face as though sensing something wasn't right.

She nodded and started to reassure him, but Ivy released a pain-filled cry, one Catherine immediately recognized as belonging to a woman in travail.

Catherine stood so abruptly that she bumped into Dylan. At the jostling, Austin's sleeping eyes flew open, and he released a startled wail. Catherine's attention stayed riveted to Ivy.

The young woman's eyes were wide and filled with fear, and her husband grabbed her hand. "Is it time?"

Catherine wanted to blurt out that yes, indeed, it was time. But if Dylan and his family thought she was Kit, how could she explain her midwifery skills?

"I'll go on to town and fetch the doc," Wyatt called over his shoulder as he took off at a jog toward the barn.

The other women congregated around Ivy, helping her up. As she made it to her feet, she wobbled.

With a growl, Jericho scooped her into his arms, his expression rigid with determination.

"We need to get on home, Jericho," Ivy said as the young man strode toward Wyatt's house. "I can't impose on Wyatt and Greta for the birthing."

"We want you to stay, Ivy." Greta practically ran to keep up with Jericho.

"It's not all that far," Ivy insisted. "We can make it there."

Jericho didn't stop, not even a falter in his steps. Catherine watched his back until he disappeared into the house. She liked him. Even though he was undoubtedly enamored with Ivy, he wasn't a pushover, was instead a wise and determined young man.

With everyone having scurried off, Catherine stood beside Dylan, helplessness rushing through her. She couldn't sit back and do nothing, not when she'd been trained in midwifery since she was just a child. Not when she'd been delivering babies on her own since she was fifteen years old. She'd lost count of how many newborns she'd helped birth.

As another of Ivy's screams echoed from inside the house, Catherine took a step forward but then forced herself to halt.

Dylan stared at the door, his eyes wide with concern.

"I could go in and help," Catherine offered hesitantly.

"Reckon she's in good hands until the doc can get here."

"That's true." From everything Catherine had learned, Greta had already gone through five birthings of her own. While one of her babies hadn't lived long, Greta was practiced enough with travail to aid Ivy for now. And Linnea was a brilliant scientist and had assisted in a few labors and deliveries.

"I suppose we should head on out. This could take a while." Dylan's voice contained a reluctance that told Catherine he didn't want to depart, that he was worried about his sister.

She didn't want to leave either. She simply couldn't. It wasn't within her nature or training to walk away from a woman in the midst of child birthing. "If you'd like to stay, I won't object."

"Maybe a short while."

"I don't mind." That was an understatement.

"Alright then." Dylan sat back down on the bench, almost as though his legs couldn't hold him a moment longer.

She lowered herself to the spot beside him in spite of everything within her urging her to go inside and take over the birthing.

"Ivy's gonna be fine, just fine," Dylan said.

"You're right. Ivy's young and healthy and strong." Even so, sometimes things went wrong that they couldn't control. But Catherine bit back the warning and let her words of assurance settle between them.

Austin had gone back to sleep in Dylan's arm, unaware of the turmoil she and Dylan were both feeling.

Dylan continued to stare at the house right along with her. His body was rigid, probably coiled as tightly as hers and ready to spring at the least evidence of a problem. With the children having been ushered off to the barn to wait out the labor, silence had settled over the ranch, broken only by the lowing of cattle somewhere nearby and the whistle of the wind through the grass.

"My ma died after childbirth." Dylan finally spoke, his voice ragged and raw.

"I'm sorry, Dylan." Catherine's hand reached out as if it had a mind of its own, and she laid it on Dylan's, squeezing gently.

He turned up his hand and captured hers, holding tight as though he needed someone to cling to.

"Flynn did his best to protect Ivy and me from all that was going on with my ma and my stepdad, but I reckon child birthing will always scare the living daylights out of me."

She glanced at their hands together. The pressure of his

THE LAST CHANCE COWBOY

fingers and the firmness of his hold wrapped around her and enveloped her with a feeling that she wasn't alone, that they would help each other get through this trial. Was that what marriage was all about? Having someone to walk with you amidst whatever difficulties you faced so you didn't have to do it alone?

She wanted him to know she was there for him. If she shared a little bit about her background in midwifery without telling him everything, would that ease his turmoil? "My grandmother and mother are both very skilled midwives."

"They are?"

"Yes, and I know for a fact that most women like Ivy come through childbearing with no issues."

"You think so?" He turned his green-blue eyes upon her, those long lashes making her want to tell him anything just so his fear would go away.

She laid her other hand on his, sandwiching his big hand between hers. "With a skilled doctor, she'll come through it fine."

Dylan's eyes locked with hers as though drinking in her confidence. "Doc's a good one. Set up an office in Fairplay about two years ago. Now we don't have to share a doc with the surrounding towns."

"Well then, there's nothing to worry about."

She waited for him to ask her more about her grandmother and mother. But he didn't seem fazed by this new piece of information about her family, likely because he didn't know—or remember—much of anything to begin with and was ashamed to admit it.

They sat outside until well after dark, holding hands and

talking more about his childhood and his family to distract him from the noises and commotion from within the house.

In the high altitude of South Park, the temperatures dropped rapidly with nightfall, as she'd discovered the previous evening when walking home after supper at the Gundersons'. Finally, she couldn't contain a shiver, and Dylan ushered her inside with the baby.

The main front room was empty except for a rocking chair and a stool near the stove. Simple handmade adornments made the room homey—lacy curtains in the window, a colorfully braided rug in front of the stove, a framed sketch of the ranch hanging on the longest wall. She guessed the room normally held the table and benches that were still out in the yard.

"I'll go wait in the barn with the men." Dylan hovered near the entrance, rubbing his gloved hands together and peering warily at the closed bedroom door.

Jericho was nowhere to be seen. Was he in the birthing chamber with Ivy? Catherine's brow puckered at such an odd prospect. Fathers-to-be usually made themselves scarce during travail. Their anxiety and interference made the birthing worse. And if something happened?

She shook her head. Maybe Dylan should remain in the house just in case they needed help with Jericho. "Perhaps you can help me feed Austin first?"

At her suggestion, he seemed relieved and set to work warming water in the kitchen off the main living area as if he were right at home there. Then while she reclined in the rocker and fed Austin, he rolled up his sleeves and scrubbed the pots and pans left from their supper.

When he finished, he lowered himself onto the stool beside

her and made no more mention of leaving. Instead, they easily talked as they had earlier. Catherine was surprised when he turned the conversation back to her at times, asking her about her childhood and family. Although she wanted to share openly and freely about who she was as well as her background, this wasn't the time to spring the news on him that she wasn't who he thought. Instead, she kept her anecdotes vague as she had during previous discussions.

As the hours passed with no sign of Wyatt or the doctor, Dylan began to pace. Finally, after one particularly long, piercing scream, Jericho barged out of the bedroom, his eyes wide, his hair disheveled, and his face taut with fear.

Sitting in the rocker beside the window and holding the baby, Catherine brought the chair to a halt.

Jericho glanced around the room frantically. "Where in the blazing smoke is the doctor?"

"Wyatt's not back." Dylan paused in his pacing.

"What's taking him so long?" Jericho's voice rose, thin with desperation.

"Maybe Doc is out on another call." Dylan gave life to the thought that had been running through Catherine's mind for the past hour.

"We need the doc! Now!" Jericho crossed the room, his boots slapping the floor hard as if he had every intention of bringing the doctor in at gunpoint.

Heart picking up pace, Catherine rose from the rocker. She couldn't stand idly by any longer. She had the skills and experience to assist in Ivy's delivery better than any doctor. And if Ivy was in trouble, then Catherine had to stop worrying about the ramifications of revealing too much about herself here and now. After all, Dylan and the McQuaids would find out who she was eventually.

"I'll help."

Jericho reached the door and opened it with a bang as if he hadn't heard her.

"I'm trained in midwifery." She spoke louder. "I can assist Ivy."

Jericho paused on the threshold, narrowing his gaze at her. "You're a midwife?"

"Her grandmother and mother are," Dylan said.

Jericho wavered, his tortured eyes studying Catherine. "The baby's arm is out but the rest isn't coming."

Alarm resounded through her, but she kept her expression calm so that she didn't worry Jericho more than he already was. "I'll take a look and see what I can do."

He hesitated only a moment longer before he nodded at the bedroom door. "Then go on in. At this point we need any help we can get."

She didn't wait for further permission. She handed Austin off to Dylan then began rolling up her sleeves.

CHAPTER

12

Catherine stepped inside and assessed the situation by the glow of several oil lanterns around the room. Even as Ivy strained with another push, Catherine could see that the birthing wasn't progressing the way it should.

Linnea sat on the end of the bed directing the delivery. Greta perched on a chair beside Ivy, holding her hand and pressing a cool cloth to her flushed face.

"Stop pushing," Catherine said.

Linnea and Greta looked up, surprise widening their eyes.

Catherine didn't offer an explanation and instead went straight to Ivy's abdomen and pressed her fingers expertly around the perimeter, feeling the baby's position. "We need to reinsert the arm and then bring the head down. But first we'll need to angle Ivy so the baby recedes a bit."

Both Linnea and Greta stood. And as Catherine rattled off a list of instructions, they hurried to gather the supplies she asked for, including possible herbal remedies. The medicines were all in Catherine's birth satchel in Fairplay, but she hoped Linnea could find a few things to alleviate Ivy's pain and anxiety.

Without waiting for Linnea's or Greta's assistance, she tugged Ivy up from the bed. "I know this will be very uncomfortable, but I need you to shift positions."

Trembling and weak, Ivy allowed Catherine to lift her backside far enough that most of the baby's arm disappeared, leaving only the hand exposed.

"Once we get your baby's arm back inside, it will get much easier."

Catherine lathered oil on her hands. Then she bent the baby's elbow and pushed up on the shoulder, guiding the baby out of the birth canal. As Ivy screamed at the pain, Catherine nodded at Greta, who was already back. "Go ahead and press the baby's head down to the right."

While Greta worked on the outside, Catherine tilted the shoulder into position so that the head moved into the pelvis.

"Now you can push, Ivy." Catherine slid her hand out and waited.

After several strong exertions, the head emerged. But even after more efforts at pushing, the baby's shoulders wouldn't budge. Shoulder dystocia. The baby's shoulders were again causing the problem, were likely too big.

Catherine attempted to manually reposition the baby and had Ivy try several birthing positions before allowing her to fall back onto the bed.

"I'll need a sterilized lancet," Catherine called out, wishing more than ever for her bag. "Or whatever you can locate closest to it."

Linnea had returned with several herbal remedies, and

Greta raced off to do her bidding. While waiting, Catherine made quick work of applying oil and working the area in preparation for the widening. All the while, the baby wasn't getting enough oxygen and was turning a shade of blue.

"Hurry!" She motioned toward Greta when she rushed into the bedroom with the knife.

Jericho was fast on her heels, his mouth set in a grim line. "What do you think you're doing?"

"I'm saving your child and your wife." Catherine took the knife, focused intently, and made the cut before Jericho could prevent her.

Ivy screamed as if she were being murdered, and Jericho shouted at Catherine to stop, but she worked steadily, easing the pressure and drawing the baby out in the same movement.

In the next instant, she swiped up the newborn, cleared the mouth and nostrils, and administered artificial breathing. After several moments, the little one drew in a raspy breath and then emitted a tiny wail.

A sob escaped from Ivy. "Everything's okay?"

"She's alive." Catherine continued a few more emergency breaths.

"A girl, Jericho." Ivy sobbed openly now. "Did you hear that? We've got ourselves a girl."

Jericho was clutching Ivy's hands and watching Catherine, fear etching deep grooves across his forehead and into the corners of his eyes.

"Her skin is turning a mottled red." Catherine clipped the umbilical cord and then handed the baby off to Greta, who was holding out a blanket in readiness. "Which means she's breathing and doing just fine."

Catherine bent to assess the afterbirth of the placenta.

The episiotomy was long and would take some stitching to repair. But from what she could tell, Ivy wasn't bleeding more profusely than expected after such trauma.

Even so, Catherine sewed her with care and precision until Ivy was finally lying comfortably, her baby wrapped in her arms. Just as Catherine finished applying a salve, Wyatt burst into the room, presumably with the doctor on his heels.

The middle-aged man was disheveled, his hat nowhere to be seen and his thinning hair standing on end. He tossed aside his coat as he plowed his way to the bedside and peppered Ivy and Linnea with questions. When Catherine attempted to inform him of the procedures she'd performed, the doctor paused and peered down his nose at her, his eyes filling with disdain. "Ma'am, your assistance is no longer necessary. I shall take over now."

She took a rapid step back, almost as if he'd slapped her in the face. What had she done to deserve such rudeness? Was he offended that she'd taken over in his stead? Or did he look down on her the same way some of the other townspeople had earlier when she'd gone shopping, believing she was Austin's birth mother and an immoral and loose woman?

Words to the contrary formed on her tongue. The need to defend herself roiled around inside, but before she said anything she'd regret, she spun and crossed the room. She had to tell Dylan her real identity before she blurted the news to anyone else. He deserved to know first.

As she reached the door, Greta intercepted her and gave her a gentle hug. "Thank you," she whispered. "You were amazing."

Catherine tried to smile her gratitude, but she couldn't get her lips to work against the hurt and frustration closing in. The moment she stepped out of the room, Dylan stopped his pacing. He was no longer holding Austin, and she glimpsed the baby sleeping in a crate and cushioned by blankets. Greta or Linnea must have made the makeshift baby bed at some point during the past hour.

Dylan watched her expectantly, his tired eyes seeming to assess her as if she'd been the one going through travail and not Ivy. "You alright?"

The simple question brought the sting of tears. No one had ever asked her if she was alright after a delivery. They inquired about the baby and the mother and the father and the rest of the family. But no one ever thought to discover how she was doing. Except now. Except Dylan.

She gave a slight shrug. "Ivy and the baby are safe. That's all that matters."

He started toward her. "Greta told me you knew exactly what to do. That you saved the baby's life. And possibly Ivy's."

"I should have gone in sooner."

"You were there when they needed you. And that's what counts."

"I could have intervened quicker and saved her and the baby the trauma."

He halted a foot away, lifted a hand as though to touch her, but hesitated. "You're being too hard on yourself."

The tears pressed hot at the backs of her eyes. This man was much too kind to her. He had been from the moment she arrived. Before she could stop it, a tear spilled over.

Mortified, she tried to wipe it away before he saw it. But his attention dropped to her cheek, and his brow furrowed.

"Hey there, darlin'." He reached for her, and before she knew what he was doing, he was drawing her into an embrace. "Come here. Come on, now."

He was turning out to be an affectionate man who seemed to thrive on physical touch. At the very least, he was holding and touching her a great deal more than she'd anticipated. She needed to resist, couldn't carry on with this man any further, not with the misunderstanding over her identity standing between them. But as he pulled her against his chest, she went to him, allowed him to fold her into an embrace.

A sense of security and safety filled her in a way she hadn't experienced since leaving Chicago and everything familiar behind. She took in a deep breath, inhaling his scent, a mixture of metal and gun smoke.

During the past two months of running and hiding and trying to take care of Austin by herself, she'd had to remain strong. But now, with Dylan's arms around her lending her strength, she let herself be weak for just a moment and gave way to the horror of the murder she'd witnessed, the fear of Rocky's accusations, and the sorrow of leaving her home and everything that had been secure. The ache she'd been holding at bay swelled into her throat. More hot tears spilled over. She couldn't stop them—didn't even try.

After she revealed the truth to Dylan, she'd have to leave. But how would she make it alone? Without anyone at all, not even Austin to keep her busy? Where would she go next? Already the bleakness of her future stretched out before her, and she wasn't sure she could move on.

She pressed her face into Dylan's chest and let his shirt capture her tears.

His arms tightened around her. "What are the tears for, darlin'? What's bothering you?"

If only this marriage to him was real. If only she'd been clearer about her identity from the start . . .

The tears flowed faster, and a sob welled up. She let her arms slide around his waist, needing someone to lean on, even if only for a moment.

"Hey now." He dipped his head down, and his voice rumbled near her ear. "Whatever it is can't be that bad, can it?"

It was. But she had to compose herself and do the right thing. "Dylan, I have a confession to make." Her conscience wouldn't let her wait another minute. She was a person of integrity just like her father, and she couldn't knowingly perpetuate a lie.

The bedroom door opened, and footsteps as well as voices told her they were no longer alone.

She wiped the moisture from her cheeks before she pulled back from Dylan. He released her, but only after she tugged to disentangle herself.

Even then, he clasped her hand with a gentle squeeze. His eyes radiated a tenderness and a kindness that reached down inside to soothe her soul.

It would be so easy to let herself fall for him. With every passing moment, her empathy toward Kit just kept increasing. She'd been with Dylan less than two days, and already she found him difficult to hold at arm's length. What would being with him any longer do to her resistance? She only had to look at Austin to know what the answer to that question had been for Kit.

Jericho and Wyatt stood outside the closed bedroom door. Jericho brushed a hand over his eyes, as though wiping away tears of his own. "Son of a gun," Jericho whispered hoarsely. "That was about the hardest thing I've ever faced. Even worse than facing down an ugly criminal."

Wyatt clamped the new dad's shoulder affectionately. "Blamed right it's hard."

"Don't know how you've managed to go through this five times. I'm thinking once is all I can handle."

Wyatt's lips turned up into a handsome grin, one that rivaled Dylan's. "You sure as cow patty ain't gonna get away with this once. Not with the way you got a hankering for your wife."

Dylan stiffened. "Don't forget. That wife is our sister."

Wyatt's grin slipped away.

"Jericho would be better off leaving her alone so she don't have to worry about giving birth again." Dylan's steely tone could have cut through ice.

Catherine sensed as before that Dylan and Jericho had a history that was causing the tension, but whatever had happened, it was clear both men cared deeply for Ivy.

Jericho pulled himself up, his chest puffing and shoulders turning rigid. "Since when have you become the expert on leaving women alone?"

Dylan's eyes flickered with something. Was it hurt? Remorse? "When I left Chicago, I left my old ways behind."

Jericho expelled a breath. "Blast it all. I know. And I shouldn't have said that."

Dylan jutted his chin.

Catherine could only imagine the mortification of having his mistakes thrown in his face day after day. She'd only had to deal with it for one day, and already it had been hard.

"Ivy's my wife now, Dylan. And I love her more than

anything," Jericho stated calmly but with an undertone of frustration. "When will you finally accept it?"

"I've accepted it."

Jericho held Dylan's gaze a moment longer before switching his attention to Catherine. "Don't know how to thank you for going in and taking charge. I have no doubt you saved both Ivy and the baby."

"I'm only sorry I didn't step in sooner."

Jericho shook his head. "You don't owe me any apologies. I'm the one who's sorry for doubting you."

"I should have explained my experience—"

"We didn't give you the chance."

"Mighty glad you were here," Wyatt interjected. "Seems to me, Dylan's got himself a fine wife."

Should she say something now? Just blurt out that she wasn't who they thought she was?

Beside her, she could feel Dylan standing taller, as if his brother's words were just what he'd needed to hear. How could she deny Dylan this moment of earning his brother's approval, something he'd probably had a difficult time gaining after his years of immoral living?

"She's real fine." Jericho echoed his agreement.

"I'm proud of you, Dylan." Wyatt gave Dylan a somber nod. "Know I don't say it much, if at all. But you're buckling down and doing what's honorable, and I admire you for it."

Dylan nodded back. "Thank you, Wyatt. That means a lot coming from you."

The bedroom door opened again, and Greta emerged. Though her face was lined with weariness, she managed a bright smile for everyone. "The doctor says everything is looking just fine."

"'Course it is," Dylan growled, slipping his hand out of Catherine's, winding it behind her back, and drawing her against him.

"It's a good thing you and Catherine stayed." Greta leaned into Wyatt, who was quick to gather her to his side and hold her up too.

"We both wanted to make sure Ivy was alright." Dylan's arm tightened around Catherine.

She didn't want to pull away, guessing he needed the accolades from his family even more than she did.

"Catherine was a godsend," Greta continued, "and we're blessed to have her as part of the family."

"Thank you." If only she truly was a part of the family.

Wyatt pressed a kiss against Greta's head, earning another smile from her. "I'm mighty glad God has a way of turning our messes around and making something useful out of them."

Catherine had the feeling he was speaking from personal experience. She'd have to ply Dylan later for information on how the couple had overcome their difficulties to stay happily married.

"Seems like God's doing the same for you." Wyatt shared another meaningful look with Dylan.

"Hope so." Dylan's attention drifted to the crate where Austin was still sound asleep. "Reckon it's time to get my wife and babe home to bed."

"Reckon so." Wyatt's comment in return contained an element of teasing, one that made everyone grin, including Dylan—although his didn't reach his eyes.

Heat rose into Catherine's cheeks. Were they insinuating Dylan was eager to return home and get into bed with her?

It was only a logical conclusion since they were newlyweds, and they had no idea Dylan wanted to wait and get to know each other first.

Now after learning of the mix-up, she was more relieved than ever that he'd come up with such a plan. She couldn't imagine how much more complicated their situation would be if they'd already spent a night together.

"Dylan McQuaid." Linnea stepped out of the bedroom and quickly crossed the room toward Catherine, her eyes shining with admiration. "I don't know where you found this gem. But you need to keep her."

The shadows lingering in Dylan's expression seemed to flit away. And as he looked down at Catherine, happiness filled his eyes. After being the black sheep of the family, he probably hadn't heard any praise for a long time, maybe not ever.

What would happen when she revealed the truth and then he had to confess to his family that he'd been wrong, that he hadn't chosen well, that she wasn't a gem after all?

A knot formed in the pit of her stomach. He'd become a laughingstock for marrying the wrong woman. Maybe they'd accuse him of more indecency and infidelity. And his job as sheriff would be in worse jeopardy than it already was since her arrival with Austin.

The knot inside cinched tighter. Heaven help her. She didn't want to hurt him further. But she couldn't possibly stay silent about who she was. Could she?

Dylan's gaze dropped to her lips, and his pupils darkened with desire.

Her pulse hopped with anticipation. Did he want to kiss her again? If so, she knew she was going to let him. And she also knew she couldn't say anything about their marriage mistake. At least not yet. Not until she figured out a way to make the revelation without hurting his reputation. And of course, she had to be careful about bringing undue attention to her whereabouts.

He leaned closer but aimed for her forehead, pressing a tender kiss there.

She held in a sigh. Abstaining was for the best . . . until she decided how to clean up this new mess she'd made.

As much as she hated the thought of allowing the mistaken identity to continue, for the time being, it was safest for them all.

CHAPTER
13

Dylan shifted the stiff steer's hair first one way and then the other. Part of the burned flesh was new. Didn't take much to see that the top of a *U* had been filled in to form an *O*.

"Them's my beeves fair and square." J. D. Otto spat a stream of tobacco into the dust. His brown hat was stained with sweat rings and age, shielding his thick, leathery face.

"The hair here is singed." Dylan pointed to the area around the top of the *O*. "And Updegraff is complaining that more of his cattle are missing."

J. D. tightened first one leather glove and then the other without meeting Dylan's gaze. The wiry rancher didn't frighten Dylan, even though he was a head taller and always as grim as a funeral-goer. "Young man, I don't take kindly to you coming out here to my ranch and accusing me of thieving someone else's cattle."

Dylan gave the steer a friendly thump against its flank. "Reckon I wouldn't have to come out if the accusations weren't true."

J. D. laid a hand on his revolver.

Behind Dylan came the distinct click of Stu cocking the hammer on his Colt. Still mounted on his horse, Stu hadn't said a word during the entire exchange. He rarely did. His severe expression was enough.

Dylan straightened the sheriff star pinned to his coat, hoping to remind J. D. and his men that he represented the law and was doing his duty. Last thing he wanted was a gun battle here on J. D.'s ranch, not when half a dozen hot and dirty cowhands were looking on, taking a break from branding calves.

With May the preferred month for castrating and branding, many of the area ranchers were in the process of or had already finished marking their calves, especially while they were small enough to handle. Even so, the job was hard and dangerous. The calves had to be roped and dragged to the fire, then thrown down before being branded.

If properly done, the searing against their hides didn't cause the creatures much pain, only a little discomfort so long as the hot iron was burned just deep enough to prevent hair from growing back but not scalding to the point of causing the skin to break open into a wound that could fester.

Dylan had branded enough cattle to know what he was looking at. And the marks on four of J. D.'s steers were fresh. 'Course, J. D. wouldn't have branded the stolen cattle openly like he was doing with the calves. Nope, he'd likely had a couple of his men do it with a saddle cinch ring. It was an easy trick that rustlers resorted to, heating the rings and then carefully applying the hot iron long enough to burn the hair away and make the alteration blend with the original brand.

The problem was, the best way to prove the tampering

was to kill and skin the steer, exposing the hide to examine it for differing scar tissue. And he wasn't about to do that, although he was sorely tempted, especially since J. D. kept on giving him the runaround.

"Fact is," Dylan said, "Updegraff's cowhands saw a couple of your men driving off the cattle."

"Can't help it if Updegraff is letting his beeves stray into the same pasture as mine. Bound to be some that get mixed up."

"And there's bound to be more opportunity to drive some into your herd and count them as yours."

"Sometimes that happens, McQuaid. You oughta know that."

"Honest mistakes happen. But outright stealing's another thing altogether."

J. D.'s spread was small, with a few corrals and a couple of hastily built cabins and barns. Although Dylan hadn't been in the area last spring, he'd learned that's when J. D. had arrived. From all appearances, the fella had no intention of making a go of ranching or using the place as his long-term residence. Dylan had speculated with Stu that J. D. was there to rustle as much cattle as possible and then make a split with the profit before heading on to another place where he could prey on local ranchers.

In trailing each of J. D.'s cowhands, Dylan had narrowed down the two who were doing the most rustling, J. D.'s step-brother, Butch, and his friend Frank. Problem was, Dylan still hadn't been able to catch them in the act of thieving.

And the other problem was that he'd found evidence another rustler was in the area. While J. D. was up to his old tricks, the new threat was taking off with the cattle and possibly hiding them in a remote location, probably with the intent of driving them to New Mexico or Arizona markets. It was even possible J. D. was behind the new batch of rustling, using it as a decoy to keep Dylan running in circles.

With more random cattle disappearing over the past couple of days, some blamed Two-Toed Joe. Dylan had heard rumors of the bear killing steers farther south. But maybe the creature had made his way north into the heart of South Park, especially if he had a hankering for beef. There was plenty to feast on.

Regardless of the presence of the giant bear, he had to find solid proof of J. D.'s rustling. And even though the fella's poor branding job made him a suspect, it still wasn't enough to lock him away.

Dylan needed more evidence. And he needed it yesterday. With every passing day that additional steers disappeared, the ranchers were only getting more sticks in their craws. Pretty soon, they'd all be agreeing with Harlan Hatfield that making Dylan sheriff had been a big mistake, and they'd vote him out quicker than a wink and a whistle.

Dylan rested both hands on his revolvers. "Listen here, J. D. I know you're stealing cattle. Maybe I can't prove it today. But mark my words, I will prove it and send you to prison for it."

J. D.'s only answer was to spit another stream of tobacco into the dirt.

Dylan took stock of each of the men, including Butch and Frank down by the ramshackle cottage, where a couple of women stood in the doorway. Some of the cowhands working for J. D. were honest fellas hired on for an honest wage. Maybe he could get one of the more upright of them to give

him inside information, details that could help him convict
J. D. once and for all.

With a final warning glare aimed at J. D., Dylan mounted
and nudged his horse around. "Two-Toed Joe's the real culprit," J. D. called after him. "Everyone knows it 'cept you."

Dylan paused.

"Reckon now you're too busy with that whore of yours
to see the difference."

Whore? White-hot anger raced up Dylan's spine. In the
blink of an eye, he twisted in his saddle and had both his
revolvers trained on J. D.

J. D. started to jerk his gun out, but Dylan took a shot,
firing right through the man's hat.

"Leave your gun in the holster, J. D." His aim was on
the man's head. "Or this ain't gonna end pretty." From his
peripheral, Dylan could see Frank starting to take aim at
him. He shifted his second revolver and fired. The bullet
zipped through the fella's hat in the exact same spot he'd
shot J. D.'s.

"Best listen to the sheriff," Stu said from behind.

Butch took aim, and Dylan shot through his hat too.
He didn't mind the comments people made about his past
lifestyle and his many mistakes. He was used to it. But he
wouldn't tolerate anybody talking about Catherine that way.
No how, no way.

He unsheathed his rifle from the scabbard on his saddle,
took aim at the steer standing farthest away. He sighted down
his rifle and pulled the trigger. At the familiar blast and
kickback, Dylan drew in a breath of gun smoke. In the next
instant, the steer released a bellow and shook his head.

"Now, hold on." J. D. had taken off his hat and inspected

the bullet hole, and now slammed the hat back on his head. "You can't come here and start killing my cattle. You'll pay for that steer."

Dylan slipped the rifle back into the carrier. At the same instant, J. D.'s protest died away as he caught sight of the hole in the middle of the steer's ear.

"You talk about my wife that way ever again"—the tension inside Dylan made each word come out clipped and hard—"I'll be shooting you just the way I did your steer."

If they hadn't already heard about his sharpshooting skills, now they knew. And now they also knew he wasn't gonna sit back and listen to anyone call his wife vulgar names.

During the past week since Ivy gave birth, Catherine had more than earned a spot of honor in the family—and in the community, for that matter. Word had gotten around about how she'd saved Ivy and the babe. Even the doc had grudgingly admitted Catherine's intervention had been skilled. He hadn't found any fault in what she'd done, said he couldn't have done it better himself.

Even without all that, Dylan liked her and was beginning to understand why he'd been drawn to her in the first place. She was kind to him—though she had no reason to be—was easy to talk to, was insightful and interesting, and had quickly turned his home into a place he wanted to be. To top it all, she was a loving ma to Austin, caring for him at all hours of the day and night.

To make things a mite easier on her, he'd been getting up with Austin and feeding and changing him so she could sleep a little later. When she began to stir, he brought her a cup of coffee in bed. Though she kept protesting that he shouldn't do it, her eyes had widened with pleasure, and she'd even smiled at him this morning, a slow, sleepy smile that had started heat burning through his gut.

Whatever the case, no matter how he felt about her, she deserved respect from J. D. and everyone else.

During the ride back to town, his anger only festered. By the time they were clattering down Main Street, he wanted to hit someone or something. Thankfully Stu didn't say a word the whole time and only cast him glances, as if gauging whether he needed to lasso and hog-tie him to keep him from doing something stupid.

As they passed by the Senate Saloon, the door stood open. In the early evening, laughter wafted outside along with the scent of cigar smoke and whiskey. Dylan breathed it in, and his mouth suddenly felt as dry as the Arkansas River in the heat of summer. A familiar longing pulled at him. All he needed was one drink to quench his thirst. Just a small one.

He let his reins hang looser, and his horse slowed its pace. More laughter rolled out into the street, beckoning him.

What harm could come from sitting down for an hour, leaning back, chatting, and sipping a beer? Was he being too hard on himself by cutting out that part of his life completely? After all, he knew plenty of good men who drank now and again.

"Trudy said yous and the wife are coming to dinner after church tomorrow." Stu's voice broke through the haze, drawing his attention away from the saloon. He tried to focus on his deputy's face, but all he could see was the open door and dark interior. The darkness and drinking had always given him solace, something he was in sore need of at the moment.

"Told me not to take no for an answer." Stu seemed to be urging his horse faster. Either that or Dylan had slowed to a crawl.

Dylan swallowed hard but couldn't get rid of the dryness and the growing need to wet his tongue.

"From the way Trudy carries on, I suppose yous better just get the wife and wee one and come on over tonight."

"Tonight?" Dylan tried to make his mind focus on what Stu was saying. "What's tonight?"

"Supper."

"What about it?"

"Yous best come on over." Something in Stu's tone needled at Dylan. And when he chanced a glance at his deputy, the scraggly brows that rose above concerned eyes told him Stu wasn't oblivious to the war waging inside him.

"I'll be alright, Stu."

"You betcha yous will. Now let's go get the wife and wee one." Stu set course toward the courthouse, maneuvering his horse so it was blocking Dylan's access to the saloon. Once they moved past the establishment, a strange sickening settled low inside Dylan.

Tarnation. He'd been tempted to stop and drink. What in the blazes had he been thinking? He couldn't remember the last time he'd seriously considered the possibility, not since those first few days after leaving Chicago when the taste of drink had still burned at the back of his throat. Since then, he'd been thirsty once in a while. But he never seriously contemplated walking into a saloon, sitting down, and ordering a drink—not the way he just had, almost as if the place would bring him comfort and peace.

What kind of crazy thought was that? How could he so

easily forget the loneliness and emptiness of his past life? And how could he so easily forget the pain and turmoil his drinking had caused not only to himself but to so many others, including Catherine?

Stu reined in at the front of the courthouse. "I'll wait while yous go get the family."

Dylan nodded, shame bridling his tongue. He dismounted, looped the reins around the hitching post, then started toward the cabin. *Lord, I thought I was doing good fighting against temptation. What's wrong with me?*

He paused in front of the door, trying to shake off the melancholy. *Please, God. I can't fail now, not when I need to be a good husband and pa.*

At a frightened squeal from inside followed by a loud bang, he fumbled at the door handle, unable to open it fast enough. As he swung the door wide, he slipped his revolver from his holster, his blood pounding with the need to keep Catherine and Austin safe. They were his now, and he wouldn't let anything harm them.

He wasn't sure what he was expecting upon entry, but not the sight of Catherine standing on the chair, her eyes wild and her face flushed. She darted a glance his way before returning it to a dark spot underneath the bed.

"What's wrong?" Was a fugitive hiding there? A feral dog? A rattlesnake? With Austin bundled up and sleeping on the bed between pillows, was the babe in danger?

"Oh my stars." She wobbled just slightly on the uneven chair. The other chair was already tipped over. Had she fallen from it?

"Whoa now." He bolted toward her. She was so flustered she was gonna crash if she wasn't more careful.

"It's under the bed." She didn't take her attention from the shadows there.

He holstered his gun and placed both hands on her waist to steady her. "What's under the bed?"

"A mouse."

The tension eased from his shoulders. She was on the chair because she'd seen a mouse? "As in a little creature about the size of one of Austin's fingers?"

"It was much bigger than that."

"How big?" He surveyed the floor near the bed. Maybe she'd mistaken it for a possum or some other critter.

"It was as big as a—" Before she could finish her description, a gray furry bundle scurried out from underneath the bed. She released a startled scream and hopped and would have fallen if he hadn't been there holding her.

"That?" He couldn't keep the humor from creeping into his voice as the creature skittered under the chest of drawers. "That mouse is smaller than an ant."

"Oh no it isn't. It's huge." She shifted her gaze to the sliver of space beneath the drawers.

Dylan's hands fit just right, spanning her middle, settling on her hips as if that's where they belonged. From her perch, she was a head taller than him, so he found himself peering up at her. With eyes rounded wide, the flecks of green and brown mingled together like spring leaves blown by the wind. Her long hair was unbound and looked darker and damper, as though she'd recently washed it.

He drew in a breath and caught a whiff of rose water. Had she taken a bath? Here in the house?

His skin prickled with sudden heat, and his thoughts flew back to the kisses he'd given her at the table outside Wyatt's house, two delicious kisses he'd hoped would prove to his family he was serious about his marriage. He didn't want them knowing or thinking he hadn't consummated and had no immediate plans to do so. That wasn't any of their business, and he didn't need them meddling.

But those kisses had about driven him crazy. Something about Catherine—her innocence, naivety, and sweetness—was alluring, did strange things to his insides, and made him crave her all the more.

As with the first kiss, she kissed like she'd never been with a man and didn't know what to do. 'Course, she'd been with him and had some experience in that area. So then why did the kisses feel so new, as though he was exploring uncharted territory?

He wished he could remember something—anything—from their time together. But he was ashamed that he still had no recollection of her at all. How was that possible?

"Can you catch it?" She made no move to get down, seemed intent on staying on the chair until the mouse was gone.

He could shoot the tail off a mouse if he had to, but he reckoned it would eventually find a way out of the cabin on its own. "Listen, darlin'. It's gonna be alright." He steadied her again and tried not to think of her hips and her tiny waist and the womanly curves too close and too tempting. He started to lift her down, but she resisted.

"Please get rid of it first, Dylan."

"That little old thing ain't gonna hurt you."

"I realize that. But it's just so . . . so creepy."

"Creepy?" His voice rose on another note of humor, and he couldn't keep from smiling up at her. "At a thousand pounds, Two-Toed Joe is creepy. But that teeny-tiny mouse under the drawers? It's just a nuisance."

She finally shifted her attention to his face. Her pert nose and full lips were right in range. All he had to do was plant her on the floor and in the process bring her flush against him. He could kiss the tip of her nose and then drop down and savor each lip.

"Trudy said Two-Toed Joe is a myth." Catherine wobbled and grabbed onto his arms to steady herself.

"Speaking of Trudy, we're heading over to the Gundersons' for supper." Stu wouldn't take kindly to their making him wait long outside. "You don't have a meal already in the works, do you?"

She glanced to the stove and an empty pot she'd likely used for warming water for her bath. Otherwise, the stove top was barren, not a drop of food in sight.

"I hadn't yet made plans regarding supper," she said. "But it would have crossed my mind at some point."

"You sure about that?" He couldn't keep from teasing her since she hadn't yet cooked a meal. He'd taken to making eggs and bacon while she sipped on her first cup of coffee in bed. When the plates were loaded with food and on the table, she eagerly climbed from bed, wrapped up in a blanket, and joined him for more coffee and the simple fare. It was a routine he liked a whole lot.

"The appearance of the mouse was delaying my efforts."

"Yep, I can see that the little critter was giving you all sorts of trouble with getting supper ready." He nodded at the open book on the table, the pages now flopping together, losing her place.

She'd been reading *Moby-Dick* a couple of nights ago

when he'd arrived home after midnight, surprising him again by not only the book but also staying up so late. She'd shyly explained that she'd traded another novel for the one at hand while passing through Denver.

When he'd dropped into the chair across from her and asked her to read to him, he'd been even more surprised when she'd turned to the beginning and seemed to happily oblige. He listened to the story for at least an hour while he cleaned his guns before Austin had interrupted with his need for a bottle. Since then, they'd made a habit of sitting and reading when he got home.

"No fair you reading without me." He'd enjoyed the story of Ishmael with his whaling plans and his encounter with a tattooed cannibal.

"Really?" Her delicate brows came together in a look of uncertainty.

"Really."

"You're not just saying so to be nice?"

"Nope. I like it." He had half a notion to caress her forehead and smooth away the worried wrinkle between her brows. And when she captured her bottom lip between her teeth, he had another notion to nibble her lip for himself.

"If you're sure."

"I'm sure."

She offered him a tentative smile, one that made him wish he could assure her that he genuinely liked being married to her. Maybe he was gonna have to try a little harder to convince her.

But at the moment, he needed to stop holding on to her waist and put some distance between them before he got carried away. "We'd best get going before Stu decides to hog-tie and drag us out."

"I can't." Her gaze darted around the room as if expecting the mouse to march across the floor and attack her. "I can't get down until the mouse is gone."

"Then you leave me no choice." He scooped her into his arms and began to carry her across the cabin.

"What are you doing?" Her cheeks flamed as they did whenever she was embarrassed.

"I'm carrying you outside."

"What about Austin?"

"I'll come back for him."

"But my hair—"

"It's beautiful, darlin'. You should wear it like this more often." The long, thick brown waves cascaded around her, softening her features, making her look younger.

Her lashes fell, the dark fringes fanning her cheeks.

As before, her innocence and her shyness were unexpected, and her reaction melted his insides faster than butter in a griddle. *Oh, Lord Almighty, help me.*

"What in tarnation is taking so long?" Stu called loud enough for half the town to hear. "Yous in there smooching?"

Dylan bumped the door open and stepped outside. He wished he'd been smooching. Instead, he grinned at his deputy still waiting on his horse by the courthouse. "Just rescuing my wife is all."

Wife. He liked saying it. In fact, he was surprised at how easy this transition to having a wife and son had been.

"Rescuing from what?" Stu's brows converged in a bushy mass.

"A mouse."

The man snorted.

"He's my hero." Catherine's voice rang with admiration.

"Hear that, Stu? I'm her hero." Even as he teased his deputy, Catherine's word settled deep inside. He set her down but couldn't seem to make himself let go. The early evening sunlight highlighted the threads of auburn in her damp hair. His fingers twitched with the need to draw her close and comb through those strands.

Stu snorted again. "Time to stop all that there *rescuing*. Some of us happen to be hungry, dontcha know."

"I know." Dylan tore his attention from Catherine to find that Stu's gaze was full of warmth and relief.

Dylan nodded his thanks. The demons that had tempted him just a short while ago were gone. The desire for a drink had dispelled, and his stomach rumbled with a hankering for Trudy's good cooking. He didn't know what had helped, but Catherine was no small part of it. Maybe this wife and child would make him into a better man after all.

CHAPTER

14

Catherine had been in Fairplay for ten days. Ten days of living a lie. She wasn't sure she could go another moment more.

She had to find a way to tell Dylan she wasn't Kit. The longer she let the misunderstanding continue, the harder it was getting to gather the courage to say something. She could reveal the truth and beg him not to speak about it to another soul. Surely he'd go along with that, wouldn't he? He'd grasp the damage it would do to his chances of getting reelected as sheriff. And hopefully he'd understand the danger it could bring to all of them if Rocky found out where she was.

"What do you think?" she whispered to Austin as she finished wrapping him in a clean diaper. "Should I inform him tonight?"

After supper with the Gundersons a couple of nights ago and then dinner again after church, she was growing too attached to the couple. She couldn't let herself, not when she might have to leave soon. Because Dylan might ask her to leave once he discovered her deception.

Austin kicked his legs and waved his arms, cooing up at her and watching her as if his world revolved around her. "You love me too, don't you, little one? I can't leave you, can I?"

As with every other time she'd admonished herself to fix the mess she'd made with Dylan, she found herself making more excuses. And staying with Austin was a very valid excuse, because she didn't want to cause him any heartache since he was so bonded with her.

She wasn't harming anyone by allowing the misunderstanding to continue, was she? It certainly solved the quandary of whether to provide her real name. She could live with the maiden name of Katherine Olson indefinitely, and no one would be the wiser. It's what she'd reluctantly penned on the marriage certificate when Father Zieber had brought it by.

With a sigh, she straightened and worked out a kink in her lower back that had been bothering her since the arduous job of scrubbing laundry the other day. She'd managed to accomplish most of the menial tasks required for managing a home. The one she still hadn't attempted was cooking. She was fairly certain if she gave it a try, she'd fail miserably.

Dylan didn't seem to mind cooking for her when she first got up. In fact, she'd grown fond of his bringing her coffee in bed every morning as well as making a simple fare for their late breakfast.

She picked up Austin and brushed a kiss against his cheek. "Your father's a very nice man."

All the more reason to tell him who she really was. He was genuinely kind. She'd witnessed him time and again over the past several days assisting people at all hours of the day and night, especially Mrs. Fletcher, who frequently sought him out for help with one thing or another.

Catherine had enjoyed getting to know the widow. Between Trudy and Mrs. Fletcher bringing food to them, Catherine hadn't needed to cook yet. But it wouldn't be too many more days before her lack of culinary skills alerted Dylan to their differing social status, and he'd realize then that she wasn't who she claimed to be.

Even if he didn't notice anything, how would he feel later if he learned the truth? Certainly betrayed. Maybe hostile. And how long would she last under such pretense? Most likely the guilt would gnaw at her until she couldn't stand living with herself.

"Ah, Momma's precious boy." She hugged Austin closer, but he wiggled against her, every day growing more alert and aware of the world around him. His personality was quickly emerging, and she guessed that not only would he be as charming and sweet as his father, but he'd also be as energetic and spirited.

Austin wiggled again.

She laid him back on the bed and then bent in and blew a kiss against his bare tummy.

He released a giggle, the first she'd heard of its kind. His face was filled with a delighted smile, one that made her heart swell with tender pressure.

Bending in again, she puckered and gave him another noisy kiss.

More of his giggles filled the air, so sweet that she couldn't keep from laughing in response. "You like that, don't you, my little one."

"Believe me, I'd like it too." Dylan's low voice rumbled from the doorway.

She jerked upright to find him leaning casually against the doorpost, arms and legs crossed, his hat tipped rakishly, and his holster low on his hip. How long had he been standing there watching and listening to her? What exactly had he overheard her say?

His smile cocked playfully, and she guessed he'd meant his statement to be playful also. But whenever he interacted with her like this, she always felt inadequate, never knowing quite what to say in response, especially with something witty.

Another woman probably would have told him to take off his shirt and let her try to blow kisses against his stomach. Or maybe she would have walked over and unbuttoned his shirt for herself. No doubt Kit would have done something like that.

But Catherine could only hurriedly turn back to Austin and press her hands against her flaming cheeks. "He just giggled for the very first time. Did you hear him?"

The scuffing of boot steps against the floor drew nearer until he stopped beside her. He stood close enough that with the slightest movement she could easily brush her arm against his. Not that she wanted to brush his arm. Or maybe she did want the contact. His presence was always so magnetic and powerful.

"His first giggle?" Dylan tugged off one of his leather gloves and reached down to let Austin grip a finger. "Reckon I can't be too proud of my son giggling, can I?"

She raised an eyebrow at Dylan. "He *laughed*. Is that better and manly enough for you?"

"Reckon I can be prouder of a first laugh than a first giggle."

JODY HEDLUND

"Go ahead." She motioned toward the baby. "See if you can get him to gig—laugh."

"Bet I can get him laughing more than you did."

She raised both eyebrows this time. "I'm not your sister, Dylan. You don't have to compete with me."

"I can see well enough that you ain't my sister." His gaze swept over her, his expression lighting with appreciation.

"Dylan McQuaid." Her insides warmed faster than honey slathered on a hot biscuit. "Focus on Austin and give him a belly kiss."

Dylan paused on his way down to the baby and glanced at her as if to say he intended to give her a belly kiss next. She could almost hear him thinking the words, but he turned his full attention upon the baby and blew a kiss on Austin's stomach.

The baby's giggles rose into the air. When Dylan laughed in turn, she couldn't keep from joining in. The joy of the moment was contagious and beautiful. They were sharing Austin's first laugh together. How could she ruin the moment by saying anything about who she really was? She had to wait until later. Maybe tomorrow.

"Thank you for that." After several minutes, Dylan took a step back. "Now I have something for you."

"You don't need to do anything for me, Dylan."

He strode toward the door. "I wanted to."

"You already do enough."

"No, I don't." Before she could argue further, he disappeared outside. A moment later, he stepped back in with a magnificent bouquet of wildflowers, one that rivaled what he picked for Mrs. Fletcher, bigger and brighter.

169

"For you." He held it out and gave her what could only be described as a timid smile.

Her breath caught in her throat. Was Dylan giving her flowers?

"Thought you needed something to fill that jar on the table."

"I do." She hadn't had an opportunity to go flower collecting since organizing the house, and without a driver and carriage at her disposal, she hadn't been able to go anywhere outside of town.

She scooped up Austin and met Dylan halfway. Taking the flowers, she bent and drew in a lungful of their fragrance. "Thank you," she murmured, letting the petals caress her cheeks. "They're beautiful."

"They can't even begin to compare to your beauty, darlin'." Like always, he was flattering her and was quite skilled at it.

A warning bell clanged inside. She needed to be careful about giving his words too much weight. Even so, she couldn't keep from liking his compliments.

Again, she drew in the floral scent. "Should we give some of this bouquet to Mrs. Fletcher? I don't want her to be disappointed that you're not bringing her flowers."

"I already delivered some to her. Those are all yours, darlin'."

She loved the way the word *darlin'* rolled off his tongue. "You're very sweet to think of us both."

"That's not all." He retreated to the door.

"But this is more than enough."

He just winked at her over his shoulder.

As he stepped outside again, she began to fit the flowers into the jar with her free hand. She wasn't familiar with the names of many flowers, but she recognized wild iris, wild geranium, and silvery lupine. No one had ever brought her flowers before. His doing so was not only thoughtful but romantic. Wasn't it?

Stop it, Catherine. He was simply being nice like he was to Mrs. Fletcher. Dylan McQuaid had probably come out of the womb with a grin and a wink.

A moment later, he returned carrying a crate. "Got something else for you."

She paused in arranging the flowers.

His eyes danced with excitement as he clomped to the table and deposited the crate. "Go on, open it up and see what's inside." Dylan extricated Austin from her arms, and he went to his daddy eagerly, his legs pumping faster.

Gingerly, she pried at the top slat. It lifted easily, and there curled up in a bed of hay was a gray-and-white kitten. It lifted its head and squinted up at her.

"Reckoned you'd need something to keep you safe from the mice when I'm not here to rescue you. This little fella seemed like he was up for the job."

Catherine stroked the kitten's head. "Aw, he's adorable."

Dylan's grin widened. "I liked this fella the best. Flynn's little girl, Flora, said he was the smartest of his litter."

"So she thinks he'll be a good mouser?"

"Yep. Said his mama trained him to catch mice real well. But promised if he don't work out, we can exchange him for another."

She'd never owned a cat before. But she wasn't about to return the kitten if he failed to live up to expectations. "I'm sure he'll do just fine here."

"Then you like him?"

"I love him."

"Good." Dylan's voice contained a note of relief, almost as if he'd been worried about her reaction.

"The only thing that concerns me—" she continued to pet the kitten, earning a loud purr—"I know Mrs. Fletcher needs a cat too."

"Already took care of that. Gave her a kitten, a black tabby."

"I'm sure she was thrilled."

"Mighty thrilled."

Austin cooed, almost as if he was happy to have a kitten as well.

"Pick up the critter and get familiar with him."

She withdrew her hand from the crate. "Pick him up?"

Dylan's handsome brow arched. "Don't tell me you've never held a cat."

"I admit, I never have." She could feel him studying her. Would he call her out right then and there and demand to know who she really was?

Instead of saying anything, he gently gathered the kitten into one hand, lifted it from the hay, and held it out to her.

She hesitated in taking it. "I don't know . . ."

"Go on. He won't hurt you."

"What if I hurt him?" She started to take the bundle but wasn't quite sure how to handle it.

"Hold on." Dylan stepped over to the bed, deposited Austin, wedging him safely with pillows, and then returned to her. He lifted one of her arms and then the other before he lowered the kitten into the crook. "There."

She stared down at the tiny face with his ears perked and eyes wide upon her. "Does he have a name?"

Dylan helped cradle the kitten with one hand and rubbed

it with his other. "Flora's always naming the kittens after plants or flowers or trees just like her ma does everything. She called this one Juniper. But you can call the fella whatever you want."

"Juniper's a fine name."

Dylan scratched the kitten's head behind the ears, and Juniper leaned into his hand, purring louder. She tried doing the same thing behind his other ear.

"You can think about it." Dylan stroked the cat's spine. With his head bent over the kitten, he was close enough that the warmth of his breath lingered near her forehead.

He hadn't tried kissing her again since the wedding supper out at Wyatt's place. Even though she'd caught him looking at her like he wanted to a time or two since then, he'd always held himself back.

She could admit she'd thought about kissing him more than a time or two. Like now. She wanted to throw her arms around him and thank him for his consideration. But she couldn't push herself on him, not even if he let her. Not until she told him the truth.

"Dylan?" she whispered as she focused on the kitten and stroked it.

"What is it, darlin'?" he whispered back.

"I need to tell you something."

"What is it?" He smiled. "And why are we whispering?"

Once again, all the excuses rose and shouted at her not to disrupt the connection they'd established, not so soon after he'd given her flowers and a kitten. But she had to push those excuses aside and do the right thing. No matter the consequences.

"Dylan," she started again.

"You wanna find a way to thank me, don't you?" His whisper was playful.

"No, that's not it." Juniper stood and started to crawl up her arm. "I mean, yes, I'd like to thank you. Of course I would. It's just that . . . I . . ."

The kitten neared her shoulder. Should she pluck it up and return it to the crate or let it run loose around the cabin or gather it back into her arms? With the tiny claws piercing through her sleeve, she tentatively gathered the creature and tried to pry it loose.

"I know how you can thank me." His whisper was low and full of promise. She barely had time to register his words when his finger touched her lips.

The second he made contact, the world around her stopped. She forgot about the kitten. Forgot about what she'd been working up the courage to tell him. Forgot about everything. All she could think about was his caress and the fact that he was asking her for a kiss. That's what he was doing, wasn't it?

Would he kiss her right here and now?

Her pulse sped with anticipation. She lifted her face and parted her lips in readiness.

Slowly, he traced her bottom lip, his pupils growing bigger and darker with the progression. When he reached the end, he let his hand fall away. She waited for him to bend in and press his lips to hers. But he didn't move. Was he waiting for her permission?

"How do you want me to thank you?" The question came out more breathless than she anticipated.

His attention was still upon her lips. "I thought tonight . . . maybe you could . . ."

Her insides began a wild flipping. What was he asking?

Was he wanting to take the next step in their relationship already? "What?" All she could manage was the one whispered word.

"Maybe you could read for two hours instead of one."

Read? As in *Moby-Dick*? The book she'd read aloud every night when he returned from duty? Heaven help her. This man was more than she'd ever bargained for.

With Juniper now sitting upon her shoulder, she gave Dylan a slight push against his chest. "Dylan McQuaid."

"What?" He grinned and stumbled back an exaggerated few steps.

"You're an absolute tease. You do know that, don't you?"

"What did you think I was gonna ask for?"

Her cheeks turned suddenly hot, and she busied herself with gathering Juniper and gently depositing him into the crate.

"Come on. Spit it out." His tone was laced with mirth. "What did you think I wanted?"

She shook her head.

"Tell me."

"Fine. I thought you wanted me to kiss you."

"I see how it is. You have a hankering for kissing. Been thinking about it a lot, have you?"

"Of course not." How could he jump to that conclusion so easily? Had her desire been written all over her face?

"Just admit it. You'd love to kiss me."

"You're impossible."

He laughed, the warm sound of it filling the cabin and washing over her with delight.

She crossed to Austin, picked him up, and hid her hot face against him. "You must have work yet to do today." There were several more hours of daylight. She needed him to take his leave so she could compose herself.

His footsteps sounded toward the door. "No sense in letting life get boring."

"I'm learning that there's no chance of any boredom with you."

He laughed again and exited. The moment he stepped outside, she realized that once again the moment had passed her by and she still hadn't revealed her true identity.

"Looking for the sheriff's wife," came a man's deep voice from the yard. "Heard she's a midwife."

"Why do you need a midwife?" Dylan's tone remained even and calm. She could picture him as casual as always, never ruffled by anything.

"I got a woman in labor up in Gully Canyon." The man spoke hesitantly. "Came for the doc, but he said she ain't the kind of woman he visits."

Catherine set Austin on the bed and drew his nightgown over his head. She knew exactly what kind of woman the doc didn't want to visit. Someone just like Kit.

"Heard your wife . . ." The man cleared his throat. "Well, heard she had some problems for herself and reckoned she might not pass judgment."

Problems herself? As in having illicit relations? And giving birth out of wedlock? Taking on Kit's identity was an exercise in humility, to be sure.

"My wife is a fine, upstanding woman." Dylan's words came out clipped and hard.

"Meant no offense, Sheriff."

"I won't put up with anyone talking bad about my wife."

"No, sir."

"In fact, I'm known for doing a little target practice on anyone who maligns my wife."

"Yes, sir. Heard that you put a shot right through J. D. Otto's hat."

Catherine didn't know anything about the shooting. But apparently Dylan McQuaid could get ruffled after all. And apparently that was over her and anyone speaking badly about her. While she wanted to take a moment to savor this new revelation, she simply didn't have the time. Every minute counted if she hoped to be of service.

She finished swaddling Austin in his blanket and then slipped her leather satchel out from under the bed. It still contained most of her midwifery instruments and medicinal remedies. She grabbed it along with Austin and started toward the door.

As she exited into the late-afternoon sunshine, she held a hand up to shield her eyes, taking in an unkempt-looking man. He was attired in beaded buckskin with a wide-brimmed hat covering long, stringy blond hair. His beard was equally overgrown, and amidst his ruddy face, his eyes held a franticness that pierced her heart.

"Are you in need of a midwife?" She strapped her bag across her shoulder.

"Yes, ma'am. Word's goin' 'round that you saved Mistress Bliss and her babe."

"You heard correctly." She hefted Austin up to shield his face from the bright sunlight. "You may tell anyone who wants to know that I will always be available to help any woman through her travail, no matter what her circumstances might be."

The man nodded, his eyes turning watery with emotion. "Thank you, ma'am. I'm obliged."

"When did her labor pains begin in earnest?"

"Earlier today."

Catherine didn't wait for more information. She turned to Dylan. "I need to go to her."

Dylan shifted his hard gaze from the man. He hesitated but a moment before he nodded. "I'll take you."

While Dylan went to the livery to retrieve his horse, she took Austin and the new kitten to Trudy's house one street over, a new clapboard two-story home. The dear woman was more than eager to watch Austin and instructed them to take all the time they needed and not to worry about rushing back.

As Catherine started down the boardwalk toward the livery, the town was growing busier as the supper hour drew near. She'd learned that many of the miners from the Platte Mine owned by Mayor Steele lived in the boardinghouses that had been built in recent years. A few other small mining operations were still in existence near the junction of Beaver Creek and the South Platte River, but most of the town gained its prosperity from supplying miners who headed up to the higher elevations to try to strike it rich.

Trudy had informed her that many in the town had wanted to change the name to South Park City, but most of the old-timers had protested. The original name had been established because the early miners had wanted the town to be upstanding and known for "fair play."

The folks still wanted their town to be upstanding. Catherine couldn't fault them for their high standards, not after the vice she'd witnessed in Chicago. But even with an effort to have a wholesome town, she never wanted to sacrifice God's call to love those in the direst of situations.

Now that she was on the other side, the one being disparaged and disregarded for her so-called waywardness, she had even more compassion for those stuck in difficult situations.

At the smashing of a saloon window ahead, she came to an abrupt halt, as did most of the other people milling about Main Street. Shouting and curses echoed through the now-open window, along with more crashing.

At the sight of Dylan crossing the street with his long stride and heading directly toward the saloon, her muscles tensed. He didn't intend to go into the middle of the mayhem, did he?

She wanted to call out to him, to tell him that they needed to leave right away—so he wouldn't have to face any danger. But before she could say anything, he halted just outside the door, pulled out his pistols, and fired both simultaneously into the saloon.

Absolute silence descended in the establishment.

With his feet planted apart and his guns unswerving, Dylan made an imposing figure. And a handsome one, too, with his hat tipped low, his jaw clenched hard, and his muscular body rigid beneath his coat and trousers.

"Whoever was involved in this fight better not make me come inside to get them." His ruthless tone was so different from the way he'd interacted with her only moments ago with the kitten. He waited several seconds before cocking the hammers on his pistols again. The clicking echoed loudly in the now-silent street.

A handful of men pushed outside, bruised and bleeding, followed by several more. The two groups took up position on either side of Dylan, glaring at each other.

One of the fellows, a big man with a rotund stomach, spit a glob of blood into the dirt.

"What's going on here, Mack?" Dylan addressed his question to the big man first.

Mack glared back. "Just tellin' these rustlers we don't want 'em in town, to get on back to where they belong."

"If they were here peacefully, then you don't have any right to rile them up."

"Well, Sheriff, maybe if you were doing your job and rounding up the rustlers like you're supposed to, then we wouldn't be having any problems, would we?"

"We've got every right to visit the saloons same as you do," said a lanky young fellow from the other group. He had curly blond hair, and his beard was patchy, as if he hadn't quite grown into manhood.

Mack snarled. "Not when you been takin' my boss's cattle."

Dylan glanced inside the open door of the saloon as if he were communicating with someone inside—maybe the proprietor?

The fellows outside started blaming each other, and within seconds, they were shouting again. From what Catherine could gather, this was an altercation between some local ranch hands and the men thought to be rustling cattle.

Catherine didn't realize she was shaking until some of the bottles in her satchel rattled. She braced the bag tighter against her body but couldn't steady herself, for the fight seemed inevitable. Dylan would be outnumbered and would surely be harmed.

"Drop it, Frank." Dylan's voice rose above the clamor. Both of his revolvers were now pointed at the lanky fellow who waved his pistol at Mack.

Once again, the commotion faded into silence. All eyes fixed upon Dylan and Frank.

One of Dylan's guns was aimed at Frank's hand and the other at his heart. "Nobody's doing any shooting here except for me."

Frank kept his gun trained on Mack.

"You know I'll shoot you before you can pull your trigger," Dylan continued. "And you also know I ain't gonna miss."

One of the other fellows standing next to Frank bumped him with an elbow. Slowly Frank lowered his gun. With a glare toward Dylan, he stuffed his pistol into his holster before he turned and stalked away. In an instant, his companions were on his heels.

Dylan didn't move, kept his guns outstretched until the fellows unhitched their horses and started out of town.

Only then did Catherine start to breathe again. She wasn't sure whether to be upset that Dylan had placed himself in the middle of the brawl or to be proud of him for being so courageous. Either way, she knew with certainty that she cared about him more than she ever believed she could when she'd first started the journey. In fact, she was beginning to dread a life without him in it.

CHAPTER

15

Dylan paced outside the shack. Darkness had descended long ago, and the temperature in the high canyon had dipped to below freezing. He stopped and blew on his fingers to breathe warmth into them.

A dozen feet away, Edwin sat on a log in front of a blazing fire, holding out his hands and rubbing them together before taking another swig from the whiskey bottle he'd brought out of his distillery that he housed in another shack a short distance up the mountain.

The trapper-turned-miner had been drinking steadily for the past hours, and Dylan was waiting for him to pass out. It was bound to happen any time, and Dylan was keeping a close eye on the fella so he wouldn't fall into the fire and burn himself.

"Come on and warm up over here." Edwin's voice slurred. "No sense in freezing to death."

The heat was beckoning to Dylan, but he shook his head and turned away from the fire. "I'll be fine."

Unlike the other day when he'd ridden past the saloon and had an unquenchable thirst, tonight the thought of indulging in whiskey disgusted him. Mainly because he'd been watching Edwin drink himself into a stupor, sinking deeper and deeper into oblivion.

All Dylan had been able to think about was but for the grace of God, he'd still be drinking and living in oblivion just like Edwin.

Thank you, almighty Lord, for kicking me in the rear and pointing me back in the right direction. The silent prayer rose to the star-studded sky, his soul welling with thankfulness to the Lord, as it had many times over the past months.

If only he didn't have to worry about his sheriff position being on the line. If Mack Custer's accusation that he wasn't doing his job to arrest the rustlers was any indication of how the other ranchers felt, then he wasn't gonna get their votes in the August election. Not unless he figured out a way to do what they'd hired him for.

Trouble was, riding out and confronting J. D. hadn't made a lick of difference. The thief just kept on taking cattle that weren't his, getting bolder with every passing day that he got away with it.

Wyatt had remarked only yesterday during a visit that he and Flynn were still steadily losing a few cattle a week. The same was true of other ranchers in the area. All except J. D.

Now that Dylan had a wife and child, he needed to win the election and keep his position. But between Hatfield campaigning against him and the ranchers getting mad at him, he was afraid he was gonna lose his badge.

What would he do if he wasn't sheriff? Go back to working for Wyatt? He'd be a worse failure than a penniless prospector.

Edwin leaned back and stared at the sky, too, his face

etched with sadness that the drinking couldn't completely drown. What sorrows was Edwin trying to escape?

Dylan studied the man's ragged appearance, stained clothing, rotting teeth, and greasy hair. Edwin was dirty and disgusting. But he hadn't turned into this shell of a man overnight. No doubt he'd worked his way to this kind of condition so gradually he hadn't even realized it.

Was that what happened when a person refused to deal with his griefs and troubles properly? Maybe if a man didn't ever stop and face his heartache rightly, he just kept on trying to bury the pain by covering it with something that never lasted and never soothed for long.

Was he guilty of the same? Had he harbored secret sorrows, buried them under liquor and ladies?

He straightened and pushed up the brim of his hat, as if somehow that could help him see into his own soul and the complexities inside. What if he needed to get down in there and do more unburdening? Would doing so keep him from feeling a need to drown his demons when the sorrows came rushing back?

'Course, he reckoned that a man would always have to stand guard against old temptations. But maybe he'd be less prone to the tripping and falling if he took the stumbling blocks from his path.

"I sure do appreciate your wife coming out here and helping like this." Edwin had spoken the same thing at least a dozen times.

At the repetition, Dylan bit back his frustration. The alcohol was turning the man's head to mush. But it wouldn't do any good to say so. "My wife's a good woman."

"That she is." Edwin sloshed another sip. "Mighty fine."

The question was, how had Dylan ended up with such a good woman? The more he got to know Catherine and see just how pure she was, the louder the question clamored. Not only was she innocent, but she was compassionate and kind and gentle and hardworking and sweet and . . . Well, shucks, he could go on all night with the things he liked about her.

"Can't rightly see how such a fine lady got herself into a predicament with you. No offense, Sheriff. But she don't seem the type."

"The blame is all on me."

Edwin paused with the bottle midway to his mouth. "You forced yourself on her?"

"What? No how, no way! I'd never do anything like that." Though he spoke harshly, he couldn't deny he'd wondered the very same thing. He reckoned Catherine would have said something by now if he'd grievously offended her in that way. She certainly wouldn't have been able to forgive him so easily, likely wouldn't have sought him out.

"I believe you, Sheriff." Edwin finished another sip. "Being a midwife and all, maybe she stole the baby from some other woman."

"The babe's my son." Dylan's hands dropped to his guns, anger starting to swirl in his gut at the far-fetched accusations. He'd hoped Edwin had gotten the hint earlier that he wouldn't tolerate anyone talking badly about Catherine. But apparently the alcohol had loosened his tongue.

Edwin put up his hands, clearly afraid Dylan planned to take up his previous threat to shoot him. Dylan had half a mind to scare the fella into silence. But what good would that do? Edwin was only speaking freely what everyone was already thinking.

The shack door opened, and Edwin stood so quickly that he stumbled and fell back onto the log.

Catherine appeared, cradling a swaddled bundle. Her face was flushed but contained a look of pleasure. "You have a son."

Edwin made it to his feet again but began to waver.

Dylan strode over to him and grabbed his arm to keep him from collapsing.

"Chipeta?" Edwin took a lurching step that would have landed him in the fire if not for Dylan's grasp.

Catherine glanced over her shoulder into the shack. "Chipeta is just fine. She's a very strong woman."

The Ute woman Edwin had taken as his common-law wife was small-boned and thin. Dylan had expected the labor and delivery to take longer and to have more complications but was relieved the babe had come easily.

"Can I see her?" Edwin's voice seemed clear of the inebriation.

"Give me thirty minutes to clean her, and then you'll be able to sit with her."

As the door closed, Edwin sagged against Dylan. The sourness of the fella's unwashed body and the heavy gust of whiskey breath hit Dylan full in the face. In the next instant, Edwin's chest heaved with sobs, and tears streamed down his cheeks.

"She's fine." Dylan patted the man's arm awkwardly. Holding a crying drunk wasn't something he'd ever done before. In fact, he'd been the blubbering drunk on more than one occasion with Bliss the one awkwardly patting and comforting him.

Was this how Bliss had viewed him? With the same mixture of frustration and compassion? If so, Bliss had been nigh to a saint for bearing with him. No doubt Dylan had put his friend through worse, and Bliss had been there through it all.

Dylan could admit, he'd never told his friend of his gratefulness for all he'd done for him. Sure, he'd thanked Ivy and Bliss for paying off his gambling debt to Bat and his gang. But the tension between Bliss and him hadn't gone away and not for lack of effort on Bliss's part.

Less than an hour later, Edwin sat on the edge of the bed next to his wife as she held the newborn. Dylan leaned against the door and tried to stay out of Catherine's way as she cleaned and organized and fussed over both the mother and babe.

The place was smaller than a shed with only enough room for the bed, the stove, and an oversized stuffed chair. It was neater than Dylan thought it would be, with a bearskin rug on the floor, herbs and other root vegetables drying overhead, snowshoes hanging on one wall, an intricately woven headdress with beads and feathers on the other. A single oil lantern hung from a low ceiling beam and cast a golden glow over everything.

What was becoming all too clear was that Catherine hadn't simply been an assistant, tagging along and helping her mother and grandmother with deliveries. Nope. She was a full-fledged midwife, moving about with the practice, ease, and know-how of a woman who'd been delivering babies for years.

The question was, why hadn't she just come out and told him about being a midwife when Ivy first went into labor? Why had she waited?

Something wasn't adding up. But with how much he liked

Catherine and how good she was with Austin, he wasn't sure he wanted to dig deeper. What if he didn't like what he found?

As she brushed past him on her way to the stove, where she was waiting for water to boil, he snatched her arm and dragged her backward, giving her no choice but to tumble against him.

The moment her body connected with his, sparks sizzled through him like the crackling of a flame touching dry wood. He wasn't even sure why he'd stopped her, why he'd pulled her in, except that for some inexplicable reason, he didn't want to lose her, and somehow he felt as though he might.

She lifted her dainty chin and peered up at him, her eyes wide and full of questions. "What's wrong?"

He didn't know how to put into words his uncertainty. All he knew was that since she'd walked back into his life, everything had changed for the better. They hadn't done anything spectacular, but that was the amazing part about it. He hadn't needed to be under the influence of alcohol to enjoy every minute of every day he'd spent with her so far. The simplicity of sipping coffee together, of watching Austin's antics, of listening to her read, of closing his eyes at night and hearing her soft breathing. He wanted more of those kinds of beautiful moments for the rest of his life.

"Is everything alright?" She dropped her tone and cast a sidelong glance toward Edwin and Chipeta before focusing on him.

What was going on inside him? Why was he having such strong emotions for this woman? Yep, he liked her. A whole lot. Was the liking already turning into love?

He'd never been in love with a woman except for Bethina.

But even then, his love had been immature and driven by his lusts.

"Everything's real fine." He couldn't stop himself from caressing her cheek with his knuckles and then tucking a strand of loose hair behind her ear. "Just wanted to see how you're holding up."

Her eyes warmed. "As long as mama and baby are healthy, then I'm happy."

"You sure?"

She tilted her head. "Are you fishing for when I'll be ready to leave? Because I warned you that I'd need to stay for a while afterward—"

He cut her off by touching his fingers to her lips. "Don't worry, darlin'. We'll stay as long as you need to."

Catherine expelled a soft breath. Her lips were soft and warm against his fingers. She didn't seem in a hurry to back away from him, almost seemed to want to linger. But when the babe released a wail, she broke the connection, nearly tripping over Edwin's legs in the process. She flushed and fumbled for several seconds before pulling herself together.

As he watched her, he couldn't keep a pleased grin from forming. He liked being able to rattle her, liked knowing he affected her, liked that she was conscious of his presence nearby.

As she picked up the babe, he kept his focus on her just because he could—and to get another reaction from her—until she finally glanced at him with a stern look, as if to tell him to stop staring. But as she ducked her head, her lips lifted into one of her pretty smiles.

Boy howdy, this woman was something special, and he wanted to be worthy of having her. But how?

CHAPTER

16

The mountain storm had arrived quickly and didn't seem to have any intention of leaving. By the time Catherine finished packing her satchel, sleet was tapping a steady rhythm against the tin roof.

The door swung open, bringing in a gust of frigid wind along with a smattering of icy droplets. Dylan stepped inside and closed the door behind him, a thin sheen of ice glistening on his hat and coat. He'd gone out to ready the horse for their return ride down the canyon, and now he shook his head. "Too icy—"

She cut him off with a nod toward the bed where Edwin was passed out next to Chipeta and the babe, who were both resting peacefully. Though Chipeta spoke some English, the native woman had struggled to understand and learn the lactation process. Edwin, who was knowledgeable of the Ute language, had been too drunk to help.

"We're gonna have to hole up here," Dylan continued in a whisper. "At least until morning."

Catherine was anxious to return to Austin, had never

been away from him for so long, but staying would give her the opportunity to assess both Chipeta and the baby one more time.

"Do you think the weather conditions will improve by morning?" The tiny home didn't have a window. Even if it had, the night had turned black as the storm had moved in, and darkness hovered in every corner.

"There's always a chance of snow in May." Dylan shrugged out of his coat and hooked it on the peg on the back of the door, followed by his hat. "But I don't think we'll get any tonight. And hopefully in the morning it'll warm up and the sun'll burn away the ice."

A yawn pushed for release, but she stifled it behind her hand. She guessed it was nearing two or three in the morning, and the long night was catching up to her.

"You should get some sleep," Dylan whispered.

She might have considered sleeping on the bearskin rug covering a swath of the hardened dirt floor if she hadn't noticed the fleas in it earlier. The only other option was the chair. But if she took the chair, that left the flea-infested rug for Dylan, which wasn't kind or fair to him.

Dylan wrinkled his nose at the bearskin as if drawing the same conclusion.

"You take the chair." She motioned toward it.

"Nope. You take it."

"I insist. You're larger. It will be more comfortable for you."

"Where you gonna rest?"

"I'll keep busy." With what? She glanced around searching for something to do with her hands to pass the time.

Dylan dropped into the chair. "I've got a solution."

"You do?"

He combed his fingers through his hair, slicking the strands back in that way that always made her wish she could be the one taming his hair. Then with a roguish cock of his head, he dropped his attention to his lap. "We'll share the chair."

"We can't. The chair isn't big enough." Even if it had been bigger, she wouldn't have been able to sleep with him sitting right beside her. Some nights it was difficult falling asleep with him several feet away.

"The chair is plenty big." He crooked a finger at her. "Come on. I'll show you."

She stepped nearer, her pulse taking up a patter that echoed the precipitation on the roof. "It won't be comfortable for you."

"Don't worry about me, darlin'." He leaned forward and circled her wrist, pulling her closer.

"I don't know, Dylan . . ."

He tugged her, throwing her off-balance. His hands spanned her waist and brought her down on his lap so that she was sitting sideways. "There."

She squirmed and tried to bolt up, mortification spilling through her. "I can't sit here."

"Sure you can." He held her in place and slipped an arm around her back, pulling her more fully against him.

She wiggled a moment longer, then froze at the realization of the indecency of her situation.

"Hey now." His voice was soft. "Stop worrying. I ain't gonna get fresh with you here and now."

He was right. She was being silly to make such a scene over sitting on his lap. They were married. Fully clothed. And in the presence of other people. What could possibly happen? Even so, she held herself stiffly.

"Just lay your head against my shoulder." He gently guided her head until she was resting comfortably against him.

"You'll grow sore very quickly with my weight on your legs." She threw out a last half-hearted excuse.

"My legs can manage a little thing like you."

"Are you sure?"

"If I get all bothered, then we'll switch, and I'll sit on your lap." His voice contained a note of teasing. As usual, she wished she had the ability to banter back with him, but she'd never been particularly humorous or quick-witted with her responses. If Dylan hadn't noticed yet, he soon would discover she was rather dull. As Chester Jones had told her upon ending their courtship, she was a kindhearted woman, but he simply didn't enjoy spending time with her because she was so serious.

She settled in, trying to loosen herself up. There wasn't any harm in sleeping here against Dylan for a little bit. Her head fit perfectly against his shoulder with his chin brushing her forehead. Her body wedged into the crook of his arm, his broad chest firm but warm.

"Comfortable?" His low voice rumbled near her temple.

"More so than I expected."

"Then I make a good bed?"

"Much better than the bear rug." She tried for a note of humor but ended up sounding forced.

"After this experience, I reckon you'll be wanting to sleep on my lap every night."

She inhaled, catching the scent of woodsmoke on his shirt and vest. She just might like sleeping beside him every night, feeling his solidity and surrounded by his warmth. But she couldn't admit that or consider it. Doing so would be much too brazen, wouldn't it?

For tonight, however, she had little choice. She'd let herself enjoy the pleasure of his embrace for a few short hours, and then she'd have to return to a mindset of keeping Dylan at arm's length.

"What do you say, darlin'?" The stubble on his chin was scratchy against her forehead, but she liked it, liked how close he was, liked how secure she felt. "Should we get rid of the bed, and you can just use me instead?"

She smiled at his jest. "Very well. But I am growing accustomed to having my coffee in bed every morning. How do you propose to handle such a dilemma?"

He nuzzled his nose into her hair and pulled in a deep breath, one that seemed to relax him into the chair even farther. "Reckon that's a real big dilemma. Can't let you go without that coffee, or you might never get your lazy bones out of bed."

She laughed. "I can't help it if I'm more suited to the night than to the day."

"It's alright with me. Some of my best talents only show themselves at night."

"And what talents are those?" The second she asked the question, she captured her lip and nibbled on it, embarrassment rushing in. She wasn't sure what he was referring to, but she could only imagine his so-called talents had to do with his previous lifestyle of drinking and womanizing.

He paused, his muscles tightening.

She needed to retract her question, but she didn't know what to say. "I'm sorry—"

"Nope, I'm the one who got carried away. Forget everything I just said."

She nodded, laying a hand against his heart. She wanted the motion to comfort him, to let him know that his mistakes were in his past as far as she was concerned. But clearly, he still struggled to put to death the thoughts and deeds of his former life.

He reached up and laid his hand over hers and squeezed tenderly, surprising her like he often did. For a moment she wasn't sure what to make of the sweet gesture. Dylan McQuaid was turning out to be more complex than she'd expected. And she was liking him more than she'd expected too.

She squeezed his hand back and then closed her eyes, letting sleep claim her.

A gentle kiss pressed against Catherine's forehead, and warmth cascaded along her nerve endings. The kiss moved to the spot between her brows and dropped first to one closed eye, then the other. The deliciousness traveled deeper and pooled in her belly.

"Mmm, darlin'." Dylan's whisper was so soft, she almost didn't hear it. "I can't help wanting to kiss you."

Oh my stars. She didn't want to wake up. Not with Dylan's declaration. But wakefulness crept through her along with all the sensations his kisses were creating, reminding her that she was snuggled up against him and sleeping on his lap.

At the nip in the air, she shivered, only to have him draw her in farther. His arms and chest enveloped her in a cocoon, and the heat of his body surrounded her. "Thank you for keeping me warm."

"Do I make as good a blanket as I do a bed?"

"Yes, I'm perfectly warm." She pried open her eyes and

wiggled her toes in her shoes. They were stiff from the cold. "Except for my legs and toes."

"Want me to warm them up?" His tone was still low.

Was he serious? He couldn't be. He was teasing her again. Or was he? After all, she'd just heard him admit he couldn't help wanting to kiss her.

"How long have I been asleep?"

"A few hours. Reckon from the light coming in under the door, it's nigh to seven or eight in the morning."

"Already?" She pushed against him, struggling to sit up. "After so long you probably cannot feel your legs in the least."

"I'm feeling everything just fine." He loosened his hold but didn't immediately release her. "Don't get up yet." His plea was earnest, and his fingers skimmed up her arm.

As his hand slid higher to the back of her neck, she closed her eyes, wanting to stay, wanting to let him touch her, wanting to bask in this closeness she felt with him.

What if after sleeping together last night in the chair, he decided to change their sleeping arrangement at home? When they'd first gotten married, she'd planned on it so she could have another child. But now the thought of sharing a bed with him anytime soon shot panic into her bloodstream. She wasn't ready. Not until she made things right.

Her eyes popped open, and she propelled herself up from his lap and away from him until she was standing.

The lantern was still lit with a low flame that seemed to shine directly on her, highlighting her wrinkled skirt and blouse, the strands of hair that had come loose from her fashionable knot, and the flush no doubt staining her face.

He stretched out his long legs, while at the same time

leaning back and crossing his arms behind his head. He watched her through heavily lidded eyes, as though he had every intention of pulling her back down and never letting her up.

Heaven help her. She pressed her hands to her cheeks. If he tugged at her, she wasn't sure she'd resist. She was afraid she'd all too easily fall into his arms.

She pivoted away from him and assessed the father, mother, and baby in one glance. They were still asleep. From what she could tell, the baby hadn't woken during the past few hours. The sleepiness confirmed what she'd suspected last night when seeing the slight yellow in his eyes. He was jaundiced.

They needed to wake the newborn up and get him eating. The mother's milk—and plenty of it—would help him through the jaundice, along with allowing him to soak in sunlight every day. With the absence of rain on the roof, she hoped the Colorado sun would show itself today, for the little one's sake.

Before she could move toward the bed, Dylan sat forward and snagged her hand. "Let me have one real kiss this morning, and I promise I won't ask you for another kiss the rest of the day."

At so audacious a request, she sucked in a breath, and her pulse raced. She didn't dare turn to face him. If she took one look at his recklessly adorable smile, she'd be helpless to resist his charm.

His fingers tightened around her, and he slowly turned her around.

"Dylan," she chided softly.

"Just a little one." His voice was equally soft but hammered deep into her body.

What was the harm of one little kiss right here and now? She'd kissed him before, and it hadn't led to anything more.

His green-blue eyes peered up at her with both desire and invitation. How could she resist him when he looked at her that way and was so handsome?

She shook her head, trying to free herself from his spell. "I thought we were intending to keep our marriage chaste for the time being."

He shrugged. "Reckon kissing is chaste enough."

"I like the idea of taking our time to get to know each other first. Plenty of time."

"Reckon I'm getting to know you well enough."

Her heartbeat stumbled. This conversation wasn't going well. Maybe she should just blurt out that he didn't know her at all. Not the real her. But before she could formulate the words, he stood and slipped his hand behind her to the small of her back.

"Truth is." The pressure of his fingers in so sensitive a spot sent a tremor up her spine. His eyes turned dark and his expression serious. "My feelings for you are growing real powerful. Don't know if it's love, but it sure feels close."

Love? She swallowed the sudden lump that wedged in her throat. How could he feel so strongly so soon? Even if they'd spent hours together, it was still too fast to be talking about love.

Yes, he was easy to like, even admire. He was the sweetest man she'd ever met. But she didn't love him yet. She couldn't allow herself to love him, not while living a lie. "Dylan, I—"

"Don't deny you feel all this too." His fingers on her back splayed, filling her with a keen longing to simply put her own past behind her and take on Kit's identity for good. It would be for the best. She could stop worrying about all the bad things that would happen to her or Austin or Dylan. She'd be safe and secure for the rest of her life with her secret. A secret she never had to share with anyone else.

His palm pressed her until their bodies met. At the slight contact of the solid length of him, she nearly gasped.

"Don't deny it." His gaze drifted languidly around her face before landing on her lips.

She couldn't. When she'd thought of marriage and sharing intimacies, she always believed the physical aspects were something to be tolerated. She'd never imagined it being like this, where she was hungry for her husband's caresses and kisses, where she actually derived pleasure from even the smallest brush of their bodies.

She wanted to believe that what she felt was simple infatuation, that it wouldn't last. But she'd seen the depth of Dylan's loyalty to his family and friends. The betrayal he'd experienced with his friend Jericho. The way he hadn't been able to tear himself away from Ivy's labor. The ease with which he'd allowed himself to love Austin. The devotion he'd shown to her so far.

She let her fingers twist at her wedding band, the one that had once belonged to his mother. Of all his family, he'd kept his mother's ring.

He might be charming and flippant at times, but underneath he was a man who felt things deeply—both the love and the losses.

He tore his attention from her lips and met her gaze directly. His brows lifted in question, and his eyes filled with uncertainty. "If you don't feel the same, I'll back off. I just thought you might be starting to like me too."

"I do." The words rushed out breathlessly. "I do feel the same. And I do like you. It's just that—"

He leaned down and cut her off, his mouth taking possession of hers both passionately and powerfully. He plied her lips, giving her little choice but to rise and respond with her own passion, a passion she hadn't known she possessed until he'd unleashed it inside her. Now, at this meshing, she was adrift in a sea of pleasure, the waves lapping against her body. It was more like severing the anchor altogether and letting the waves toss her where they would in an entire ocean.

This connection with Dylan was much more than mere liking. Dylan said it felt close to love. And she wasn't sure yet either. But she wanted forever to find out.

Would that be possible?

She longed to wrap her arms around him, slide them up his torso, and run her fingers through his hair. But the idea of being so bold made her hesitate.

He didn't let her end the kiss so easily and angled in as though he had no intention of bringing the ship to shore. He made a soft groan at the back of his throat and skimmed his fingers up to her neck. As he deftly pulled the first pin from her hair, a hot current swept her along with a new, delicious bliss. She wanted him to keep going, wanted to see where this tide took them.

At a cough on the bed behind them, mortification burst through her, and she broke away.

She peeked past him to see that Chipeta was awake and watching them with wide eyes.

Dylan reached for her again, his breathing labored and his gaze fixed upon her mouth hungrily.

Her knees were weak, her head hazy, and her whole body flushed. But as he began to tug her close again, she pressed a hand against his chest. "You said one kiss. And promised you wouldn't ask for another the rest of the day."

He twisted her pin in his fingers. "You never made a promise to me. Reckon you could kiss me all day if you wanted to."

She started to push him, but her fingers clung to his shirt. For an interminable moment, she wavered, longing to dig in and draw him back but also knowing she had to keep some semblance of sanity.

As if sensing her desire and his sway over her, he grinned slowly, which only fanned the heat inside.

She gave him a final push and released him before turning to the mother and baby. "Good morning, Chipeta. How are you feeling this morning?"

She began to unwrap the newborn from his snug, warm blanket, trying to explain that they needed to waken the baby to nurse, entirely too conscious of Dylan watching her while he put on his coat and hat.

A moment later, he stepped away from the door and leaned into her. "Just you wait, darlin'. You'll be wanting to kiss me soon enough. You'll see."

She paused, and as he spun away, her gaze trailed him, and she couldn't keep from admiring his broad shoulders and muscular torso.

As soon as he opened the door, he glanced at her, then winked, as if he'd known she was ogling him.

Quickly she shifted her attention to Chipeta and the baby.

Oh heaven help her. What new mess had she gotten herself into with Dylan? Clearly a mess she had to clean up as fast as possible. The trouble was, she didn't want to.

CHAPTER

17

Dylan could think of nothing but trying to kiss his wife again. He squinted against the sunshine glistening on the icy layer covering the grass and rocks.

His wife. Catherine was his wife. He had every right to kiss her whenever he wanted. He didn't need to feel guilty about it, did he?

He tipped up the brim of his hat and glanced behind him. She clung to the horse while he led the creature down the steep path. It was still slippery in spots, and he hoped by walking ahead, he could avoid any dangerous steps.

"Doing alright, darlin'?"

Her sights swept over the scenery—the dark pine boughs frosted with a light layer of ice, the few finches and nuthatches and sparrows flittering about, searching for seeds and insects in the frozen landscape. "It's beautiful, Dylan." Her breath rose as a puff of white into the crystal-clear air.

"Yep." He inhaled, and the cold air stung his lungs. "It's mighty fine."

The sky above the gully was as bright a blue as a robin's egg. The rain and clouds had moved on. That was something else he loved about Colorado. Each day had the potential to be clear and beautiful.

Same with his life since he'd been back. He might hit a storm, but the clouds never stayed for long.

As with every time he was out in the wilderness, he sent up a prayer of gratefulness that God had led him back. He hadn't deserved the second chance, which made him all the more grateful. He didn't deserve the second chance with Catherine either, but he was mighty glad she'd given it to him.

That kiss earlier this morning . . . He hadn't stolen that kiss from her like he had on their wedding day or at their wedding supper out at Wyatt's. Nope, she'd admitted she liked him, had all but handed herself to him for the kiss. Not with words. But he'd seen the desire flickering in her eyes. Desire she hadn't hidden or denied.

His blood heated again, and fresh longing for her speared his gut. The longing had been building in him all the hours he'd held her while she slept, her supple body right there against him. He'd dozed on and off, always keenly aware of her presence.

Whenever his hands had itched to roam, he'd given himself a stern warning. 'Course, it was natural for them to start craving each other, especially after how close they were getting. But he wasn't gonna use her for his own gratification, and he didn't want his selfishness to gain the upper hand. He was gonna do things the right way this time.

But what was the right way?

Fact was, his feelings were different from any other situation he'd been in before. Drunkenness and lust and fornication weren't driving him. Instead, the more he got to know and like her, the more he wanted to truly love her in a way that showed how much he respected and cherished her. Like his pa.

He didn't recall a whole lot about his younger years when they'd still been a family, before his ma had married the lowlife Rusty in order to keep from losing the family farm in Pennsylvania. But he'd never forgotten the way Pa had doted on Ma—bringing her flowers, bending in and kissing her neck when she was cooking at the stove, buying her peppermints—her favorite—every time he rode to town. And then there'd been that one time Dylan had found him dancing with her in the barn.

Pa had tended to her like she was an exquisite flower garden. Dylan reckoned that's why she'd withered up and died once he was gone.

He might not be like his pa yet. But he aimed to get there, one way or another.

"Real proud of you, darlin'," he said over his shoulder.

"You are?" Surprise tinged her voice.

"Yep. You worked hard last night."

"It was a relatively easy delivery compared to some."

"Still, you're a hard worker. And you had a lot of compassion to come on up here and help Chipeta and Edwin when the doc didn't want to."

"I'm glad I could help." She was silent for several clopping steps of the horse. "I guess I've always seen assisting the less fortunate as my place since most women prefer to have an older midwife with more experience."

"Don't take much to see you've got plenty of experience."

"Yes, but women want midwives who have already had babies of their own and can empathize with their travail in a personal way. Not someone young like me who can't relate to the pain and difficulty of child birthing."

She sucked in so sharp a breath that he halted, slipping as he did so. When he straightened, he placed a gentling hand on his gelding's muzzle to calm him. At the same time, he peered up at Catherine. Her eyes were round with what he could only describe as guilt.

He hadn't been to many child birthings, but from what he could tell, it didn't take a whole lot more than having one child to be able to empathize with the pain other women were experiencing. "Reckon you're doing just fine."

She shook her head and pressed her lips together in a tight line.

"Don't be too hard on yourself. Everyone starts in the same place, without any experience. But it comes with time."

She didn't say anything and instead stared off into the distance down the canyon. Her shoulders stiffened, and her expression only seemed to grow more agitated.

What had he done?

Before he could formulate a question, the crackling and crashing of brush brought his attention around, only to find a brown bear lumbering toward them, grunting and snorting.

In an instant he had his revolvers out. But the bear picked up its pace, and Dylan had the sinking feeling he wasn't gonna be able to scare it off with a couple of shots. It already had them in its sights and, for whatever reason, had decided they were a threat. Or dinner.

He swiftly placed himself between the horse and the charging beast and shot above its head, hoping the blast would cause it to rear up and stop.

But other than a slight hiccup in its run, it didn't veer off course and continued straight toward them, its grunts and snorts growing louder.

Behind him, Catherine released a soft gasp that she caught behind her hand. He had half a mind to send her and the horse on down the trail ahead, but he was afraid if the bear saw the motion, it would start chasing her and leave him behind. And that's the last thing he wanted.

"Soon as it gets to me"—he tried to keep his tone calm— "you ride on outta here."

"I'm not leaving you behind—"

"Do it!" This time he couldn't keep from shouting. He took aim at the bear's head. He didn't like to kill a creature if he didn't have to, but in this case, he reckoned he wasn't gonna have a choice.

He squeezed the trigger and the click was followed by a blast. The bear hit a dip in the ground and the bullet only knicked its head. It was gaining ground. And fast. Only a dozen paces away.

With a strange sense that this might be his end, he shot at the grizzly again, hoping he could at least stun it and slow the attack. But before the bullet could make an impact, the bear barreled into him, roaring with a fierceness that sent chills up Dylan's spine.

The momentum of the hit sent him flying backward. He landed against the ground hard, thankful it was grass and dirt and not rocks. Even so, the force of the impact knocked the air from his lungs.

The bear rose and snarled, taking a swipe at Dylan with

one of his front paws. Dylan scrambled backward. But claws snagged his trousers, ripping them and digging into his flesh.

Pain and heat seared his legs, but he pointed his revolver again. He didn't have time to aim. All he could do was fire and hope to injure the creature.

As the bullet hit the grizzly, it stood to its full height, towering over him and roaring, its mouth wide, revealing yellowed teeth.

Behind him, the horse released a shrill whinny and shied well away from the bear. Any second the gelding was gonna throw Catherine. She had to get out of harm's way now before it was too late.

Dylan's pulse spurted with fresh determination. Ignoring the pain searing his legs, he jumped up, took another shot, and then ran toward the horse. He needed to slap it and send it running. But as he neared the horse, Catherine reached out while clinging to the pommel.

"Come on!" She motioned for him to latch on to her hand. "Get on!"

"We can't outrun him."

"We can try."

Dylan hesitated. The bear had taken a step backward and was lowering to all fours. So that it could come after him again?

"Please, Dylan!" Her skin was pale and her eyes wide, but her face was set with the same look he'd seen when she'd gone into each of the deliveries, one filled with purpose and determination that couldn't be swayed. "I refuse to leave here without you."

"Blast it all, woman!" He ignored her outstretched hand and hoisted himself up onto the horse behind her with an ease he'd developed over the years from practicing trick riding with Bliss and Ivy. As he situated himself into the saddle behind Catherine, he was already kicking the gelding forward.

While he grabbed the reins, he glanced over his shoulder to gauge how much of a lead they had on the grizzly. Thankfully, it hadn't moved from the spot of the attack and had instead dropped to its haunches and was sniffing at the dark, wet stain in its shoulder above its heart.

Dylan didn't allow himself a moment of relief. He urged the horse onward as hastily as the conditions would allow, which wasn't fast enough for his liking. They still weren't out of danger. The bear might be stunned for the moment, but it could easily get up and charge after them, angrier than ever.

He kept casting glances over his shoulder until they lost sight of the creature. Even then he didn't let up.

During their descent, Catherine frequently looked behind them, too, her eyes still wide.

When they reached level ground, he nudged the gelding into a gallop. His heart and head were both pounding as hard as the horse's hooves, but he wouldn't take any chances with letting the wounded animal catch up. Not while Catherine was with him. If it had been just him, he might have circled back around and tried to kill it to put it out of its pain. And to ensure that it didn't attack and hurt anyone else who might be up in Gully Canyon, especially Edwin and Chipeta and their newborn.

"We need to stop," Catherine finally called above the beating hooves.

The landmark ahead, the lone pinyon pine growing out of the crevice in the rocks, was the sign they had only a couple of miles until they left the mountainous area and were on the open plains. "We ain't got long now, darlin'. Can you hold on?"

"It's not me I'm worried about." She touched his knee. "It's you. We need to stop your bleeding."

Fiery pain had been lapping at his legs. But he'd gritted his teeth and forced himself not to think about it, to focus on everything else.

"I'll be alright until we get back to town." As soon as he spoke the words, the world around him began to spin, and he felt himself slipping.

Catherine yelped and in the same moment grabbed his arm, clutching at him until he somehow managed to right himself in the saddle. "Please, Dylan. You're getting weaker. Let me take a look at the wounds. I may need to tie a tourniquet. At the very least I can bandage them to staunch the blood loss."

As black dots formed in his vision, he gave a curt nod. The bear wouldn't chase them this far. Fact was, the grizzly was no longer their biggest problem. His injuries were.

He tugged on the reins and brought the horse to a halt. He slid down before he toppled off. As his feet made contact with the ground, agony ricocheted through his body. He bit back a groan and clutched the saddle to keep his legs from buckling.

Then, inhaling a steadying breath, he pivoted to aid Catherine's dismount.

"You don't have to be strong any longer, Dylan." She ignored his outstretched hand and climbed down by herself. "You're injured, and now you can let me help you."

Dizziness swirled around him again, and he rested his head against the saddle and closed his eyes. The bear's claws had dug into his flesh deep and torn him up bad. He could feel the blood running from his wounds down to his ankle. His trousers—or the remaining shreds—were saturated with blood and stuck to his leg. His socks and boots were drenched with blood too.

As Catherine crouched beside him and examined him, her lips pursed tightly. She stood and threw open the flap of the satchel she wore diagonally across her body.

"Can't be all that bad, can it?" He tried to make his tone light, but it came out strained.

"Your worst injuries are below your knee, and the flesh is torn to the bone." She withdrew a roll of linen and an ointment. "I don't think any of your major veins or arteries are severed, but you're still bleeding profusely."

More black dots clouded his eyes, and he wavered.

She slipped an arm around his back and braced him up. "Maybe you should lie down while I do this."

He leaned into her and nuzzled his nose into her hair. "What are you gonna do to me, darlin'?"

"I'll try to make you feel better so you can make it home without passing out."

"I know how you can make me feel better." He brushed his lips across her ear.

"Dylan McQuaid. Don't you ever stop your flirting?"

"Nope." He had the urge to capture her lips right then and there in a long kiss, but he wasn't gonna break the promise he'd given her earlier in the day. "I could sure use a distraction right about now."

"How about if I tell you a story?"

"That wasn't the kind of distraction I had in mind. But sure, tell me a story."

She knelt next to him and peeled away his pant legs.

He sucked in a steadying breath, then gritted his teeth.

"I'll tell you about the first baby I ever delivered." As she kept up a steady stream of conversation about riding out with her mother in the middle of a storm and racing against time to deliver the babe before relatives arrived to steal it away, he only half heard her story above the roar of pain in his head.

All the same, he was grateful for her conversation and the gentleness of her touch. She didn't say anything more about the condition of his wounds, but from the crease in her brow as well as the worried lines at the corners of her eyes, he guessed they were worse than she'd let on.

Somehow he managed to keep standing while she slathered on the ointment and covered his legs with the bandages. He made it back into the saddle. He even kept his wits about him the rest of the ride to Fairplay. Only when they halted in front of the courthouse and he dismounted did he allow himself to collapse and fall into oblivion.

CHAPTER

18

"Dylan McQuaid, you're a terrible patient." Catherine crossed her arms and stood next to the bed, frowning down at him lying next to Austin and the kitten, who were both sleeping soundly. She'd caught him climbing back into bed when she opened the door and had no doubt he'd been up the entire time she was out purchasing more baby formula.

Dylan peered up at her with his beautiful, mischievous eyes. "And how am I so terrible?"

"You know how."

"Can't help it if I need to walk around once in a while."

"The doctor said you need to spend two weeks off your feet." Dylan had only made it four days before he started to rebel. On the fifth day, yesterday, he'd only disobeyed the doctor's order a few times. He'd been so excited that two of J. D. Otto's cowhands had stopped by with details about J. D.'s operation and the stealing. The two were moving on, hadn't wanted to work for a crook any longer. Before leaving, they'd decided to give the sheriff the testimonies he needed to put together a solid case against J. D.

Dylan had wanted to go to the courthouse office for the meeting with the two, but Catherine had convinced him to stay abed while she took Austin outside. The meeting hadn't lasted long, since the cowhands were eager to get out of town before J. D. could catch and punish them.

Now today, she could hardly keep Dylan down, knew he was feeling better, which was a relief after seeing him so pale and weak.

Nevertheless, he wasn't fully recovered and needed to let his wounds heal. So far, his flesh hadn't putrefied. But with dozens of stitches—so many she'd lost count—his risk of infection was all the greater.

She bent and pulled his covers back up. Although he was wearing a cotton undershirt, he was only in his drawers. The indecency was necessary for tending his wounds, reapplying salve, and changing the bandages. But the thought of his unclad state made her stomach cinch with a strange nervousness.

Since the bear attack, he'd been in too much pain to bring up any mention of the physical attraction that had simmered to the surface that night of delivering Chipeta's baby.

Catherine alternated between being mortified for so easily giving in to his request for a kiss and being pleased that he'd wanted to kiss her. No man had ever shown her so much attention or desired her the way Dylan seemed to.

After she'd blurted that she hadn't experienced childbirth for herself during the ride down the canyon, she'd waited for him to ask her to clarify what she'd meant.

Of course, he'd been slightly busy outrunning the bear

and battling his wounds. But now that he was recovering, she expected he'd broach the subject any day. If he asked, she wouldn't lie. But she didn't want to bring it up again. After watching him get mauled, she finally understood how desperately she didn't want to lose him and how much she wanted to protect him—and Austin—especially from her past.

She was surprised at her contentment with the simplicity of their existence, how little she actually missed the luxuries and conveniences of her previous life. She certainly didn't miss her parents' busy activities and parties and the constant comings and goings with the pressure to please them and keep up appearances and make sure she wasn't detracting from her father's public image.

Yes, her parents had loved her dearly and showered upon her every conceivable blessing. Even so, she'd often felt lost and alone amidst all their aspirations.

But here . . . she felt needed, even wanted. She was no longer a liability. Instead, Dylan made her feel like an asset.

Of course, she hadn't had any expectations about her new life because she'd never intended to stay in Fairplay, much less end up married. But her hasty marriage of convenience was turning out to be different—full of so much more excitement and wonder than she'd counted on when she'd agreed to Dylan's proposal.

Even when he was being a difficult patient . . .

She tucked the sheet up to his chin and then did the same for Austin before giving Juniper an affectionate pat. "Your brothers both offered to come and tie you down if I need them to." Wyatt and Flynn had rushed to town the instant they'd gotten the news Dylan had been mauled by the bear, and they'd ridden in every day since to check on him.

Dylan stretched his arms over his head and grabbed the rods of the metal headboard. "No need to call them, darlin'. I'll let you tie me up."

Her stomach fluttered, and she blushed at the prospect of the comments Dylan would likely make if she bound him to the bed. He'd tease her to no end.

His bantering always ignited sparks inside her and lit the air between them with a strange sizzle. Like now. That slow-burning heat crackled, drawing her like it had since the first time she'd met him. It tugged hard so that her body was taut with a need she didn't understand.

She turned away from him and fanned her face as she crossed to the table, where she'd stacked the medicinal supplies. "Time to change your bandages."

Taking a look at the wounds in his legs would cool her down and remind her of how awful the attack had been, how helpless she'd felt atop the horse as the bear slammed into Dylan and knocked him to the ground. She'd tried to scream, but fear had clogged her throat. As she'd watched him fire his revolvers, her fingers had fumbled after his rifle in the scabbard. But she'd hardly been able to unbuckle the leather strap before he was standing and trying to send her on her way without him.

Retrieving what she needed, she squared her shoulders and approached the bed again.

Dylan turned his face away, but not before she caught sight of the pain there. He tried to mask the suffering from his injuries, but he couldn't fool her, not a midwife who was intimately familiar with all facets of pain.

As with the other times she changed his bandages, she distracted him by making conversation, this time talking about the doings around town. Even if Stu had already been in that morning to update him on the brawls and disturbances of public peace he'd had to attend to last night, Dylan's eyes lit with interest as she shared about the teamsters arriving that morning with wagonloads of supplies for the mountain community along with a stack of mail and newspapers from Denver.

When she finished caring for his wounds, she poured a mug of coffee, set it on the small chest of drawers that served as a bedside table, and then reached for one of the pillows to help prop him up.

"Sure do miss bringing you coffee in bed." He leaned forward and sat up, allowing her to fluff the pillows.

She'd slept on his pallet the past few nights with the kitten even though he'd protested that he wanted her to have the bed. She had no trouble falling asleep, but she had to force herself up much earlier than she was used to. "It's a good thing you can't bring me coffee. You were spoiling me and making me lazy."

"I like spoiling you. And sometimes it's okay to be lazy."

She finished arranging the final pillow behind him.

"In fact"—his arm slipped around her waist—"reckon now's a good time to be lazy."

At his touch, delight tingled through every nerve. Nevertheless, she tried to wiggle free. "It's almost noon, and I have things I need to do."

He twisted her around and drew her down so that she was sitting on the bed beside him, half on his lap. "The things can wait while you rest with me."

He was so near she could feel his warmth and hear his thudding heartbeat.

"I can't rest with you." She pushed against his chest, but he circled his other arm around her.

He bent nearer, his cheek brushing against hers and enticing her with the scratchiness of his overgrown stubble. When his lips touched her ear, she nearly hopped up with the current that charged into her.

His fingers splayed at her hips and kept her in place. "Please?" His whisper echoed in the hollow of her ear.

Oh my stars. What this man could do to her with just one word. She closed her eyes to ward off the sweet pleasure suddenly pulsing through her.

"Let me hold you for a little while." The warmth and sincerity in his whisper made her tremble.

This closeness with him was heavenly. And yet what did he have in mind with a *rest*? Did he really just want to hold her? Or would he expect more?

"Dylan," she started. "I'm not sure."

Now that he was feeling better, she wasn't surprised he was taking up where they'd left off the last time they'd kissed. As with then, he had apparently abandoned all resolve to remain chaste or even to take things slow.

He pressed a kiss into her ear that nearly made her swoon. She leaned back, tilting her head and giving him permission, even though a part of her urged caution.

His fingers skimmed up her arm, shoulder, and slid to the back of her neck. Maybe all he was intending was another kiss.

Heaven help her. She loved his kisses, hadn't stopped thinking about the kiss he'd given her at the cabin, had dreamed about it, had hoped for another. If he kissed her now, she wouldn't be able to resist him. And why should she?

"Lie down with me, darlin'." The soft pressure of his mouth brushed the spot below her ear.

She had to bite her bottom lip to refrain from releasing a gasp.

"How's my cutie-patootie today?" A cheerful voice sing-songed from the doorway.

Catherine scrambled to break free of Dylan. "Oh my, oh my." She was still tangled in his arms and on his lap when she twisted to see Trudy Gunderson bustle into the cabin carrying a basket.

The hefty woman stopped short at the sight of them, and her mouth fell open.

"Reckon you might need to learn to knock," Dylan said wryly. "Or I'm gonna have to make sure to lock the door when we're home."

Nearly panicking with mortification, Catherine stood, giving Dylan little choice but to release her. She smoothed her skirt, tugged down her bodice, and then combed stray hairs back into the usual knot. "I was tending to Dylan's wounds." The excuse came out wobbly and breathless.

Trudy gave her a once-over, then shifted her attention to Dylan reclining against the pillows, one arm crooked behind his head, looking as satisfied as if he'd just won a grand prize.

"Okey dokey." Trudy closed the door and nodded vigorously. "If you say so."

"I was teaching Catherine the best kind of medicine." Dylan's tone was serious, but the sparkle in his eyes gave him away and made Catherine duck her head.

"Well, now." Trudy placed her basket on the table. "I always did say that a good round of smooching can work wonders for the body."

"That's what I say too." Dylan's grin kicked up.

Catherine slipped her hands over her cheeks to hide the burning.

Trudy surveyed the bed, where Austin was still sleeping. Juniper was now sitting and sniffing the air.

A delicious aroma filled the room and wafted from the basket on the table, making Catherine's stomach rumble with hunger.

Trudy opened the lid and lifted out a pan covered in towels. "I brought you one of my favorite hot dishes—scalloped potatoes and ham. Stu raves about it almost as much as he does about my plum pudding."

Catherine was afraid to let go of her cheeks for fear they were still blazing red, but the polite thing was to compliment Trudy and thank her for her generosity. It was the second meal the woman had delivered to them since the bear attack. Greta had brought one she'd prepared. And Linnea had delivered a meal her housekeeper had cooked up for them. Mrs. Fletcher had dropped off a cake. And several other families had come by asking after Dylan and delivering baked goods.

Most in the community seemed to accept her as a midwife, and word of her deliveries was spreading. Only two days ago, a miner had called on her for help with his wife, who was in travail. Stu had taken her out to the mining camp, but by the time she'd arrived, the baby was already delivered stillborn.

Yes, there were still those who believed she was a fallen woman. But even as she'd shopped that morning, she could sense a growing respect.

Home. This was her home now. Even if her place in it had come about in a most unusual way, perhaps God had ordained it all anyway.

Trudy took plates from the cabinet and scooped up heaping helpings. "You need to eat more to regain your strength. And your pretty little wife might be good at smooching, but she needs to work on her cooking skills."

Catherine stiffened, waiting for Dylan to acknowledge that her cooking skills were actually nonexistent.

"Nobody can cook like you, darlin'." Dylan's compliment was sincere toward Trudy and at the same time avoided making Catherine look bad. How was he so adept at such social skills?

"That's right." Trudy crossed to the bed and pushed the plate in front of Dylan. "But I'll whip Catherine into shape soon enough. Dontcha worry."

As Dylan took his first bite, he winked at Catherine. She let her shoulders relax and smiled in return.

Before she could get too comfortable, Trudy thrust a pail into Catherine's hands. "Fetch a pail of water, and I'll show you how to make ham bone soup." The older woman nodded at the bone she was unwrapping, along with an assortment of vegetables. "Dylan likes it, and it's easy to make."

As Catherine headed outside and crossed toward the well, she couldn't contain another smile. Maybe everything would turn out alright after all.

"Mrs. McQuaid?" said a youth coming down the path past the courthouse, a lad about the size of Ty, Dylan's nephew. But whenever she'd seen any of Dylan's nieces and nephews around town or at church, they'd politely addressed her as Aunt Catherine.

The boy strolled toward her, a swagger in his step as he admired a silver coin in his palm. "You Mrs. McQuaid? The sheriff's wife?"

"Yes. That's me."

"Got a letter here for you." He held out a folded sheet of tattered paper. It wasn't a proper letter in an envelope. In fact, it was nothing more than a ripped scrap of paper.

She took it from him and turned it over. "Do you know who it's from?"

"Nope." He tossed the coin and then caught it as he started on his way. "A fella just told me to see that I put it directly into your hands."

And likely had been paid to do it if the coin was any indication.

"Thank you." She unfolded the scrap, the bright sunshine illuminating the two lines written in neat cursive. *"I figured out who you are. Tell your husband to drop out of the race for sheriff, or I'll have to tell everyone the truth."*

Her pulse dropped like a bucket into the bottom of a well. For a moment she could only stare at the warning. Someone knew about her identity. But who?

With a start, she called after the boy, "Wait!"

But he only picked up his pace and disappeared around the courthouse.

Catherine didn't have to question the lad. She could guess who the letter was from. Harlan Hatfield. Somehow he'd determined that her identity was Catherine Remington and not Katherine Olson. How? And if he knew who she really was, did that mean he also knew about the crime she was being accused of?

Her hands began to shake.

This was terrible. She was bringing trouble to Dylan—exactly what she hadn't wanted to happen.

She glanced toward the cabin and prayed Trudy hadn't

seen the exchange. Then before anyone could catch her with the note, she tore it into tiny shreds, crumpled the pieces, and stuffed them into her pocket. She would burn them in the stove the first chance she had.

If only the problem itself could go away as easily.

CHAPTER

19

Dylan limped out of the cabin in the early morning light and closed the door so that he didn't wake Catherine and Austin. No how, no way was he lying around for another blasted day. He didn't care what the doc ordered. He was well enough to walk and work and didn't need any more pampering.

'Course he wasn't complaining about the extra time with Catherine and Austin. The past week of being with them while recuperating had been mighty fine. He'd held and fed and played with the little fella and could almost believe Austin was taking a shine to him.

And when Catherine wasn't busy with chores, she read *Moby-Dick* to him and let him teach her a game of cards with the one deck he'd kept from his days of gambling. He'd enjoyed every minute with her, even the simple moments of talking or watching Austin or playing with the kitten.

But the trouble was, spending time with her only increased his craving for her instead of taking it away. Not that he wanted it to go away. But when he'd pressured her to go to bed with him the other day right before Trudy's visit, he'd sensed her hesitancy, even her shyness about it, and he'd pushed her anyway. He'd been a selfish scalawag.

He paused outside the door and took a deep breath of the cool air. Even just a few minutes ago while sitting at the table and watching her sleep, all kinds of longings had swamped him. He'd been tempted to cross over to the pallet, gather her into his arms, kiss her, and never come up for air.

Even with the attraction growing, and even if it felt natural to move things along, he had to put her first this time, had to make sure she knew he would never use her and leave her again.

If he rushed her, he'd only hurt her, perhaps damage the fragile relationship they were building out of the ashes of the past's mistakes.

The truth was, he wanted her to be good and ready for the next step, maybe even be the one to suggest they take things further. Until then, he had a heap of self-control to learn.

He slicked back his hair and placed his hat on before gazing to the east and the pink and red still lingering in the wispy clouds from the sunrise. *Lord Almighty, help me to steer clear of trouble. Already messed up something awful once and don't wanna do it again. Especially not with Catherine and Austin.*

With a half grunt, he pushed forward across the yard toward the courthouse, each step jarring his wounds and shooting pain up his legs. Even if the gashes still hurt, they were healing without infection. At least that's what both Doc and Catherine told him each time they dressed his injuries.

He straightened his sheriff badge on his vest and then

polished it with his sleeve. Stu had managed alright by himself for the past week, but it was high time Dylan got back in the saddle and scouted the lay of the land.

With that fight between the Elkhorn ranch hands and J. D. Otto's fellas, he knew time was running out for him to solve the rustling problem. Next time someone got mad at the rustlers, there was gonna be more than broken windows and busted barstools.

Besides that, the ranchers were fast losing confidence in his abilities. According to Stu, they were as restless as caged coon dogs and were considering their other options for putting an end to the rustling, options that would involve the old-time vigilante committee and the hanging tree.

Dylan didn't want to see things get that far out of hand. He wanted justice served the right way, to show the people of Fairplay that the law would prevail, that they had to be patient. Even so, the need to do more had been building all week and even more now that he had the testimony of two of J. D.'s cowhands.

There had also been more sightings of the bear rumored to be Two-Toed Joe. Dylan couldn't be sure he'd faced Two-Toed Joe. He'd been too rushed and panicked to get a good look at the bear's paws. But Doc claimed a couple of the scratches on his leg had the marking of two claws rather than the usual five. Whatever the case, that bear had to be put down before it hurt anyone else.

As he stepped onto Main Street, he took stock of the businesses beginning to open and the few early risers making their way down the plank sidewalk. He raised a hand in greeting to several of the fellas before he pulled his keys from his pocket and headed inside.

Without the benefit of full sunlight, the room was too dark to see much. After he lit the lantern, it illuminated the heap of mess he'd been expecting—a mound of mail, discarded newspapers, half-full coffee mugs, several dirty bowls and plates, loose change, and crusty handkerchiefs. The floor was caked with dried mud and dead flies. And the trash can was overflowing.

Dylan didn't consider himself to be tidy, but Stu took the meaning of *disorganized* to a new level. With how perfect Trudy kept her house, Dylan reckoned his deputy needed a place he could let go and be himself. But after the past week, the office was starting to look and smell worse than a pigsty.

He lowered himself into the desk chair. He'd have to tease Stu to no end when he came in. For now, he was just glad to be back and busy. Once he took stock of the mail and news, he aimed to write up the information from Smiley and Rube.

He'd learned from them that there wasn't another rustler in the area after all, that J. D. was the one with a hideaway near Tarryall, where he was taking the majority of the stolen livestock. Hopefully Stu would confirm everything during his ride to Tarryall today to check out the location of the hiding spot.

Once they compiled the evidence, Dylan would finally be able to arrest J. D.

One thing was for certain—he wasn't giving up. Not until he locked J. D. behind bars or ran him out of Colorado for good.

"Yep. You ain't gonna last here, J. D.," he whispered. "You wait and see."

And it wasn't just about keeping his job as sheriff either. He really did want to see criminals held accountable for breaking the law. He might have wandered far and wide during the past years, but he'd never compromised living as a law-abiding citizen.

Even in Chicago, when faced with bribes from certain aldermen and bosses, he'd always stayed on the right side of the law and never turned a blind eye to crime. He thanked the Lord Almighty he hadn't headed down that path. He'd seen the corruption firsthand with fellow police constables and knew that once sucked into the mire, it was nearly impossible to get out alive.

Drawing in a breath of resolve, he began sorting through the mail, mostly correspondence from the main police headquarters in Denver. He sifted through the open cases that still needed to be resolved, men committing thieving and street violence in Denver. A handful of wanted posters sat at the bottom—the worst of the worst criminals, usually those passed on from departments around the country.

He always tacked new ones up outside next to the door. Doing so was a means of communicating with men passing through town, warning them of danger but also seeking information on the criminals. Most of the wanted sheets had descriptions rather than photographs. He preferred the picture because it made the identifying easier. Even then, the criminals were difficult to track down. That's why the government and private agencies hired bounty hunters like Bliss.

As he shoved aside the wanted posters, his attention snagged on one with a picture of a woman.

With a start, he grabbed the sheet and moved it closer to the lantern. When the glow of amber fell across it, his heart slammed to a halt.

The likeness resembled Catherine. She was wearing a fancy

hat and attired in a fashionable gown, standing next to a person who had been cut out of the picture.

With an eerie silence settling around him, he read the title printed in bold letters above the picture: *Reward of $200 for the capture of Catherine Remington.* The description next to the picture was in smaller plain print: *"Wanted for murdering Alderman Stretch Watson and Katherine 'Kit' Olson. A pretty, petite woman of five feet, four inches tall. Hazel eyes and dark brown hair. A midwife."*

"What in the blazes?" His pulse took off at double speed, galloping wildly. What could this possibly mean? It had to be a mistake.

He scanned the photograph again, taking in Catherine's unsmiling face, familiar pert nose, rounded chin and cheeks, and full lips. She was as serious and earnest in the picture as she was most of the time in real life. Her expression contained the same intelligent look he'd come to expect from her as well as a softening kindness around her eyes.

The names had been mixed up. His wife was Katherine Olson—yes, Kit. He'd likely once called her by that nickname.

But why had someone confused her for Catherine Remington, a woman who was wanted for murder? Of Alderman Stretch?

His thoughts flew back to everything he remembered about Stretch, a crime boss who'd wheedled his way into political power over a red-light district called Little Cheyenne, its streets lined with nothing but saloons, gambling houses, and places of ill repute. It had been one of the most depraved areas of Chicago, and Stretch had often paid the police to turn a blind eye to crime.

If someone had murdered Stretch, then he'd finally met his due after all the violence and vice he'd perpetrated. Dylan doubted a single person had shed a tear at Stretch's funeral. Most likely there had been widespread rejoicing that he was gone.

Even so, murdering Stretch was still a crime. And this Catherine Remington was being accused of it. The question was, who was she? And why was Kit mixed up in this?

Remington. A big name in Chicago. Paul Remington, the alderman.

Dylan sat back in his chair and stared at the picture. Was Catherine Remington the daughter of Alderman Paul Remington? That would make sense, especially because Alderman Remington had been vocal in his stand against corruption in Chicago politics. He'd wanted to bring about reform and started a movement to that effect. In the process he'd gained many enemies, including aldermen like Stretch who used their political careers to profit themselves.

But that still didn't answer the question of why Catherine Remington had killed Stretch. What motive could she have for doing so? Perhaps she'd hoped to take revenge for something Stretch said or did to her father. More likely she'd been at the wrong place at the wrong time.

His racing thoughts petered to a halt. The wanted sheet said Catherine Remington was a midwife. That meant Kit Olson wasn't, at least not that he recalled. Even though he didn't remember much about her, surely he wouldn't have forgotten that fact—or the fact that her mother and grandmother were also midwives. After all, he'd had no trouble remembering her father owned a store.

Was it possible the woman he'd married wasn't Kit Olson,

the daughter of a grocery store owner? What if her real name was Catherine Remington, the midwife daughter of an alderman?

He let the paper drop to the desk and swallowed hard to fight against the rising panic. It couldn't be true. How could he have made such a big mistake?

But what about everything else that didn't match up? As a woman from the working class, Kit wouldn't have had such fancy clothing, probably wouldn't have had much education, and most likely wouldn't have picked up a novel like *Moby-Dick*. Would she have saved money for her fare to the West? Her father didn't pay her to work at the store, not when everyone in the family was expected to contribute.

On the other hand, a wealthy woman like Catherine Remington might have had savings to draw from, would have behaved and talked like a lady, and likely had many years of schooling—more than he had. She would have grown up with servants waiting on her hand and foot, which would account for why she knew so little about preparing meals. While it was unusual for a woman of her class to be a midwife, it wasn't unheard of, especially since the skills had been passed down.

Then there was everything about their relationship that had been different. He hadn't exactly attracted virtuous women in Chicago. Most had been somewhat loose. Whatever the case, Kit wouldn't have been so naïve and shy, would have been bolder and more enticing.

Catherine, however, was hesitant in their relationship, especially physically, had let him lead and teach her. Her embarrassment and tentativeness had been endearing. Her willingness to go slowly and get to know each other made more sense for a lady of means who'd most likely been treated with the utmost respect by the gentlemen in her life.

It didn't take much sorting out of the facts to see that he'd married the wrong woman. Why hadn't he realized it sooner?

Dylan released a low whistle. "Oh, Lord Almighty, what have I gone and done now?" He buried his face in his hands and tried to come up with an answer. But only one clanged through his head. The wanted ad hadn't mixed up the women. He had.

If he'd married Catherine Remington, then what had happened to Kit? Had she died? The poster said that Catherine had killed Stretch and Kit, but Dylan guessed Kit's death had been an accident.

What if Catherine had been helping Kit give birth? After the way she'd gone without hesitation to help Chipeta, he could easily picture her venturing into Little Cheyenne or any other destitute place to assist the poor women with birthing. In fact, she'd even said she often helped the less fortunate because other women preferred a midwife with more experience. She'd all but told him she hadn't suffered through child birthing herself. Why hadn't he realized that?

No doubt she'd helped Kit as best she could but hadn't been able to save the poor woman. Was it possible Kit had known she was dying and told Catherine about him, even asked her to deliver the babe to him? That would account for how Catherine had known a few things about him as well as where to find him.

Why, then, had Catherine lied to him about who she was when they'd first met? Why had she pretended to be Kit? Unless she hadn't . . .

Technically, she'd never made any claims to be Kit. She'd gone by Catherine and had every intention of handing Austin over to him and leaving. With how much she loved Austin, such a parting would have been excruciating for her. But she'd brought the babe anyway.

He'd been the one to persuade her to stay and marry him. He'd acted rashly, stupidly. A pattern he seemed destined to repeat.

"Why, God? Why can't I ever learn?" He bent over further to quell the queasiness roiling around inside.

Even if Catherine had truly believed he was proposing to her, surely she'd realized his mix-up at some point. And if so, why hadn't she said anything?

He'd practically dragged her into bed with him, believing they'd already shared intimacies, that they weren't strangers in that regard. He'd kissed and teased and made no secret of his growing desire for her. He'd made a fool of himself and been much too forward with her.

In all likelihood, she'd made a fool of him, too, by allowing him to go on believing she was the mother of his child. Why had she been so cruel and careless?

Betrayal stabbed him, making him want to yell out. Instead, he sat up, grabbed the wanted sheet, and read it over. Was Catherine running away from these charges of murder? Was that why she'd come to the West?

Not only had he married the wrong woman, but he'd married a murderer.

As soon as the thought filtered through his mind, shame slapped him in the face. Catherine might have deceived him, maybe perpetuated a lie. But he knew her well enough to realize she'd never kill another person, not willingly with malice. In fact, he couldn't see her even killing anyone in self-defense. She was a caring, sweet, loving mother and midwife who went to great lengths for others.

Since she wasn't a killer, what had happened? Why was the reward so huge? Like she was a dangerous bandit, bank robber, or war criminal? Because she wasn't those things any more than she was a murderer.

He stood and began to pace. What should he do? Tear up the sheet and pretend he'd never seen it? If anyone ever asked, he'd deny knowledge of it.

Yet, even if he ignored the poster and the truth in the short term, deep inside he'd know that what had developed between them was based on a lie. He'd always question whether he could trust her.

Besides, even if he chose to rip up the wanted poster and act like it didn't exist, that wouldn't change the fact that other posters were still out there. If he'd figured out who she was, it wouldn't take long for others to either. Word that they had a new midwife up here in Fairplay might eventually filter down to Denver. A woman by the name of Catherine. Someone, somewhere was bound to link Catherine's description to the one on the poster.

Expelling a sigh through tight lips, he palmed the back of his neck and rubbed it hard. With the rarity of women criminals, the notice would draw even more attention. Especially for that kind of reward.

He paced away from the desk to the bookshelf, spun, and crossed back. Catherine wasn't safe—not in Fairplay, not in Colorado, maybe nowhere in the United States. As long as those posters were tacked up around the country, she'd always have to look over her shoulder and be wary of bounty hunters or other zealous citizens intent on doing their duty to report crime.

And if the time ever came that someone did level an accusation, how could he sit back and allow it? Especially when his gut told him she was as innocent as a newborn babe? He couldn't fathom her having to stand trial for murder. With the corrupted justice system in Chicago, she'd have no guarantee of a fair hearing.

Yet, how could he stop another law officer from arresting her?

For that matter, how could he keep his career as sheriff if he was married to a woman charged with murder? His job was already on shaky ground. Something like this could be the ruin of him. He'd never get reelected with her by his side.

A part of him wanted to go directly to her, confront her with the truth, and then send her on her way. He could easily file for an annulment. But such a move wouldn't help his career either. Even if he tried to explain the predicament to the public and his family, he'd taint his reputation, this time irreparably.

Besides, if he confronted her, he'd risk frightening her away. She might pack up and flee at the first opportunity. Not that he was worried she'd steal Austin. If she'd come all this way to deliver the babe to him, she wouldn't take off with his kid. No, he was more worried about her running off without a word.

With a growl of frustration, Dylan swiped up the wanted poster and folded it into squares until it fit into his trouser pocket.

Just when he'd thought the gossip over his child and hasty wedding was starting to die down. Just when he figured he might be able to put an end to the rustling. Just when he was showing Harlan Hatfield that he deserved to be sheriff, a new storm was hitting him, a storm that threatened to be the worst one yet.

How would he survive?

CHAPTER

20

Something was wrong with Dylan.

Catherine paused in slicing the potatoes Trudy had set in front of her and glanced toward the open door. Not only had he been gone most of the day, but during the brief interactions they'd had, he'd been strangely aloof, almost angry.

When she'd awoken that morning to Austin's hungry crying, Dylan had already been absent. She hadn't been overly surprised to find him gone, since the previous day he'd been restless as well as eager to return to work.

"Now then, you need to get them a little thinner." Trudy stood at her spot of command in front of the stove, browning the beef. "Or they'll take too long to cook."

Positioned at the table within full view of the open door, Catherine resumed her chopping, trying to focus on the potatoes, but her sights kept straying outside to every passing shadow. Dylan was due back any time for supper. On the one hand, she hoped he wouldn't return until she finished preparing the simple fare of fried beef and potatoes. On the other hand, she wanted to see him and assure herself that he was back to his usual charming self.

"Let me show you again." Trudy held out her hand for the knife.

Wordlessly, Catherine relinquished it to the woman.

Trudy picked up one of the peeled potatoes and sliced it so fast, she was done with the entire plump vegetable in the amount of time it took Catherine to cut one slice.

"Dontcha worry your little heart. You'll learn soon enough." Trudy passed the knife back to her. "Just keep trying."

Catherine was grateful for the cooking lesson. She truly was. She couldn't rely on meals from family and friends any longer, had to learn the skill for herself.

If only she knew what was bothering Dylan, then she'd be able to concentrate better. Even so, she'd managed to make fluffy biscuits and a cabbage salad to go with the meal. Trudy had promised she'd show her how to bake a cake tomorrow.

Austin was cooing contentedly on the bed, recently fed and changed. Catherine was having to keep a better eye on him, since he was wiggling more every day and had managed to shift closer to the edge of the bed. What he really needed was a cradle of his own. She'd hesitated to suggest such an item to Dylan for fear he'd tease her about moving the baby to make room for them to be together.

He hadn't pulled her down onto the bed again, hadn't asked her to rest with him. But his low, breathy suggestion to let him hold her for a while had lingered in her thoughts, sending tingles over her skin every time she allowed herself to dwell on the possibility.

Had her hesitancy in the moment pushed him away? He

hadn't touched her again, had kept a proper distance. Of course, he'd been as sweet and friendly as always, never passing an opportunity to flirt or make suggestive comments. Until today . . .

Was he starting to lose interest in her already? She'd suspected it might happen eventually.

Perhaps it was for the best. At least until she figured out what to do with Harlan Hatfield's cryptic note. She'd been analyzing the situation from all angles so she could make the threat go away.

Since Dylan believed Harlan was a decent man and only wanted what was best for South Park, she'd decided the best thing to do was to try to reason with him. If she wrote to him and arranged a meeting, she could explain all that had happened to her. Maybe if he knew she wasn't really a criminal, he'd let the issue go.

She sighed.

Trudy's clanking of the spoon around the cast-iron skillet came to a halt. "I can tell something's bothering you. . . ."

Catherine paused, the blade halfway through the potato in front of her. Did she dare bare her heart to Trudy? The woman had proven herself to be a kind and caring soul from the moment they'd met. She'd likely have words of wisdom. "I guess I'm just worried Dylan will get tired of me. Maybe he's already sorry he married me."

"Uffda." A hint of censure filled the word. "It doesn't take much to see that man is completely daft in the head over you."

"Do you really think so?"

"I know so."

The spoon began scraping again, and Catherine continued

her meticulous potato slicing. She tried to let Trudy's words settle inside and comfort her, but she still couldn't shake the feeling something wasn't right.

"It's just that when men get to know me, they decide they don't like who I really am. And they end up leaving me." There, she'd spoken the truth aloud. With her doubts out in the open, she kept her attention riveted to the potato even as Trudy's spoon grew idle again.

"Now, I'm no expert on men, mind you. But I say if a man decides he doesn't like you after he gets to know the real you, then he isn't worth crying over."

"But what if the issue lies within me? The fact that I'm plain and dull. What if I'm simply not exciting enough for Dylan?"

"That man doesn't need exciting. He needs levelheaded and down-to-earth, which is exactly what you are."

"He might not think so. Especially compared to the other women he's known."

Before Catherine knew what was happening, Trudy crossed to her. "Now, you listen here. You're exactly who God intended you to be." Trudy's expression radiated earnestness so much so that a lump formed in Catherine's throat.

"Thank you, Trudy."

Trudy took the knife from her hand, set it on the table, then grasped both her hands. "We women have to stop defining ourselves by lining ourselves up against other women. Instead, we need to define ourselves the way our Creator does."

Could she stop worrying about her shortcomings and comparing herself to other women? That was hard to do, especially when men seemed to like other women better than her.

"Our Creator says that we are fearfully and wonderfully made. Dontcha ever believe anything else. Do you hear me?"

Catherine nodded. She'd thought of that verse from the Psalms from time to time after helping with a delivery, especially when the mother held her newborn for the first time, caressing the baby's little nose and mouth and fingers. Catherine never doubted that each child was fearfully and wonderfully made. It was so obvious at birth.

Such a truth didn't change with the passing of time. If it was true at birth, then it was as true at age twenty as it would be at forty and sixty. Why, then, was it so hard to accept God's definition?

Footsteps sounded on the doorstep, and in the next moment Dylan ducked inside. She quickly reached for the knife and half-cut potato. She was almost afraid to look at him for fear she'd see the same aloofness as earlier in place of his usual charm and friendliness.

"You're a mite early, Dylan." Trudy had returned to her sizzling pan at the stove. "But dontcha worry your little head. I've been teaching Catherine everything I know. And she'll be able to cook tasty meals in no time at all."

Dylan didn't reply with one of his usual comebacks and was instead strangely silent.

Catherine shot a glance his way to find his expression grave and his eyes wary. Her stomach dropped. She'd been right. Something was really wrong.

Trudy paused and glanced at Dylan, too, clearly waiting for his response.

"How long before it's ready?" he finally asked, his tone as serious as if someone had died.

As Catherine cut the last potato, Trudy reached for the

cutting board and the potatoes. "Not more than half an hour. Why?" She dumped them into the skillet with the beef and stirred the mixture together.

"Need to speak to Catherine privately. That's all."

That's all? Catherine wiped her hands on the apron Trudy had given her. It sounded like he was a judge about to hand her a death sentence.

"Okey dokey." Trudy gave the skillet a final stir before she turned around and handed the wooden spoon to Catherine. "Then I'll leave you to it. Just stir it several more times, taste, and salt. If it starts to stick to the bottom of the pan, add more lard."

Catherine didn't want Trudy to leave, didn't want to face Dylan alone. But she took Trudy's place in front of the stove and gave the mixture a stir for good measure.

Trudy untied her apron, set it in the basket containing the baking supplies and utensils she'd brought along, and then put on her hat, taking her time to situate it on her head just so and tying it underneath her chin.

After looping the basket over one arm, she gave Catherine a long, meaningful look. And although Catherine wasn't quite sure what the look was supposed to mean, she nodded at Trudy as though she did.

When the woman stepped outside, Catherine swiveled to the stove, buying herself a little more time. She scooped up a spoonful of lard from the ceramic crock and tossed it into the pan, even though the potatoes weren't sticking.

Dylan cleared his throat.

She prodded the melting lump as if the meal depended upon it.

Another minute passed. "Catherine, we need to talk."

She drew in a deep breath, preparing herself for whatever fault he was going to find with her. As she started to turn, a knock sounded on the doorframe, followed by a child's voice. "My mama needs the new midwife."

Catherine rushed to the door, eager to escape Dylan. A barefoot girl with large brown eyes and curly brown hair peered up at her. Wearing a threadbare dress that was frayed along the hem, the girl couldn't have been more than eight or ten years old.

"I'm the midwife. How can I help you?"

"My papa sent me. Told me to ask if you'd come help mama have her baby."

"Of course—"

"He said to tell you we can't pay the doctor's fee."

Trudy stepped back inside, obviously not having gone far. Catherine wouldn't have been surprised if the woman had been standing right outside the door waiting to hear what Dylan wanted to talk about.

"This is Maria Rossi," Trudy said. "Her papa is among a new batch of immigrants working in Steele's mine. Her mama has four other little ones."

"We can't pay the doctor's fee," Maria persisted, as though she'd been instructed to make sure Catherine understood their financial situation.

Catherine offered the child a smile. "Then it's very lucky for you that I'm the midwife and not the doctor, since I don't require a fee."

She never had worried about payment. Had never needed to in Chicago while living with her parents. Of course, some women had paid her. But she never charged anything.

How would Dylan feel about her philosophy? Of course,

it hadn't come up when she'd assisted Ivy since the young woman was now family. And Edwin had been passed out drunk, leaving Chipeta to press a beaded necklace into Catherine's hands. At first she'd tried to make Chipeta understand that she didn't need to give her anything. But at Dylan's nod, Catherine realized she would only insult the native woman by not accepting the small offering.

Catherine moved the pan off the burner. "How long has your mama been having pains, Maria?"

"All day. She woke us up with them last night."

The woman had been in labor for a long time. Catherine wanted to ask if Mrs. Rossi was leaking fluid and how far apart the pains were. But she wasn't sure how reliable the information would be from the little girl. She'd wait to ask Mr. Rossi.

As Catherine crossed the room and reached for her satchel under the bed, her gaze snagged on Austin wiggling his arms and legs. Should she bring him with her?

"Dylan, you stay with Austin since the doctor will be by soon to dress your wounds." Trudy cut in, as if sensing Catherine's question. "I know Mrs. Rossi a little bit, so I'll take Catherine out there and lend a hand."

As Catherine stood and strapped on her satchel, she expected Dylan to protest. Instead, he crossed and picked up Austin. "Come here, little fella. We'll get along fine."

Somehow the words seemed final, as if Dylan planned to get along fine without her forever. A chill slipped into her blood. So she'd been right. He didn't want her anymore. That's why he was eager to talk to her, so he could end their marriage.

She tried to meet his gaze, but he bent his head and buried his face in Austin's body, kissing the baby and earning a squeal. Her heart squeezed as she watched them. Yes, the two would get along fine without her. But that didn't mean she wanted them to. Now that she had them both, she didn't want to lose them.

CHAPTER

21

Another new life. Catherine paused outside the cabin door and gazed up at the sky, her heart overflowing with gratefulness. The stars were fading, and the air contained a quiet peace that came only at the predawn hour when the town nightlife tapered to silence.

She breathed in the coolness, still fully awake and crackling with energy, even though she'd been at the Rossis' for most of the night. The feeling would evaporate with the rising of the sun, and fatigue would finally overcome her. But she always loved the few hours after a successful delivery when she reveled in the beauty of the birthing process.

Of course, the situation had been precarious when she and Trudy had first arrived the previous evening at the one-room shanty on the outskirts of town. With little Maria's help translating for Mr. Rossi, they learned his wife had lost her fluids hours earlier and had been in heavy labor since, but something was keeping the baby from coming.

Catherine ran her hands over Mrs. Rossi's abdomen and

discovered the baby's head was too high and out of the pelvis. The internal exam confirmed the baby was presenting cross lying. The good news was that Mrs. Rossi was fully dilated and there wasn't anything—no afterbirth, cord, or growths—in the lower wall of the womb preventing the baby from coming.

After having already birthed seven children—two who died in infancy—Mrs. Rossi's womb and abdominal muscles had become flaccid so that her baby had too much room and wasn't dropping into position. Compounding the problem was the fact that Mrs. Rossi had become so exhausted that her contractions had weakened, further preventing the baby from moving where it should.

With Trudy's help, Catherine had managed to maneuver the head down without trapping the cord. As soon as the baby's skull reached the cervix, Mrs. Rossi gained fresh momentum and was able to bear down. After only fifteen minutes of active pushing, the newborn made its way into the world.

Afterward, Mr. Rossi had insisted on Catherine and Trudy staying while he cooked an elaborate Italian supper. The meal had taken hours of preparation, and midnight came and went before they sat down together around the tiny table and enjoyed the spicy pasta dish and crusty loaf of hot bread while Mrs. Rossi rested comfortably in bed. She encountered no trouble getting the newborn to nurse, and when she fell asleep and supper was cleaned up and the other little ones were put to bed, Catherine and Trudy left.

Since they'd passed the Gundersons' house first, Catherine had walked the remainder of the distance home alone with Trudy's parting words warming her heart. "You were so calm, efficient, and decisive with an equal measure of tenderness. I'd say God gave you all the qualities that go into making a miracle-working midwife. You're very special. Dontcha ever compare yourself to any other woman again."

A miracle-working midwife. That might be a slight exaggeration, but the affirmation washed over Catherine. Was it possible God had given her the exact qualities necessary to carry out her work? She'd always found herself lacking. But maybe she'd been wrong and was just the way God wanted her to be.

What about Dylan? Could he learn to accept her for the way she was? Or was he bound to reject her like all the other men in her life?

Her attention shifted to the closed door. She still didn't want to have the conversation he'd intended to have last evening. At least she'd put it off. Maybe she'd have the day while he was away at work to figure out how to prove to him she was worth keeping around. Because she was. She had to believe it.

Through the square window, the interior of the cabin was dark. When she slowly opened the door and stepped inside, she tiptoed, praying she wouldn't wake Dylan or Austin.

As the door closed behind her, she swiped off her hat and set it with her satchel on the floor. She'd put them away in the morning.

Turning, she started across the room, only to stop short at the sight of Dylan sitting in one of the kitchen chairs. It was almost too dark to tell he was there, except for the slight slant of moonlight shimmering in past the curtains.

He was slumped over, elbows resting on his knees with

his face buried in his hands. Defeat and dejection rolled off him in waves, crashing into her and sending her back a step.

She wanted to retreat all the way outside, but she held herself in place. She couldn't avoid this confrontation forever, and she might as well get it over with now.

Swallowing the fear threatening to make her mute, she forced herself to whisper, "What's wrong?"

He didn't move.

After several long moments, she swallowed again. "Dylan, you're scaring me."

Slowly, he sat up, dropping his hands away from his face and sliding something forward on the table. Through the darkness, it looked like a piece of newsprint or maybe a letter.

Did he want her to read it?

He sat back in his chair and crossed his arms. "Want to explain that?"

Why wasn't he calling her *darlin'* like usual? Hesitating, she stared at the item, wishing he'd just tell her what it was. But after a moment more, she crossed to the table, picked it up, and scanned it. The darkness prevented her from making out anything.

At the scratch of a match, a flame flickered to life, and Dylan touched it to the wick of a candle on the table. While only a faint light, it was enough for her to see the strain in his expression. Was his leg paining him, or was it something else?

Her gaze dropped again to the sheet, and this time she sucked in a breath at the picture of herself centered on the paper. The photograph had been taken over a year ago at a political rally she'd attended with her father and had ended up in the *Chicago Tribune*. What was it doing here?

As she read the words above the picture, her blood ran cold. *Reward of $200 for the capture of Catherine Remington.* She skimmed the rest, her horror swelling with each passing second. Rocky was behind this. Apparently he wasn't satisfied to simply pin the blame for his crime on her—he was intent on ruining her family in the process.

Nausea welled up, and she pressed a hand against her mouth to keep from being sick.

"Well?" Dylan's whisper was harsh, demanding.

Did Dylan think she'd committed the two murders? What could she possibly say to defend herself? "I don't know what to say—"

He shoved back and stood, tipping over his chair. It clattered to the floor. His chest heaved in and out, and his nostrils flared. "You betrayed me."

Betrayed? She glanced at the wanted poster again, her attention zeroing in on Kit Olson's name.

He knew who she was. Finally.

She almost breathed a sigh of relief to have the mix-up out in the open. But at the glare he was leveling at her, she straightened. Surely he wasn't blaming her for everything. After all, he'd played a part in this too.

"Why did you deceive me? Why weren't you just honest?"

"I didn't set out to deceive you—"

"You didn't tell me the truth about who you really were." The anguish in his whisper and in his eyes ripped through her.

No good could come of arguing with him. It would only stir up more hurt. The fact was, she should have cleared up the misunderstanding. Her own conscience had told her so on a multitude of occasions. But instead of listening to that gentle prompting, she'd plainly ignored it. And in the process, she'd hurt Dylan terribly.

"I'm sorry, Dylan. Truly I am. I wanted to tell you, but I let my own selfish desires keep me from it."

"I can't believe you thought you could get away with this."

She wanted to hang her head. She had no excuse for what she'd done. It had been wrong.

"So was that your intention? To come here, take on Kit's identity, and drum up my sympathy so I'd marry you?"

"What? No." His accusation stung. Did he think so low of her that he believed her capable of entirely contriving their marriage? "I didn't take on Kit's identity, at least not purposefully."

"You sure acted like it." Their whispers were getting louder. She didn't want to wake Austin, but the pressure inside was piling up.

"I never claimed to be Kit. I told you I was Catherine."

"You knew I wouldn't know the difference."

At the arrogance in his tone, she bristled. "I assumed you would take one look at me and realize I was a stranger, someone you'd never before met, which is exactly what I was."

His response stalled.

She continued as her frustration mounted. "How was I to know you were so inebriated during the few times you spent with Kit that you had no recollection of what she looked like?"

His mouth hung open a second longer before he clamped his lips closed, pressing them together in a tight line.

She fisted her hands and placed them on her hips. If he wanted to argue with her, then she wouldn't back down.

"You must've wondered why I was pushing a complete stranger for a wedding. Didn't that seem odd?"

"Strangers get married sometimes out of convenience. I believed you needed a mother for Austin and concluded I was a logical choice."

"You should have made your identity clearer." His accusation lacked the same fervor from a moment ago.

"And maybe you should have been able to recognize that I wasn't Kit."

They were no longer whispering.

Thankfully Austin remained asleep and blissfully unaware that his life was about to change forever. Now she understood why Dylan had been angry the past evening when he'd come home, why he indicated that he and Austin would get along fine without her. He had no intention of keeping their marriage now that he knew the truth, just as she'd predicted.

Dylan blew out a breath before cramming his fingers into his hair. "Aside from how this whole thing started, you figured out the mistake and didn't tell me."

"As I said previously, I am truly sorry for letting the mix-up continue without saying anything. I should have done so the moment I realized what you believed—"

"And when was that?"

"The night of the wedding feast at Wyatt's ranch, when you spoke of my father owning a store."

His long lashes framed his tortured eyes. "That's almost the entire three weeks we've been married."

"Yes." A dozen excuses clamored through her mind, but all of them were weak in light of the hurt in his expression.

"So you planned to keep on deceiving me forever? Is that it?"

"I started to tell you a few times, but I was afraid of this happening, of you getting angry."

"Blast it all! Of course I'm angry." He practically yelled the words but then caught himself and ended on a half whisper. "You can't expect me not to be."

"I know." Oh, heaven help her. Why hadn't she been honest all along?

He rubbed his eyes wearily.

The last thing she'd wanted to do was hurt him. But she should have known deceitfulness could never bear good fruit.

He dropped his hands and nodded at the wanted paper crumpled in her fist. "What about the crimes?"

After scanning the notice again, she tossed it back to the table. "Do you believe I'm a murderer, Dylan?"

"How do I know what to believe when you've been lying to me all along?"

The comment stung as if he'd reached over and slapped her cheek. But she didn't flinch. She deserved his censure.

"Tell me the truth."

"It's a long story."

He righted his overturned chair and then sat, waving at the one across the table. "Tell it to me."

She pulled out the chair and collapsed into it. "I was the midwife who delivered your son."

CHAPTER

22

At some point in listening to Catherine's tale about witnessing Rocky Rogers Kenna murder Stretch, the anger escaped from Dylan's body, leaving numbness inside.

"Kit made me promise to bring you Austin," she finished quietly. "During the entire two months of traveling and trying to keep from being followed, I told myself I would hand him over and walk away. I never realized how challenging it would be to carry through with my resolve."

He scraped absently at a spot of candle wax that had dripped onto the table, trying to take in all the details and make sense of everything. In spite of her living out a lie for most of their short marriage, he believed her description of Kit's death, Stretch's murder, and Rocky's threats. Catherine was an innocent victim. He hadn't needed to hear her tale to come to that conclusion. But now that he had, he was even more convinced she'd been framed.

Any judge who took on the case would easily see she wasn't capable of murder, and a jury wouldn't have enough evidence to convict her. But that was in a perfect world. And Chicago was far from perfect, and Rocky's influence and money were too far-reaching.

Even though Alderman Remington was also a powerful man, he wouldn't stoop to dishonest tactics to free his daughter. His integrity and determination to play by the rules, while noble, would put Catherine in jeopardy of a lifetime jail sentence if not the death penalty.

She'd done the right thing in running away. Dylan could give her credit for that. No doubt she'd come to the same conclusions he had that she had no guarantee of justice and that she was better off sparing her family the disgrace of a trial that might end in her conviction.

Even so, his gut clenched in knowing Rocky was getting away with such corruption. It wasn't fair to Catherine or her family.

Dylan had spent the better part of the previous evening and night thinking on the accusations of murder. And now that he knew Rocky was involved, his mind spun off in a hundred different directions.

Part of him wanted to go with her to Chicago, enlist the help of the honest people he'd gotten to know while living there, and fight with everything they had to convict Rocky of the murder.

But at the same time, he reckoned the wisest course of action was sending her to Canada, where she could take on a new identity and live without worry of anyone tracking her down. He'd provide her the name of a family he knew who'd moved to British Columbia. She could seek them out until she established herself.

She leaned back in her chair. "Even before I realized you'd

mistaken me for Kit, I wasn't planning to tell anyone about my past. I wanted to stay hidden so Rocky wouldn't be able to find me."

"Makes sense."

"Once I was aware of the mix-up, it just became easier to withhold the information about who I really was. I've been afraid that if word spreads about my true identity, I'll bring danger to you and Austin."

"I can handle danger."

"But when I realized how precarious your sheriff position is with the election and how much it means to you and your family that you're on a righteous path now, I didn't want to cause more problems for you."

He understood what she was saying. "Still, you should've told me."

"I know. It's just that I worried that once you discovered I wasn't Kit, you wouldn't want me to be your wife anymore and wouldn't let me be with Austin."

What would he have done if he'd known she wasn't Austin's mother that first day when she was sitting in his office? Her fear wasn't unfounded. He reckoned he wouldn't have married her so quick-like. Maybe he would've even sent her on her way.

"Austin's in good hands now." Her eyes glistened with tears as she watched the sleeping infant. "I can leave with that knowledge."

So she knew she had to go away. "Yep. He'll be just fine here with me."

She ducked her head and swiped at her cheek.

What kind of lowlife rat was he for saying something so hurtful? Maybe he had every right to be angry at her for deceiving him, but he didn't want to see her suffer.

"It's for the best." He tried to gentle his tone.

She nodded. "I understand that as sheriff you have an ethical obligation to turn me in. And I won't resist your arrest."

"Arrest?" he barked out the word before he glanced at Austin to make sure he hadn't awoken the fella. He'd had trouble getting the infant to fall asleep last night. The babe had been as cranky as a cricket in a corner. And Dylan sure as sunrise didn't want to go through that ordeal again.

"Listen, Catherine." He spoke in near-to a whisper. "I ain't gonna arrest you, not when you didn't commit a crime."

"Then you believe me that I didn't murder either Stretch or Kit?" Her eyes widened, revealing the flecks of brown in her green eyes. Her long lashes were damp and looked even darker.

"Knew from the minute I saw the accusation that it wasn't true."

"Thank you, Dylan." She started to reach for his hand but then pulled back. "You're a good man. Kit was right."

The same guilt hit him as before. He hadn't been good to Kit. Catherine knew it more than anyone. She'd been there at Kit's last moments, watching her die uncared for and alone, cast out and rejected by her family because of him. And yet, both Kit and Catherine had still accepted him. How could they forgive so easily? Forgiveness didn't come as naturally to him, and he wasn't sure he'd ever be able to forgive or forget Catherine's deception.

"Everyone else is gonna realize you're not capable of murder."

She released a tired sigh. "Maybe some of the folks who've gotten to know me. But most will see the poster and assume the worst about me, especially since they already think I'm a fallen woman."

She had a point. Even so, he had no intention of doing anything but trying to protect her. He picked up the wanted poster, creased in a dozen places from where he'd folded it and kept it in his pocket all day. He lifted it to the candle flame, and the fire licked the edge. "They won't see it."

Her eyes rounded. "I'm sure there are many other notices out there. We can't burn them all."

The paper ignited, curling and smoking as the flames spread. He held it away from the table so it wouldn't catch anything else on fire.

As the flame moved closer to his hands, he let the charred remains fall to the floor. The last of the fire finished consuming the paper before flickering out. As far as he was concerned, that's what needed to happen to each of the wanted posters with Catherine's picture on them.

He wished he could hunt down every single one and get rid of them, but for the rest of her life, she'd have to worry about someone seeing the poster, recognizing her face, and making the connection.

"Even if no one else finds out," she said, "Harlan Hatfield sent me a message that he figured out who I am. He wants you to step down from being sheriff."

"Don't worry none about Harlan."

"I'm truly sorry that I might ruin your chances at keeping the sheriff job, Dylan. You're good at it, and you deserve it."

As much as he wanted to get reelected, this wasn't her fault. Ultimately he'd been the one to set the whole thing in motion when he'd slept with Kit. And sins always had a way of catching up with a person no matter how far they might run from them.

She stifled a yawn. "I know I need to leave. I just wish I

could do it in a way that doesn't create more scandal and embarrassment."

There was no way around this causing him a heap of trouble.

With her eyes upon him full of so many questions, his heart pinched in his chest. He didn't want to imagine her having to run off, trying to hide, constantly looking over her shoulder. She'd be alone without anyone to help and protect her or take care of her, at least until she reached his friends in Canada. Even then she'd be in a foreign place and wouldn't know anyone, would be a lifetime away from home, from him, and from Austin.

A strange sense of panic wound into his muscles that he didn't understand. He pushed up from his chair and stood, needing to get away from the confusion.

It oughta be easy to let her go. She'd lied and hurt him. If that wasn't enough, he wasn't under any moral obligation to her since they'd never shared any intimacies and Austin wasn't her child. Even if Austin did need a mother, it couldn't be her. Not with danger hot on her heels like a pack of hunting hounds.

If it was so easy to let her go, then why was the very thought of sending her away making him as tight and stiff as an old leather boot?

She stood, too, and glanced at her carpetbag shoved under the bed. "I guess I'll pack. . . ."

He stuffed his hands into his pockets. To keep himself from grabbing hold of her? "Listen. There's no need to rush off. Ain't anywhere you can go right now. Might as well get some sleep after being up all night."

She hesitated, still staring at her bag. "I can get a room at the hotel."

The frustration and confusion inside only pummeled away at him. "Naw. No sense in that." He pressed his fists deeper into his pockets.

"I don't mind—"

"Shucks, Catherine. Just go to bed for now, and we'll talk again when we're both rested."

She twisted at his ring on her finger, twirling it around for a few seconds before she pulled it off. Without a word, she set it on the table and then walked to the pallet and began to unroll it.

"Take the bed."

"No, with your injuries—"

"I'll be fine on the floor."

She stood a moment, then nodded. Without even taking off her boots, she climbed into bed, gathered Austin against her, and pressed a kiss to his head.

A lump rose swiftly into Dylan's throat. He couldn't see her face, but he could see the rapid rise and fall of her shoulders and knew she was fighting against her emotions just like he was his.

The parting was gonna be hard. He had half a mind to tell her to forget about leaving, tell her she could stay and they'd work things out. But he clamped his jaw to keep from saying anything more.

It was for the best if they went their separate ways now, before it got even harder—maybe even impossible—to do so.

When Catherine awoke, her eyes were swollen and her nose stuffy, as though she'd been crying. At the wiggle of the little body snuggled into hers, reality came flooding back along with the tears. The reason she felt as if she'd been crying was because she had been. Off and on for hours. Apparently, she'd finally fallen asleep.

She tugged Austin closer and kissed his fuzzy head again, desperate to hold him for as long as possible before she had to leave him behind forever. Only this time, he pushed back and released a grunt that ended in a half cry.

She tensed, waiting for Dylan to say something or to offer to take Austin. But silence prevailed, a silence so stifling, she sensed Dylan was gone even before she rolled over.

Bright sunlight streamed in past the curtain. It was well into the morning, and a coffee mug rested on the table next to an empty bottle. That meant Dylan had already fed Austin and placed him back into bed with her. Maybe she'd slept so long that Austin was already due for another feeding.

The baby fidgeted and made a few more grunty cries. Yes, he was working at telling her he was hungry again. She needed to get out of bed and make the bottle before he decided he was angry about being hungry.

"Alright, I'm going." Pushing her hair out of her face, she sat up and moved to the edge. She stopped short at the sight of a second but full coffee cup on the bedside table.

Had Dylan put it there? For her?

She glanced again at the mug on the table where he usually left it after draining it dry, then shifted her attention to the mug waiting for her. There wasn't any steam rising from it. It was likely cold after sitting for so long. But that didn't change the fact that he'd brought her coffee in bed.

Her throat constricted.

Why had he done such a kind thing for her after how terribly she'd deceived him?

Tears stung the backs of her eyes. How could she have any more left after how much she'd already cried?

She pressed her palms against her eyes to keep tears from flowing. She had to pull herself together. With as much as she needed to do in a short amount of time, she couldn't allow herself to wallow in self-pity.

First, she needed to tend to Austin, then she had to pack as well as sell off several pieces of her jewelry to have enough money to purchase a stagecoach ticket to Denver. From there, she'd wire her father and ask him to help pay for the rest of the return trip.

She'd had plenty of time to think about her choices during the hours of crying and holding Austin. And she knew now what she had to do, the thing she should have done all along—stand up for herself and the truth, that she was innocent of murder. Even more than that, Rocky had committed a crime, and because of her cowardice, he was walking around free to hurt or kill more people. If she didn't at least try to expose him, their deaths would be on her conscience.

Maybe she'd lose her fight for justice and end up hanging from the end of a noose. Maybe she'd ruin herself and her family's reputation even further. But it was past time to stop ignoring her conscience and do what was right no matter the consequences.

Even now, she wanted nothing more than to pack her bags, pick up Austin, and run away someplace new. It would be easier this time. But that was only because after a person

262

gave way to temptation once, the justifications came a lot quicker the next time.

She'd seen that happen with her lying to Dylan. The more she'd given in to the urge to hide the truth, the easier it had gotten to let the deception continue, until it hadn't bothered her as much anymore. In fact, she'd been well on her way to accepting that what she'd done wasn't all that wrong.

She sighed, remorse for the past night and past weeks filling her.

Standing firm and sticking to the truth was the hard way but the right way. She should have done it with Dylan. And also with the murder accusations.

Austin released a louder wail.

The sound prodded her up. She arranged the pillows so Austin wouldn't roll off the bed, and then she crossed to the stove and shook the kettle. It needed more water.

Austin's cries began to escalate, enough now to disturb Juniper, who'd been stretched out on the floor, lying in a spot of sunshine. Now the kitten sat up and put his ears back.

She aimed for the bed. "You're not going to let me get changed into fresh clothing first, are you?" She didn't want to miss catching the stagecoach, but she also didn't want to give up holding the baby every chance she had until she left.

At a knock on the door, she changed directions. Hopefully no one was calling for her help with delivering a baby. Although she needed to leave town, she'd make time just as she always did. In fact, she wished she could pay Mrs. Rossi a visit before departing. Even if the woman was an expert in childbearing, anything could go wrong, as it had last night.

"All I can do now is pray for her," she whispered as she opened the door.

A tall man stood on the step, wringing the brim of his hat in both hands. With his curly blond hair and youthful face, she recognized him as one of the cowhands who'd been a part of the brawl outside the saloon. Dylan had called him Frank.

His brows pinched together above serious eyes. "Mrs. McQuaid?"

Should she respond to that title anymore? For Dylan's sake, she guessed she ought to hide her real identity a little while longer. Once she was gone, he'd have to figure out a way to tell everyone the truth about what had happened and who she really was. But until she was well on her way to Denver, she'd have to keep up the charade.

"I'm Mrs. McQuaid." It wasn't a lie. They were legally married, just not for much longer. "How can I help you?"

"You're the midwife?" He gave her a once-over, his brows rising.

She probably looked a fright. "Yes, I'm the midwife. I was out most of the night helping deliver a baby." She had to offer some kind of explanation for her swollen eyes, splotchy face, untidy hair, and wrinkled garments.

"I've got an emergency. With my woman. Was hoping you could help."

"What's your woman's name?"

"Minnie."

Catherine went through her mental list of pregnant women in the area, a list she added to every time she heard of someone new. Of course Trudy had given her information about most of those women.

Catherine tried to remember as much as she could about Minnie—a young girl of only seventeen who'd run away from a bad home life back east to be with her man, who'd come to Colorado to work as a cowhand. The two had gotten married as soon as they realized Minnie was pregnant. But if Catherine remembered correctly, Minnie wasn't due for a couple more months.

"What kind of trouble is Minnie having?"

"Don't rightly know." His gaze shifted nervously around as though he was afraid of anyone seeing him here.

Catherine held back a tired sigh. Like most men about to have a child, he was clearly scattered and uncertain. The only thing she could do was go with him and check on Minnie for herself. The problem was, Frank worked for J. D. Otto. How would Dylan feel once he learned she'd gone out to J. D.'s?

On the other hand, Catherine couldn't turn down a woman in need of a midwife, not even her worst enemy. "I need to grab my satchel." And take care of Austin. His cries were growing more insistent.

"Thank you, ma'am."

She nodded and stepped inside. Her satchel sat on the floor where she'd left it last night with her hat. As she bent to pick them up, her visitor's footsteps thudded behind her, and his shadow fell over her.

He must be in a hurry to follow her inside rather than waiting on the doorstep like a gentleman would.

"I'll be ready in just a minute." She straightened, but before she could turn, a hand clamped over her mouth. A rag pressed against her nose, and the pungent ether-like scent of chloroform assaulted her.

What was this man doing? What did he want from her?

She struggled to break free. But his other hand gripped her wrists behind her back. "Don't fight me, little lady." His tone was hard, having lost all the worry from moments ago.

He shoved the rag against her nose and mouth more firmly, nearly cutting off her air supply. Somewhere her brain warned her not to breathe in the anesthetic, that doing so would render her weak, possibly even unconscious.

But he was too strong to resist, and when he wrenched her arms more painfully, she couldn't keep from sucking in a sharp breath. Her head grew lighter, and her vision wavered.

Austin's cries only seemed to grow louder. And her need to get to him swelled with an urgency that made her draw in another breath.

In the next instant, everything went black.

CHAPTER
23

A faint baby's cry drifted in the air. Was that Austin crying?

Dylan stepped through the back door of the courthouse and released a long, noisy yawn. He hadn't been able to get more than a couple of hours of shut-eye last night. Every time he'd heard Catherine sniffle or shudder with a sob, the pain in his chest had swelled until he thought he might be having a heart attack.

When finally she'd fallen asleep, he'd rested uneasily, getting up at daybreak with Austin, then heading to work.

He squinted in the noon sunshine, the air temperature having warmed up a whole heap in the hours he'd been finalizing the testimonies he'd gotten from Smiley and Rube. The two had given him plenty of incriminating evidence against J. D. Otto.

Stu's trip to Tarryall was the final nail in J. D.'s coffin. The deputy found the cattle right where Smiley and Rube said they'd be. Stu hadn't gotten close enough to check the brands, but it didn't matter. The fact that J. D. was holding cattle in the remote location was proof enough.

Problem was, J. D. wasn't gonna surrender himself without a fight. And Dylan had been pondering all morning the best way of capturing the man without anyone getting needlessly hurt.

Angry, almost hoarse wails again wafted toward him.

Dylan bit back a second yawn and strained to listen. The sound was definitely a babe. And Austin was the only babe in the vicinity he knew about.

He glanced across the backyard to the cabin only to find the door wide open. That wasn't unusual. Catherine sometimes left the door and window open to allow in fresh air. But she never let Austin cry for any length of time. She was always quick to comfort him.

Why wasn't she comforting him now?

Dylan strode down the narrow dirt path past tall clumps of grass that were now green but wouldn't stay that way for long in the dry and dusty town. As he reached the cabin, Austin's wails rose pitifully, as though he'd been at it for a while.

"Catherine?" Dylan ducked inside, the dark interior a stark contrast to the brightness outside. He blinked and tried to focus. Catherine was nowhere in sight.

His heart picked up speed, and he crossed to the bed and picked up Austin. "Hey there, little fella. I'm here."

Red-faced and with his legs twisted in his nightgown, his cries tapered off. He peered up at Dylan and was quiet for a few seconds before he released another hoarse wail.

Dylan took in the empty bottle sitting on the table right where he'd left it earlier. Hadn't Catherine given him his next feeding? She'd been the one to teach him that Austin needed to eat approximately every three to four hours. The babe would have been due at least an hour ago.

"Let's get you your dinner, little fella." All the while he worked to prepare the bottle, he jostled the frantic Austin in the other arm. Finally, as the babe started greedily sucking and gulping the milk mixture, silence descended.

Dylan glanced again to the open door, waiting for Catherine to step through, breathless and flushed, her eyes bright, her expression serious as she explained where she'd been. No doubt with a nearby neighbor helping with something.

Even as he rationalized where she was, fear wrapped tight fingers around his heart.

"Maybe you were sleeping when she left." He lowered himself into the same chair he'd been in during the conversation last night, the kitten rubbing against his leg, hungry and begging for milk too. "Maybe Mrs. Rossi had an emergency, and maybe your ma didn't think she'd be gone for so long."

Your ma. Dylan closed his eyes to push down the sorrow that simmered just below the surface. Catherine wasn't Austin's ma. At least not in the biological sense. Even so, she'd been a loving ma, caring for Austin as if he'd been her own. In fact, Dylan couldn't imagine any other woman taking an illegitimate child as she'd done and loving him so much. Most would have shunned Austin, maybe would've taken him to an orphanage.

What would've happened to his son if Catherine hadn't had the courage and the determination to make the journey west? What if the babe *had* ended up in an orphanage instead? Or what if Catherine had decided against bringing Austin to Fairplay, especially since she hadn't known anything about him as the pa? With as deeply attached as she'd grown to Austin, she could've raised the child alone.

Fact was, he owed Catherine a debt of gratitude for protecting Austin and connecting him to his son.

Dylan opened his eyes and brushed his thumb over Austin's plump cheek. The babe paused in his ravenous eating, his eyes finding Dylan's. Tears rimmed his lashes, and his brow was furrowed as if he was as puzzled as Dylan about why Catherine had left.

How was Austin gonna react when Catherine was gone for good?

Dylan had been putting off coming back to the cabin, hadn't wanted to discuss the next steps—which included her leaving. He wanted to hold off on it as long as possible. But the sooner he could send her on her way to Canada, the safer she'd be.

Maybe she could stay another day . . . maybe two. But beyond that, she had to go. Especially since Harlan knew who she was. Dylan had half a mind to ride up to Como and beg Harlan to keep quiet. But Harlan would see it as his civic duty to inform everyone of this newest problem in Dylan's personal life. Once Harlan went public with the news, Rocky's men would be in Fairplay faster than hornets on honey.

Would Harlan stay silent if Dylan promised to resign as sheriff? Dylan didn't want to give in to the pressure, but if doing so would protect Catherine, then he'd turn over his badge in a heartbeat.

But his thoughts circled like a wagon train back around to the wanted poster. Even if he surrendered his badge, someone somewhere would eventually connect Catherine to the crime.

Breathing out a tense sigh, Dylan slumped back. Catherine's betrayal still hurt. And he was still angry. But disappointment was rearing up more than anything else. He'd stepped up and taken responsibility for his child, thought he was being noble by offering to get married. He'd done his duty without complaint, wanting to make the best of his mistake.

But the truth was, marriage hadn't been all that hard, had even been fulfilling. Now the prospect of Catherine not being here every day wrenched his heart out. He loved her quiet, sensible ways and her calm, unruffled spirit. He loved how adaptable she was with her time, willing to stay up late, even lose a whole night's sleep if necessary. He loved how easy she was to be around, how he could be himself and not have to impress her. And he loved her companionship during all hours of the night and day.

She'd brightened his life and made him realize how beautiful a relationship could be. After his failures with so many other women and his problems with lust, this different kind of relationship with her—one not fueled by physical needs—was satisfying in a way he'd never realized was possible.

The relationship had so much more substance and depth because it was based on friendship and mutual respect and sacrifice. Maybe it had even renewed his faith in the possibility of having a committed marriage—something he'd never believed he deserved. Even though his flesh was weak at times, the marriage had challenged him to grow in self-restraint.

Yep. Marriage had been making him a better man. *Catherine* had been making him a better man.

"It don't matter," he whispered.

Austin paused in his sucking as though he might challenge Dylan's comment. But then he grunted and resumed his meal.

"I mean it. It don't matter." The words came out more forcefully this time but left a big, empty hole inside. "I can find another wife. I'll get you another ma."

Except that he didn't want another wife. He couldn't imagine himself with anyone but Catherine. She was the only one he wanted. And she was the only one he wanted as a ma to Austin.

"Reckon we can get along fine without anyone." He repositioned the bottle so Austin could drink the last ounce. "Just you and me, little fella. That's all we need."

The words fell flat. Aside from all the logistics of raising a babe alone while trying to work, Austin needed a ma and not just a pa. Sure, he could enlist his family's help, and Trudy would jump at the chance to take care of Austin. But none of that replaced having a ma who would raise him up right.

He was suddenly hungry to see Catherine, hungry for her soothing presence, hungry for her practicality, hungry for her wisdom. She'd know what to do to make this situation turn out right. And that's what he wanted more than anything, to work things out between them and figure out a way for her to stay.

But the doorway was as empty as it had been since he'd stepped inside. Where was she? She hadn't run off, had she?

At the possibility, his heartbeat crashed to a halt. His gaze shot to her carpetbag under the bed. It was still there, which meant she hadn't gone yet. Besides, Catherine wouldn't just up and leave Austin and him. Not without a good-bye.

His sights darted around the room, taking in her satchel

and hat where she'd dropped them last night. If she'd gone out to the Rossis'—or any other place to offer her midwife skills—wouldn't she have taken along her supplies?

A piece of paper was shoved between the satchel and the wall. Maybe it would give him a clue of her whereabouts.

He stood, let Austin finish the last couple of sips, then set the bottle on the table while propping the babe upon his shoulder for burping. Thumping the little fella's back, Dylan crossed to Catherine's satchel then snatched up the paper.

As he flipped it around, fear gusted through him and froze him to the spot. It was the wanted poster with Catherine's picture on it. How had it gotten here? It couldn't be the one he'd carried around yesterday in his pocket. He'd burned it in the candle flame last night and swept up the ashes this morning. He'd been all too anxious to get rid of every trace of the blasted thing.

This—he crumpled the sheet—was obviously a different poster from some other place.

What in the blazes had happened?

His hand stilled on Austin's back at the same time the world around and inside him stilled to nothingness. There was only one explanation. Catherine had been captured. Most likely by a bounty hunter who was even now hauling her to Denver to lock her up.

CHAPTER

24

Dylan rummaged through the mess of supplies for extra am-
munition, pulled out the box, and then slammed the drawer
shut.

"Yous sure she didn't run off for herself?" Stu stood by
the office door and exchanged a worried look with Trudy,
who was bouncing Austin. "Maybe she was afraid you'd
lock her up."

"She wasn't afraid of me, Stu." Dylan practically shouted
the words but then ducked his head with remorse for taking
out his worry and frustration on his deputy. The man had
done everything he could to help him over the past months,
had been a steady and true friend.

When Stu had walked into the office a short while ago to
find Dylan rushing around while holding Austin, who was still
fussing, all he'd had to do was show Stu the wanted poster,
and he'd run right out and grabbed Trudy off the street.

Trudy had marched over, taken the babe, and demanded
to know what was wrong. Dylan had explained everything

as briefly as he could while he tucked a knife into his boot and strapped an extra gun at the small of his back.

Now he flipped open the box of bullets and counted out enough to fill each of his revolvers so they were ready for when he needed them.

"Catherine wouldn't have left Austin to fend for himself."

"I agree. Catherine wouldn't have just left." Trudy swayed back and forth, the rhythm calming Austin so that his eyelids grew heavy, although he kept fighting sleep, his eyes popping open every few seconds, almost as if he knew something had happened to his ma and he couldn't rest until she was safely back. "That lady wouldn't hurt a bedbug. There's no way in high heavens she committed murder, and there's no way she ran off anywhere without you and Austin."

After the cold and callous way he'd treated Catherine last night, Dylan wouldn't blame her for running off without telling him. But she'd never do that to Austin.

As embarrassing as it had been to admit the marriage mix-up to Stu and Trudy, one thing had become clear in the retelling. Catherine didn't deserve a single ounce of blame for the misunderstanding. He'd been the idiot to mistake one woman for another. If he hadn't been such a drunkard those last days in Chicago, then maybe he would've been more careful not to seduce a young woman like Kit. Maybe he would've gotten to know her better.

At the very least, from the moment he first saw Catherine sitting in the office with Austin, he would've recognized she wasn't Kit. When she'd offered to be his housekeeper and nursemaid in order to take care of the babe, that should've been another clue. What true ma would make that kind of offer? Most likely a real mother would have been more demanding, might have even been the one to suggest marriage without waiting for him to bring it up.

All he knew now was that he couldn't stand back and let some greedy bounty hunter take her to Denver to collect on the reward.

"I'm going after her, plain and simple." He crossed to the bag he'd packed, opened the flap, and stuffed the box of bullets inside. "If I head out now, there's a good chance I can catch up to the bounty hunter."

"Criminy." Stu shook his head while smoothing a hand over his mustache and down his untamed beard. "Yous don't even know which pass he's taking."

"I'll track him." At least Dylan hoped so.

"And yous don't know if he's working alone or with others."

"Don't matter." Dylan didn't care if he had to fight an entire army of bounty hunters to free Catherine. He was gonna get her out of trouble, and that's all there was to it.

"I don't see this going anywhere good." Stu spread his feet and crossed his arms, as if he planned to prevent Dylan from leaving.

"Now, Stuart Gunderson." Trudy's voice dropped to a loud whisper as she glanced at Austin's face and found that he'd finally surrendered to sleep. "You be more supportive of Dylan. Dontcha know he's a man who just lost the woman he loves? And he's desperate to find her."

Stu grunted.

"It's so romantic." Trudy offered a big-toothed smile and fluttered her eyelashes. Dylan guessed she meant to appear romantic herself but instead looked like she was trying to blink something out of her eye.

At any other time, he would have teased Trudy back. But

not now. Not when the woman he loved was in so much danger. Yep. Trudy was right as usual. He loved Catherine. He'd felt it coming, sensed it growing. Even if he was angry at her for lying to him, it didn't change the fact that he'd fallen in love with her.

He'd fallen in love with his wife.

The thought only stirred his insides into a frenzy of need. He had to go after her and get her back. Then he'd figure out what to do next.

The courthouse door swung open, and Dylan walked over to the desk and grabbed the wanted poster. He crumpled it again and stuffed it in his pocket before the newcomer could catch sight of it.

"Sheriff. Just the man I was hoping to see." The voice came from the open doorway and belonged to J. D. Otto.

Dylan stiffened, his hands dropping to the handles of his revolvers. What was J. D. doing in town? Maybe he'd gotten wind that his cowhands had stopped by on their way out of the area and told him everything they knew. And maybe he was coming to warn Dylan not to believe the two men.

Well, it was too late. Dylan not only believed them, he had half a mind to arrest J. D. right here and now.

"You best keep those six-shooters holed up this time." J. D. spoke with a little too much confidence. "Or I'll make sure you regret it."

His hackles rising with a sense of unease, slowly Dylan pivoted, his grip tightening on the handles. Stu's hands twitched above his guns, and the air crackled with tension. Behind J. D., right outside the courthouse door, a couple of his cowhands stood with their hands on their guns.

This was gonna get ugly. Fast.

Dylan nodded at Trudy with his sleeping son and then at the back door. "Go on. Get to the house."

She didn't need a second invitation to leave. With wide eyes, she bustled out of the courthouse, letting the door slam closed behind her.

For a long second, no one spoke. Dylan didn't want to have a shooting brawl. Someone would get killed, and it'd probably be J. D. Best to work this out as calmly as possible. "I can guess why you're here."

"You can?" J. D.'s brow rose.

"Yep. You came to let me arrest you."

"Came to tell you that whatever those cowhands told you ain't true." Again, J. D. spoke with too much self-assurance, as if he'd already solved a riddle that Dylan was still working on.

"Reckon we all know it's the truth."

"Nope. And I have a feeling you'll be agreeing with me soon enough."

"I have a feeling I'll be arresting you soon enough."

"My man Frank came back from Denver yesterday." J. D. nodded at the taller of the cowhands standing outside the door. "And now it looks like you're the one who needs arresting for hiding an outlaw."

Hiding an outlaw? What was he talking about?

"Frank keeps tabs on notices that get posted at the police station."

"Why? So you know when your crimes catch up to you? Give you some time to cut and run?"

J. D.'s lips curled into a half smirk. "A notice of a woman caught his eye. Mighty fine reward being offered, and we're aiming to cash in on it."

The crumpled poster in Dylan's pocket began to burn. The heat of it licked his skin and went straight to his chest. He'd known it was just a matter of time before someone else saw the wanted poster for Catherine. But he'd hoped to have things figured out by then.

"Always good to do our civic duty and rid the area of anyone who's a menace, especially a criminal who's murdered two people." J. D. met Dylan's gaze. The glint in the man's eyes told Dylan everything he needed to know. He'd had a part in taking Catherine.

Dylan tensed and didn't realize he'd pulled out both of his revolvers until the clicks of the other guns told him everyone else had followed suit.

Raw anger sliced through him. He'd never felt the need to take down another man as much as at that moment.

"Where is she?" Dylan's tone was lethal.

"She's locked away where she can't hurt anyone."

His blood ran cold. What had J. D. done to Catherine? Had he already sent her to Denver? "She ain't an outlaw or murderer."

"Denver police ain't gonna feel the same way."

Dylan kept his revolvers focused straight on J. D. "You best hand her over."

"Why? So you can obstruct justice? I don't think so."

"She's as innocent as a babe. Been accused of things she didn't do."

"Guess that's up to a judge. Not you."

"Sometimes a man has to take justice into his own hands."

"My sentiments exactly." J. D.'s smirk slipped away, replaced by cold, hard resolve.

Take justice into his own hands. The words reached out

to taunt him. Was a person ever right to evade the law? If he started taking justice into his hands whenever he wanted, what was to prevent crooks like J. D. from doing the same?

"What do you want, J. D.?" It was obvious now the man had come to bargain. Maybe that's why he'd captured Catherine in the first place.

J. D. lowered his guns and holstered them. "Want you to leave me and my ranching business alone."

Dylan's gut twisted into a noose. J. D. had seen quick enough that day on his ranch just how much he cared for his wife. All it had taken was one insult and he'd been ready to punish the rustler. Now J. D. was aiming to leverage that affection and make him a pawn.

This was exactly the kind of corruption Dylan had stood against in Chicago. 'Course, at the time he hadn't had a wife or son for any of the crooks to use against him. He hadn't had anything to lose but his own life. And he hadn't cared much about it, had been willing to risk it.

But he wasn't willing to risk Catherine.

Desperation flooded his gut.

From the corner of his vision, Dylan saw Stu give a curt shake of his head as if to warn him not to give in to J. D.'s ploy. But Dylan ignored his deputy, kept his focus on J. D.

Truth was, he'd do whatever he had to in order to get her back and keep her from harm. Including bargaining with the devil himself.

J. D. nodded at Dylan's legs, the outline of the bandages evident through his trousers. "Two-Toed Joe's the culprit with the cattle. Reckon you know for yourself how vicious that bear is."

Dylan held himself motionless as J. D.'s meaning sank in.

The crook wanted him to blame the cattle loss on the bear. After being attacked, Dylan had every reason to play up the bear's role in making off with cattle in South Park.

Could he really turn a blind eye on J. D.'s crimes, especially now that he'd finally gained enough evidence to arrest him? What would the other ranchers say? How would he explain his change of heart toward J. D., especially to his brothers? They wouldn't accept his excuse about Two-Toed Joe for long.

Whatever the case, he had to play along with J. D. for the time being . . . at least until he figured out the best way forward.

Dylan let his guns drop to his sides. "Yep. Two-Toed Joe's become a real menace."

J. D.'s shoulders loosened almost imperceptibly, but it was enough to know the man had been worried.

Dylan holstered his guns and tried to keep J. D. from seeing just how ruffled he was. "Reckon people's identities get mistaken all the time, especially when comparing to a likeness in a poster."

J. D. nodded. "Reckon they do. Sure is hard to tell from a black-and-white photograph who's who."

"Then you'll let my wife go?"

"Yep. We can put this whole misunderstanding behind us as long as we're seeing eye to eye on how things stand."

Dylan allowed himself to look J. D. in the eye, figured that's what the man wanted to seal their deal. "I don't think anyone's gonna blame me for wanting to focus my attention on Two-Toed Joe for a while."

"Good. Might as well focus on the real threat, especially when regular folk are all still at risk with that bear on the loose."

"We don't want anyone else getting hurt."

"Looks like we're both thinking the same thing." J. D.'s slight smile fell back into place.

Dylan couldn't manage a smile in return even if someone paid him a stash of gold to do so.

From outside, Frank cleared his throat.

J. D. glanced at his cowhand, the two communicating an unspoken message, before leveling another shrewd look on Dylan. "Only seems fair to compensate Frank for the reward he's passing up, don't you agree?"

Dylan bristled against the insinuation. J. D. had another thing coming if he expected him to pay Frank two hundred dollars, but he had to keep telling J. D. what he wanted to hear. "You best figure out a way to keep your men silent same way I'm gonna have to."

Even now, Stu was shaking his head again and muttering under his breath.

"I told Frank you'd be more than happy to cooperate, especially knowing he's been doing a real good job keeping the other fellas from having some fun with your wife."

A shard of fear stabbed at Dylan. This new threat was the worst one yet. How could J. D. even think about allowing his men to abuse Catherine? It was downright evil.

J. D.'s gaze dropped to Dylan's holster and his hands gripping his revolvers. Dylan's knuckles were white with the need to defend Catherine.

"You're right." Dylan forced himself to speak levelly even though he wanted to cross over to J. D. and Frank and arrest them both. "You bring Catherine here safe and sound without touching a hair on her head, and I'll hand over the money then." He didn't have two hundred dollars just sitting around. Who in tarnation did?

"You bring the reward out to the ranch." J. D.'s tone grew arrogant. "All two hundred dollars. Then once we count it, Frank'll be willing to make the exchange."

The lanky cowboy nodded his agreement.

"It's gonna take me some time to get that kind of money." Even if he intended to hand J. D. two hundred—which he didn't—Dylan had to buy himself some time to come up with a plan to get Catherine back.

"Reckon Frank can hold strong till this time tomorrow. After that, no tellin' what might happen."

For the first time in his life, Dylan considered falling on his knees and pleading. He'd never pleaded when he'd gotten himself into trouble in the past. He hadn't even begged the time Bat and his gang had taken him captive and threatened to kill him if he didn't pay back his gambling debts.

Before Dylan could drop down and start groveling, J. D. spun and pushed his way past his cowhands outside.

Dylan took several steps, hot pressure building in his chest with the need to do something or shoot at someone. Before he made it halfway across the room, Stu shoved the door closed and barred it with his body.

"Get out of my way," Dylan growled.

"You're not going anywhere until yous have time to calm down."

"I am calm. As calm as I'm gonna be 'til I get Catherine back." He kept going, fear and frustration making each step hard and rigid.

Stu held out a hand and stopped him. "Hold on, now. We'll get her. But we'll do it the right way."

"You heard the whole conversation, Stu!" Dylan balled his fists but held his arms at his sides to keep from barreling into his deputy. "What in the blazes am I gonna do? What if I don't have any other choice but to give in to J. D.'s demands?"

"We always have a choice—a choice to do what's right in our own eyes, or what's right in God's."

"But I can't let her suffer. I can't." Just the thought of any man laying so much as a pinky on her tore him up worse than bull horns hacking into a hide.

"You betcha. And we'll do everything we can to help her. But it's got to be without breaking the law or breaking our convictions."

Stu was right. Deep down Dylan knew he couldn't give in to the need to do whatever it took—like lying, cheating, and killing—to get her back. He couldn't turn around and start down a dark trail after walking these past months on the straight and narrow. But he also couldn't leave Catherine at the mercy of J. D. and his men.

Stu was watching him, likely reading his thoughts. "When we do what's right, then we can trust the good Lord for the outcome of His choosing. Might not be exactly what we want, but when we honor Him, He blesses us for it."

From the earnestness of Stu's tone, Dylan suspected the deputy was speaking from personal experience.

Dylan didn't know everything that had happened in Stu's life, but Trudy had divulged enough for him to understand that fighting in the war, losing so much of his family, and not being able to have children had been among his difficulties.

Yet, through it all Stu had remained a man of principle, hadn't wandered the way Dylan had. Maybe he needed to take his friend's advice to heart.

But what about Catherine? He pictured her as he remembered her only this morning, sprawled out in bed, her hair a tangle of dark brown waves, and her lashes resting against her cheeks. She was his wife, the woman he'd pledged to love and honor and protect. But this was about more than just honoring his vows. This was about her. She was beautiful and talented and kind and deserved to have a life that wasn't haunted by a crime she hadn't committed.

"I've got to find a way to save her, Stu." His voice cracked over the words.

Stu clamped a hand on his shoulder. "We will."

Dylan could only pray his deputy was right, but he couldn't shake the terrible feeling he was wrong.

CHAPTER

25

Hay tickled Catherine, waking her from what seemed like an endless, dreamless sleep. She pried open one dry, gritty eye and then the other to the sight of a rough-hewn log wall without chinking.

Gradually she became aware of the gentle low of a nearby cow, the clucking of hens, and the rattle of wind in the shingles overhead. She breathed in the strong scent of manure and animal flesh and guessed she was in a barn.

Wakefulness prodded her more forcefully, and as the memories of all that had happened came rushing back, she sat up—or tried to—but found that her arms were bound tightly together in front of her. And her legs were tied together too.

"Austin?" The word was trapped in the rag tied around her head and through her mouth. What had happened to Austin after she'd been kidnapped?

Distress reared up, making her almost frantic. What if he

was alone and crying and hungry? Or what if he wiggled past the pillows and rolled onto the floor and hurt himself?

She attempted to push up again and managed to get to a sitting position. Even though the place didn't have much natural light, she could see that she was in a horse stall. Across the haymow, a lone dairy cow swished her tail back and forth. Saddle tack and ropes and other livestock equipment hung from beams and walls. A cat sat in a patch of sunlight streaming in from a high open square window and was giving itself a bath.

There was no question about it. She was in a barn. But where? J. D. Otto's ranch? Did it have to do with the wanted poster?

She could think of no other logical explanation. And it was clear now that Frank hadn't wanted her to come and help Minnie after all. He must have used it as a ploy to lure her into a false sense of security.

The fellow was likely holding her until he could take her to Denver and turn her over to the police to cash in on his reward. Once there, she'd ask to telegram her parents and explain her predicament. Hopefully she'd be able to return to Chicago and have her trial there.

She allowed herself to sink back into the hay and prayed she was right and that her captor didn't have more sinister plans for her. A shudder rippled through her even though the barn was warm, and she forced herself to think on something else. Like food.

Her stomach growled with the need for a meal. From the angle of the sunlight, she guessed it was late afternoon or early evening, which meant she'd gone all day without sustenance.

At the steady pounding of horses' hooves drawing nearer, she again sat up. Someone was coming. Maybe it was Dylan. Rescuing her.

As soon as she allowed the bubble of hope to float up, she just as quickly burst it. Dylan had made it very clear he didn't want anything to do with her. She didn't blame him. If he'd been having doubts about her before last night, now he wouldn't want her at all.

The litany of her shortcomings began to play through her head, all the reasons why she wasn't a good match for the handsome, charming young man. The townspeople might have been able to accept her when they believed she'd had a baby outside of wedlock. But they'd never be able to forgive or accept her when they discovered the charges of murder leveled against her. Even if she could somehow prove the charges weren't true—which would take a miracle—the blemish would stain her reputation forever. He'd be better off without her.

Yes, her leaving was for the best.

If only the thought of separating from him wasn't so painful. After the other rejections from suitors, she ought to be used to the hurt. But if anything, the parting with Dylan stabbed deeper.

Of course she'd spent more time with him than anyone else and had experienced a vulnerability and openness that was new for her. He was a comfortable companion and an enjoyable friend. Not only that, but her attraction to him was undeniable. The least contact with him physically—and even sometimes just the thought of his touch—made her breathless with longings she couldn't explain.

The horses slowed to a stop outside the barn, two of them, if not three. Men's voices rang out, along with that of a woman.

At the squeal of the barn door opening, she lay back down and closed her eyes. She didn't know what her captors intended to do with her. But maybe if she pretended to be unconscious, she could delay them.

More voices and calls filled the yard outside the barn, but muted footsteps crossed the haymow and came closer.

"Think he'll come up with the two hundred dollars, Boss?" It was Frank.

"Yep. No doubt about it." The boss spoke with a rougher voice and an air of authority.

Were they talking about Dylan? And why did he owe them two hundred dollars?

Two hundred was the reward on her wanted poster. Maybe these men were bargaining with Dylan, requiring him to give them the money in exchange for her freedom. But where would he get so high an amount?

"And if he ain't got the cash?" Frank asked, clearly wondering the same thing she was.

"Don't matter. Bought enough time for Butch to herd the extra beeves out of here. Once they're gone, the sheriff won't have nothin' but the hearsay of a couple of cowhands aiming to retaliate for being fired."

"Thought Smiley and Rube up and left. Didn't realize you fired 'em."

"Did now."

She guessed this was J. D. Otto. And she couldn't let him get away with his rustling. Not with how badly Dylan needed to put an end to it to get reelected as sheriff. Maybe in his solving the rustling problem, folks would be able to forgive him more easily for his mistake in marrying her.

One of the men slapped a gloved hand against the stall

gate before heading away. "Don't worry, Frank. We'll get your money one way or another. Reckon we can double our money if we play our cards right."

"That so?" The younger man perked up.

"We'll collect money from the sheriff and then haul her on down to Denver and cash in on the reward there."

"The sheriff'll kill us for double-crossing him."

"Won't be able to accuse us of nothin' without showing himself to be a crook for attempting to keep her out of jail."

Oh, heaven help them. The situation was going from bad to worse with every passing moment. Not only was J. D. using her kidnapping to distract Dylan from the rustling, but he was also coercing Dylan into doing what was wrong.

She couldn't understand why Dylan would take such a risk for her, not after what she'd done to him. Regardless of his motives, she had to find a way to free herself. If she could get away—far away—then Dylan would have no need to resort to unlawful means to save her.

She waited until both men were gone, then she wiggled her hands. The stiff hemp of the rope chafed her skin, but she worked against it anyway. She wouldn't rest until she escaped and was no longer causing problems for Dylan. The fact was, she loved Dylan too much to let him do any harm to himself on account of her.

Yes, she loved him. She knew she needed to deny the feeling, but why bother, not when she would be leaving soon.

CHAPTER

26

The desire for a shot of whiskey burned Dylan's throat, growing hotter the longer he stared across the street at the saloon where Stu had disappeared. In the twilight, the bright lights and merry music pouring from the open windows beckoned to him, whispering of the pleasures he'd find inside, pleasures that would help him forget about the pain radiating through his chest.

The bulge of coins in his pocket weighed heavily and was tempting him more with every passing moment. Gambling again would be a real easy way to solve the problem with J. D. He could win the two hundred dollars. Then he'd be able to get Catherine back without putting her or anyone else in danger.

"Lord Almighty, I'm still struggling." Dylan grabbed onto the hitching post outside the courthouse to hold himself back. "Thought I was getting stronger, moving beyond my past. But just look at me. I'm still so weak and need your strength in a mighty way."

He and Stu had wrangled over what to do for most of the day. And Stu was sticking to his guns to resolve this crisis the lawful way without giving in to J. D.'s demands.

Dylan couldn't just ride out to J. D.'s ranch and shoot up the fella and every last one of his crooked cronies like he wanted to. And he couldn't rush out and demand that J. D. hand over Catherine, not when it was within anyone's right to answer the call on the wanted poster.

But he could arrest J. D. for rustling and in the process hopefully free Catherine. The problem was, J. D. wasn't gonna give himself up nice and easy. Nope, handcuffing J. D. was gonna take a posse of ranchers, a heap of gunfighting, and a whole lot of trouble for everyone involved.

Stu was hoping to dredge up enough help from the cowhands who'd come to town for the evening, had told Dylan to wait for him outside, that as soon as they had enough fellas, they'd ride out under cover of darkness and try to take J. D. by surprise.

Dylan's aim was to keep Catherine from getting hurt, but his gut told him he wouldn't be able to and that he needed to find a different way to free her.

Like with the gambling . . .

The urge to cross the street rose swiftly and strongly again. He dug his fingers against the post and resisted the itch to stick his hand into his pocket and run his fingers through the coins.

"Oh, Lord Almighty. Please, Lord. I need you." As the hoarse whisper wafted into the night air, his sights shifted heavenward.

"When we do what's right, then we can trust the good Lord for the outcome of His choosing. Might not be ex-

actly what we want, but when we honor Him, He blesses us for it."

Stu's words from earlier in the day had been banging about in his head like a loose shutter on a windy day. And now the clamoring started up again real loud, pounding hard, reminding him that as tempting as it might be to calm the storm in a way that made the most sense to him, he'd only messed things up in the past whenever he'd tried. Maybe this time he needed to leave the storm calming to the only One who'd ever been able to rebuke the wind and waves.

"Lord, I need you," he whispered again, standing up taller and taking in the first stars starting to make their glorious appearance in the endless purple-blue sky. "I don't wanna go back to my old ways. But right now, I don't see how I can save Catherine if I don't do what J. D. wants of me."

The irony wasn't lost on him, that he'd resisted consorting with criminals for years, that it was the one thing he'd never done wrong. But here and now, when he was sober and restrained, he was wrangling with the desire to give in to the underhanded dealings.

Maybe allowing him to face bribes and the temptation to gamble was the Lord's way of helping him grow—challenging him to resist, and in doing so, strengthening his character and resolve all the more.

"Alright, Lord. I need to get Catherine back. But I need you to help me do so honorably."

He spun around so he was no longer facing the saloon. That was the first thing he had to do. Turn away from the things that were enticing him. He had to put them behind him and move forward choosing what was right.

And what was right wasn't avoiding the problems or

running away from them. Instead, he had to telegram Alderman Remington in Chicago. Maybe somehow the politician would know what to do and how to help Catherine. He likely had many connections, even in Denver. Certainly a lawyer who could come to Catherine's defense.

He expelled a deep breath, and the pounding of approaching horses drew his attention toward the south end of town. Four men were galloping fast, bringing a halt to the pedestrian traffic as well as the few other wagons and horses rambling through town.

Dylan's hands dropped to the handles of his revolvers and his muscles tensed, but when he recognized the broad shoulders, the muscular bodies, the confident bearings, he relaxed his posture as the four neared. What were his three brothers and Bliss doing in town?

No doubt they'd heard the rumors about all that had happened today. Even though Dylan had tried to keep things under wraps, news spread faster than wildfire in these parts.

Brody was with Wyatt and Flynn, which meant he'd arrived in the high country sometime in the past day or two. Dylan respected Brody but wasn't close to him and certainly didn't need him coming now to hear him confess how he'd been a fool to marry a stranger. And not just any stranger, but one wanted for two murders.

Although he'd tried real hard to be worthy of the family name over the past months and had thought he was becoming respectable, he was gonna disappoint his brothers. Again.

As the four big men reined in near him, their horses snorting from the ride, Dylan steeled himself.

Wyatt tipped up his hat at Dylan first, revealing his serious brown eyes.

Flynn and Brody both nodded at him. And Bliss regarded him with a guarded expression, one that never revealed much.

For several long moments, nobody spoke. And the men didn't dismount.

If they were waiting for him to invite them to get down, they were gonna get blisters on their hind ends first. He hadn't asked them to come and didn't need a lecture tonight.

He started to sigh when Wyatt finally spoke. "You gonna stand there all night down in the mouth, or are you gonna get up in the saddle?"

"Get up in the saddle for what?"

"We're fixin' to ride on out to J. D.'s and get your wife back."

Dylan's breath caught, and his lungs squeezed. What was Wyatt saying? He'd obviously heard about Catherine being kidnapped today. But maybe he didn't know about the wanted poster yet.

"We're champing at the bit to get going." Flynn peered at him with his usual intensity. "Figured you might be itching to join us."

"Blamed right." They were offering to help him fight against J. D. and get Catherine back? How could he turn them down?

"Quit your yammering," Wyatt said, "and let's go."

Dylan's blood zinged with fresh energy. Was this God's answer to his prayers? He lifted his foot to his horse's stirrup, then halted. If they knew the truth about Catherine, they wouldn't be so eager to help him rescue her.

"Listen." He planted both feet on the ground and squared his shoulders. "You won't wanna help the likes of me once you know everything—"

"Already heard it all," Flynn interrupted. "Trudy Gunderson told Greta every last detail and then some when Greta was in town this afternoon."

"Then you're aware of the wanted poster and that Catherine's being accused of murder?"

"Yep." Flynn exchanged a glance with Wyatt.

Dylan wanted to slink away and privately bear the shame of his mistakes, including this most recent one with Catherine. Even so, he had to defend her. She was an innocent victim, and people needed to know it. "She didn't do it, if that's what you're thinking."

"Nope." Wyatt spoke quickly. "Not what we're thinking at all."

"She's a real good woman."

"Ain't arguing with you there."

Then what in the blazes were they arguing about? Did they know he was to blame for the marriage mix-up? "I take complete responsibility for our hasty wedding. She didn't realize I thought she was someone else. And by the time she figured it out, we were both getting along just fine." More than fine, actually.

"Everyone can see she's the perfect woman for you, Dylan." Flynn's tone gentled as he studied Dylan with the green-blue eyes they had in common. "And we ain't blind to the fact that you've fallen for her real hard."

"Yep, I love her more than I thought I could ever love any woman."

This time Brody nodded. "When a McQuaid man loves a woman, there's no going back. It's fast, furious, and forever."

They were a powerful and passionate group of men. And Dylan couldn't deny what Brody said was true. When he'd finally fallen in love, it had been fast, furious, and it would be forever. Even if he and Catherine still had a lot to work through and a heap of obstacles to overcome, he wasn't letting her or their marriage go. After all, God hadn't given up on him when he'd done far worse things. How could he give up on Catherine? He not only forgave her, but he needed her forgiveness too—for lots of things, both recent and in his past.

Was the same true of Bliss? Had Dylan held on to old grudges long enough?

He cast a glance at his friend. If Bliss had found this kind of enduring love with Ivy, how could Dylan hold it against his friend for breaking a vow he'd made when they were both kids? Maybe the vow had been worthwhile long ago in keeping Ivy and Bliss from jumping into a relationship too soon. But if Bliss felt for Ivy even half of what Dylan felt for Catherine, then he understood why Bliss had done it.

Wyatt's spurs jangled as he adjusted himself in his saddle. "Are we gonna stand here all night jawing? Or we gonna go turn J. D. Otto and his men into crowbait?"

For the first time, Dylan noticed the extra firearms each man had. His heart pinched with affection for these men who had been a part of his life for as long as he could remember, the only family he'd known. They'd been there through the worst parts of his life, loving him anyway. And they were still here when he needed them most.

A lump rose swiftly in his throat.

Before Dylan could answer, Stu stepped out of the saloon across the street with at least a dozen men following after him. He stopped short at the sight of the McQuaid men and Bliss on horseback.

"It's about time," Dylan called. "We're riding on out to
J. D.'s place and aiming to fight to get Catherine back."

"Good," Stu called, "because I've got a posse of men who
are fed up to their eyeballs with J. D. Otto and are willing
to stand up to him."

Dylan took in the cowhands from the various ranches that
had suffered from J. D.'s rustling—Stirrup Ranch, Elkhorn,
Updegraff, and more. Stu had been a busy man, rallying a
small army.

Dylan nodded at his deputy, trying to convey his thanks.
This man, these people, his brothers, his friend—they were
all willing to help him. Even now, when they knew the worst
about Catherine and him.

His chest burned and his eyes stung. Even if things didn't
go the way he wanted them to tonight, he couldn't doubt
the love and loyalty of his family and friends again. Most
of all, he couldn't doubt God's love to an undeserving sin-
ner like him.

CHAPTER

27

Catherine flexed her sore wrists, wishing she had her salves or a compress to ease the pain where the rope had broken through her skin leaving bloody scratches.

At least she was free. . . .

She knelt behind a water trough, praying the darkness of the night would hide her until she was well away from J. D.'s ranch. With the late hour, the men were finally trickling toward the bunkhouse, and as soon as the path was clear, she'd be on her way.

Frank had already checked on her for the night. She'd made sure her bindings looked secure and pretended to be asleep when he'd lifted the lantern over the horse stall. As he'd walked out and given instructions to another cowhand standing guard at the barn door, she'd sat up and shed the bindings that she'd loosened throughout the evening.

Then she'd piled several crates in front of the high window. She'd managed to climb up and drop out the other side without notice. Ever since, she'd been hiding and waiting for the chance to flee.

While she wanted to take a horse, she couldn't risk the noise or commotion. The walk to town would be long and navigation would be difficult, but she was determined to return to Fairplay and demand that Stu lock her up until a marshal could come up from Denver to provide her a safe escort to Chicago.

All she wanted to do was get away so J. D. couldn't use her to manipulate Dylan. Hopefully she'd also make it back to town in time to warn Dylan and Stu that J. D. was moving the stolen cattle.

If she'd once cared about her future, she no longer did. If she had to go to jail or suffer worse, she would as long as she could prevent harm from coming to the man and child she loved.

The moon overhead squatted low, as rounded as a mother at full term and glowing with the radiance of expectation. On any other night, Catherine would have admired the pregnant moon, would have risen on her toes to see it better.

But tonight, the moonlight might be her greatest enemy. She needed the darkness to shelter her during her getaway, especially if Frank and J. D. noticed she'd escaped and began to search for her.

She surveyed the ranch yard again. It was finally deserted. Time to make a run for it. She crept to the end of the trough and began to rise. But the door of the main cabin opened, and a long wail from inside spilled into the night, raising the hairs on her arms.

The light from inside illuminated Frank as he stumbled out.

Catherine stiffened. What was he doing? Hopefully he wasn't returning to the barn to check on her. If he did, she wouldn't have a long enough head start. Frank and the other cowhands would catch up, unless she could get away now and find another place to hide.

She glanced to the north. Though she'd been unconscious during the trek to J. D.'s ranch, she imagined the land spread out much like the rest of South Park—a few hills and rocks dotting the countryside but little else than prairie dog mounds, brush, and grass.

Even so, she had to go. She couldn't waste another minute.

Praying the darkness would provide enough cover, she moved along the fence rail surrounding the barn, slipped underneath, and darted toward the nearest scraggly juniper.

Another cry wafted from the cabin, and Catherine halted, recognizing the universal wail of a woman in travail. It was followed by Frank's frantic call toward the guard at the barn door. "Minnie needs the midwife!"

Catherine lowered herself behind the bush, her heart beating hard enough to give away her location. She had to keep going, had to run.

But even as she rose and pivoted, her steps weighed her down along with her conscience. She couldn't run away from a woman in need, not even when the woman belonged to the man who'd kidnapped her and was holding her for ransom.

Yet, if she went with Frank into the house to help Minnie, she'd seal her fate. Frank would tie her up tighter next time and place a heavier guard around her. And she'd never get free to warn Stu and Dylan.

The warring inside hurt Catherine's stomach, and she pressed a fist against it to stave off the worry and pain. She was under no obligation to stay, especially after how Frank had already deceived her into thinking he needed her help. It would serve him right to suffer.

"Heaven help me." She'd made excuses for her deception with Dylan. And here she was making more excuses instead of loving her enemy as Scripture commanded.

Standing straight, she started across the way she'd already come. "Frank, I'm here."

Halfway to the barn, he halted. In the darkness she couldn't see his face, but his hand dropped to his revolver.

Did he think she'd had assistance in escaping? Was he worried she had an army about to attack him?

"I'm alone." She continued toward him but more cautiously.

"How'd you get out?"

"I freed myself."

"And you were running off?"

"Yes, but I'd like to help Minnie."

He remained stiff and unmoving. "Why would you do that instead of making your escape?"

"Because it's the right thing to do."

Another wail, this one louder, came from the cabin. It jabbed Frank into action, and he backtracked toward the open door. "She started having her pains tonight but says it's too early. Maybe you can tell her what to do."

Catherine hastened after Frank, wishing for her birth satchel and praying she wouldn't fail to be of assistance. If Minnie really was in premature labor, then the situation was precarious. Babies born too early always had a difficult time surviving.

And tonight, with the wanted poster accusing her of

murdering two people, what would happen if Minnie or her baby died? Would Frank accuse her of another murder?

As Catherine entered the cabin, she quickly assessed the mother-to-be in the bed, thrashing and panting, her face contorted, her skin slick with sweat, her hair plastered to her head. The cabin was lit by a single lantern, but it was enough to see that the place was sparsely furnished with the bed and a few chairs. It reeked of vomit and stale booze.

Another young woman rose from the chair beside the bed, her anxious eyes beseeching Catherine. "Help her. Please. You've gotta do something to stop the baby from coming."

The woman was stout but attired in a flamboyant gown of bright peacock blue with the neckline cut revealingly low. She wore a headdress of equally bright blue feathers, and her face was painted with rouge. Had she come out from one of the brothels to help Minnie? Was she a friend of sorts?

It didn't matter who she was. Catherine had to enlist her help. She rattled off a list of supplies she needed including hot water, a clean bowl, lard, and towels. As the woman bustled around the cabin to gather the necessary items, she introduced herself as Becky, J. D.'s mistress.

With Minnie in too much pain to answer any questions, Catherine plied Becky, but she couldn't offer much insight about the thin, pale girl, who looked too young to be having a baby.

Catherine didn't waste time, but instead got busy examining Minnie. The cervix was already halfway dilated. Minnie was having the baby tonight whether anyone was ready or not.

Lying on his belly on the slight ridge above the ranch, Dylan sighted down his rifle. He was as tense as a tangled horse's tether, ready to disable Frank and another fella, now loitering near J. D.'s cabin. The light pouring out the door illuminated them well enough that Dylan could easily make each shot.

But Wyatt and Flynn and Stu and several others were working out a new plan of attack now that Catherine had gone into the cabin to help with the delivery of a babe.

If only she'd kept coming. From their position surrounding the ranch buildings, they'd watched her drop from the barn window and creep behind the trough and out of the corral. When she'd started running away from the ranch, Dylan had nearly leapt to his feet to race to her. But Brody and Bliss had held him in place, urging him to stay down until she was far enough away not to draw any gunfire.

But she only made it a dozen paces before turning back. They'd heard the entire conversation about Frank's woman being in labor, and Catherine's response about wanting to help.

Again, Brody and Bliss had wrestled him to the ground to keep him from calling out to her and telling her not to go into the cabin. Deep inside he knew she couldn't say no to a woman in need, but how could their posse attack without putting her in more danger? The second Frank or J. D. realized they were being ambushed, they'd grab Catherine and use her as a shield, forcing him to back off or risk her life.

As much as he wanted to find a way to bring an end to this conflict without losing any lives, all along he'd suspected that wasn't gonna happen. And right now, with some of the cowhands congregating outside the cabin, likely awaiting the outcome of the birthing, Dylan wanted to take control.

"Once the birthing's over, it's gonna be too late," he whispered.

Beside him, Bliss sighted down his rifle. "We'll act here soon."

"Not soon enough."

"Give them a few more minutes."

"I can't."

Bliss shifted, and Dylan could feel the man watching him, no doubt trying to decide if he oughta wrestle the gun away. "Sometimes love can make us act crazy." Bliss's statement didn't contain any accusation. It seemed more like a confession.

"You don't need to apologize to me again, Bliss." Dylan didn't move his aim from Frank but loosened the pressure against the trigger. "You didn't do anything wrong by falling in love with Ivy."

"I should have told you—"

"I didn't understand what it meant to love a woman the way you love Ivy. But now I do. I know what it's like to love that woman so much that you'll do anything—anything at all—to be with her."

Bliss was silent. The cadence of crickets played in the background.

"I should have released you from your promise not to go after Ivy long before we ran away from Colorado."

"You just wanted to keep Ivy safe."

"But I went about it all wrong." Dylan drew in a breath that smelled of dust and sage. "I'm asking you to forgive me, Bliss. I was a blasted fool."

"Thank you, Dylan. Means a lot that we can fix things between us."

"Just sorry I didn't do it sooner."

Dylan shifted his rifle barrel as Frank poked his head in the door. When he stepped back out a moment later, his shoulders were slumped. "They're distracted. This is a good time to hit."

Bliss laid a steady hand on Dylan's gun, lowering the barrel. "Don't matter how much you sweet-talk. I'm not letting you shoot anyone. At least not yet."

Dylan should joke back with his friend. But ever since Catherine had been taken, he'd lost his humor. Now he was nothing but an angry, frustrated man, ready to lash out.

"I can't lose her, Bliss," he finally whispered, his voice raw with all the desperation that was tearing up his insides.

"We'll get her back." Bliss spoke firmly enough that Dylan could almost believe him. But even if they got Catherine back safely tonight, Dylan was afraid he'd only end up losing her in the long run anyway.

CHAPTER

28

"Try not to push and instead relax." Catherine positioned herself as the head crowned, holding it back so it didn't come too fast and split the perineum.

Minnie released a moan. After the past two hours, the end of the delivery was underway.

"Blow out breaths, Minnie."

With the next contraction, Catherine eased the head out, giving her a view of the puckered face. She quickly wiped the nose and then the mouth. But the infant didn't make a sound. Wasn't it breathing? What if it was stillborn?

"The head is born. On the next contraction, you can push."

Catherine checked for the baby's heartbeat but felt none. "Heaven help us," she whispered.

Minnie released a guttural noise and thrashed, already in the throes of another contraction.

"You're doing wonderfully. Keep breathing and push hard." Catherine pressed the head down and delivered the presenting shoulder. The other shoulder and arm followed. In the next instant, the baby—a boy—slid the rest of the way, slippery with mucus and blood. He was silent and motionless, his skin a blue-gray like a Chicago sky in winter.

Becky held out a towel, and Catherine laid the infant there, checking quickly for deformities, peeling skin, or any other signs the baby was decomposing, which could happen if the baby was stillborn in the womb for more than a week. But she didn't notice any signs of distress. And she couldn't see any other issues. His body was perfect—his hands and feet and legs and arms and little nose and mouth.

But he was tiny, half the size of a regular newborn, and Catherine could only guess that he just wasn't ready to be born. Maybe his heart had stopped, or his lungs weren't fully developed.

Catherine started to tie off the cord.

Becky watched the unmoving infant. "Is it dead?"

"Dead?" Minnie's raspy voice rose on a screech. "My baby is dead?"

In the next instant, Frank was stomping inside. "What do you mean, the baby's dead?"

In a flutter of her bright skirt and feathery headband, Becky shooed Frank. "Get on out with you! This is no place for a man."

With the stillborn infant in one arm, Catherine quickly draped a sheet over Minnie, still needing to deliver the afterbirth, but it could take another ten or fifteen minutes before Minnie's uterus contracted again and began the process of separating and expelling the placenta.

At the sight of the tiny blue infant in Catherine's arm, Frank halted just inside the door, his face contorted with worry and anger. His towering stance reminded Catherine of the bear that had attacked Dylan.

"You're a murderer!" Frank shouted, going for his revolver. "I should've never let you near Minnie!"

Catherine took a step back. She'd feared this might happen.

In the next instant, he drew out his gun and pointed it at her.

She needed to explain that the baby had been born too early and that the death was no one's fault. But the wildness in Frank's eyes told her he wouldn't be able to listen. He was too distraught.

Shouts erupted from outside, along with gun blasts. Before Frank could react, a shot rang into the cabin, hit the revolver in Frank's hand, and sent it clattering to the floor.

Catherine startled, and Becky squealed with fright.

"Don't move or you're a dead man." The terse voice from the other side of the door belonged to only one man. Dylan.

Catherine's pulse jumped. Dylan was here? Why?

Frank turned to look outside and then froze as Dylan stepped through the doorway, both revolvers out and aimed at him.

Dylan's face was as rigid as sandstone, his jaw clamped taut, his eyes glittering with anger. Several other men poured into the cabin around Dylan, including Stu. With Dylan's guns trained upon Frank, the others crept around him until Stu lunged for Frank and grabbed his arms.

Minnie started sobbing, and Becky rushed to her side.

"You won't get away with this, McQuaid!" Frank shouted as Stu handcuffed him. "Your wife's the murderer, the one needing to be arrested, not me. I ain't done nothin' wrong by trying to bring her to the authorities."

Through the commotion, Dylan's cold gaze swept over the room, halting upon Catherine. With her hair hanging in disarray and her garments soiled and unkempt, she felt her inadequacies all the more. She wasn't a raving beauty, wasn't anyone special or charming or vivacious. She was a practical, no-nonsense, no-frills woman. With charges of murder leveled against her, charges that would forever haunt her, as proven by Frank's unfair accusation.

Even so, Dylan's gaze took her in, assessing her with an urgency that made her breath hitch. He'd been concerned about her, was still worried. Did that mean he cared, that maybe he could even find it in himself to forgive her?

As soon as the hope blossomed, she stomped it out. It didn't matter what Dylan did or didn't feel for her. She was going back to Chicago to face her charges, and she refused to drag him into her problems.

Stu began to haul Frank toward the door, the other two men prodding him along with the barrels of their guns.

"She killed my baby!" Frank shouted.

At a soft shudder in her arms, Catherine glanced down to find the baby's eyes open. Though squinting, he looked around even as he struggled to draw in a breath.

"He's alive!" Catherine laid the infant on the end of the bed, pried open his small mouth, and bent in and offered the babe some of her own air. She continued the artificial respirations for several more moments, heedless of the commotion around her.

Beneath her hand, she could feel the rise and fall of the baby's chest growing steadier. She found his pulse and counted his rapid heartbeat. The blue was fading, replaced by the healthy mottled red of a newborn. The baby peered up at her, then scrunched his face and released a thin wail, like the mew of a kitten.

Tears stung Catherine's eyes.

"My baby, my baby, my baby." Minnie was sobbing and reaching her arms out for the infant.

Catherine watched the boy a moment longer to ensure that he was indeed breathing normally. Then she lifted him carefully and situated him in Minnie's arms.

Tears ran unchecked down the girl's cheeks as she met her son. "Oh, Frank, he's beautiful."

Only then did Catherine become aware that Frank was still in the cabin, handcuffed and held back on either side. He'd grown motionless and was watching Minnie with their baby, his expression tender. In fact, everyone was watching Minnie as she smiled down at the newborn. Everyone except Dylan. His attention was fixed upon Catherine, his green-blue eyes taking her in as if he couldn't get enough of her, his gaze asking her if she was alright.

She nodded and wiped her hands on her skirt. Had he forgiven her? Even if he hadn't, she wanted nothing more than to fall into his arms and let him hold her and tell her everything would work out just fine. But deep inside she knew that nothing would be fine, at least not for a long time, if ever.

CHAPTER

29

Dylan leaned against the corral fence, his attention on J. D.'s cabin unswerving, both hands resting upon the handles of his revolvers. The intensity of the morning sunlight made his head hurt, and he tipped his hat lower, hiding his tired eyes in the shadows.

Stu and the rest of the posse had herded J. D., Frank, and the handful of remaining cowhands into town to await transport to jail in Denver. Another posse had headed up to Tarryall to try to catch up to Butch and the rest of J. D.'s rustlers before they made off with the hidden herd.

Meanwhile, Wyatt and Flynn and other area ranchers had congregated at the break of day and were now out among J. D.'s cattle, returning the steers to their owners as best they could determine.

Dylan had decided he wasn't going anywhere until Catherine finished tending to the new mother and babe. For added precaution, Bliss and Brody had remained with him. Bliss sat on the top rail, his boots hooked against a lower post, and Brody leaned against the cabin next to the door, his rifle cradled in his arm.

For once, Dylan was glad Bliss and Brody were the silent types, because he wasn't in the mood to talk to anyone except Catherine. And she'd been busy for the past hours trying to keep the new little fella alive, clearly using every trick she'd ever learned to do so.

No doubt she was desperate to find a way to save the babe's life.

"She killed my baby." If Frank's emotional accusation was playing through Dylan's mind over and over, he could only imagine how it was affecting Catherine. Even though everyone knew Minnie had gone into labor early and the babe was a runt, too tiny to survive easily on his own, Frank's charge of murder still lingered.

Catherine would have to live the rest of her life with people speculating about her innocence and guilt. It wasn't fair, and he wanted to shout from all the balconies in town that Catherine hadn't committed the crimes being leveled at her. But when it came right down to it, people were gonna believe what they wanted. Frank was proof of that.

The frustration swirling in Dylan's gut ate at him. What was he gonna do next? A part of him wanted to run off with Austin and her someplace new where no one would know her and she could live without judgment. But the other part of him knew running wasn't gonna solve the problem.

He had to keep on doing the right thing.

After all, God had shown him last night in a mighty clear way that even though staying strong was difficult, the results were well worth the struggle. His friends and family and other fellas had come out in droves to help him get Catherine back as well as bring the rustlers to justice.

He cleared his throat and tossed a glance at his friend resting casually. But he knew Bliss well enough to realize the casual look was only a pose. Bliss was probably as tense as he was on the inside. "I know I don't have any right to ask you, but you'd be doing me a big favor if you stepped in as sheriff until I can get back to Fairplay."

Beside him, Bliss unhooked his boots and hopped down. "Reckon Stu can fill in since I'll be going with you."

Dylan pushed away from the rail and bumped up the brim of his hat. "You can't go with. You don't even know where I'm going."

"You're heading to Chicago to prove Catherine's innocence."

Dylan could only stare at his friend in surprise. After the cold way he'd treated Bliss, he didn't deserve his friend's help.

Bliss peered at the mountains in the distance. "Been thinking long and hard about everything you told me about Rocky Rogers and his accusations against Catherine."

Dylan swallowed the lump of fear that swelled every time he thought of her going to trial against Rocky. There was no telling how many judges and lawyers were on his payroll. And even if they weren't, Rocky would find a way—either through threats or bribes—to make sure they did things just the way he wanted.

Bliss had questioned him more last night as they'd waited to make their attack. As an agent for Pinkerton Detective Agency, Bliss and his father both had connections to Chicago's seedy underworld. Even if Bliss's father was a terrible drunk, he'd still managed to retain his reputation as one of the best Pinkerton agents.

"You'll need a good detective or two," Bliss continued, "to gather enough evidence to convict Rocky. I'll cash in on a few favors owed me and get you the help you need."

Dylan couldn't let his friend make that kind of sacrifice. "Don't reckon you'll want to be away from Ivy and the new babe—"

"Ivy'll be fine. Can't keep that woman down for anything. Besides, Judd's there for her."

"Naw." Dylan's throat tightened at his friend's loyalty. "It's too much, Bliss. Can't let you do it."

"Ivy would tan my hide if I let you go off by yourself."

Dylan attempted a smile but couldn't get his lips to crack.

Bliss finally looked at him, his gaze serious. "While we're gone, Catherine and Austin need to stay out at Wyatt's, where the family can keep her protected from anyone else hoping to cash in on the reward."

"I was planning to take her with. But I like your idea better."

"No sense dragging her into the den of thieves unless we absolutely have to."

"Agreed."

A motion in the cabin doorway drew their attention. Catherine stepped through. She turned and spoke to J. D.'s woman, who'd followed and was now filling the doorframe with her bulky body and dress.

Brody pushed away from the cabin and stood alert.

Catherine gave a parting word to the woman before she turned and smiled tiredly at Brody. Brody didn't smile in return. Smiling wasn't something Brody did often. Instead, he cocked his head toward the fence rail and him and Bliss.

Her gaze shifted their direction.

Dylan's stomach did a nervous jig.

She tucked her long, loose hair behind her ear and then smoothed down her skirt.

He reckoned now was as good a time as any to say what he needed to. He took a step forward, then stopped. After he'd all but told her he didn't want to be with her the last time they were together, he didn't deserve her forgiveness. But he wanted another chance to make things right, even if it was his last.

"Go on and talk to her." Bliss's voice was low and filled with understanding. "Brody and I will saddle the mounts."

Dylan nodded and started across the yard. She stayed rooted to the spot just outside the cabin while Brody ambled off, giving them privacy.

When Dylan neared her, he had the overwhelming need to wrap his arms around her, hold her, and reassure himself that she was safe. But she stared at the ground, as though expecting him to chastise her. It was no wonder after how angry he'd been with her.

He stuffed his hands into his pockets to keep himself from touching her. "How's the babe doing?"

"He's nursing. It took some time to get the hang of it, but if he keeps at it, he may have a chance at surviving."

"Good."

She peeked up at him, her eyes wary.

He had so much to say, but where did he start? And where was his smooth-talking charm when he most needed it?

At the flash of a blue dress just inside the doorway, Dylan grabbed Catherine's hand and tugged her with him as he strode away from the cabin. He didn't know where he was going, only that he had to be with her alone without anyone looking on or listening in.

As he reached the bunkhouse, now eerily silent and empty, he rounded the back side. She allowed him to lead her, although he could sense a reluctance in her stiff posture. In the shade of the building, he finally stopped, the grass up to their knees and bright with big yellow flowers and daintier purple ones. Both would look pretty in a bouquet.

She didn't pull away. And he tightened his hold on her hand, trying to figure out the right words to say. But before he could formulate his thoughts, she spoke in a rush. "I will always regret that I deceived you, Dylan. It was wrong. And I had no excuse for doing it. I only hope one day you can forgive me for it."

"The mix-up was my fault, darlin'. All mine. And I shouldn't have gotten angry at you."

"Yes, you had every right to be angry. I deceived you—"

"I forgive you. As long as you forgive me for being a self-righteous scalawag."

"You didn't do anything wrong." Her statement was strong and certain.

"The list of my transgressions and shame could drown me in the depths of the sea."

"Then let them drown, but without you."

The green in her eyes was as warm as a summer meadow, a place he wanted to bask in forever. Was she right? Did he need to let go of the guilt and shame he'd been carrying around? Let them drown so he could finally be free to live without always thinking about his past mistakes?

He'd still be weak at times, still would need help from his

friends and family to hold him accountable. But he had to stop beating himself up and move forward.

She studied his face, almost as if she were trying to memorize it. "You'd make me very happy knowing that we're parting ways on friendly terms."

"Parting ways?"

"Yes, I'm going back to Chicago and turning myself in."

"Nope."

"I have to, Dylan. I have to stop running away. In fact, I never should have run. And now I need to try to bring about justice. I can't let Rocky get away with hurting anyone else."

She jutted her chin and started to pull away from him. But instead of letting go, he grabbed her other hand. "Bliss and me are going without you. We've both got connections there. We'll pull together all the evidence we need to clear your name."

Her eyes widened and filled with tears. "I can't let you do that for me."

"You and Austin are staying with Wyatt while I'm gone."

"No, Dylan. That's too much."

He cut off her objections the best way he knew how. He bent down and captured her mouth with the kiss he'd been aching for. He drank in the sweetness of her lips, and as he did so, his entire being tightened with longing for her.

At first, he sensed her shyness or maybe her hesitancy at their kissing. But he wanted her to know just how much he needed her in his life, how much he wanted her to stay with him. He laced their fingers at the same time he angled to take the kiss deeper, pushing them both into an abyss.

The timidity of her response fell away as she met him stroke for stroke, opening herself up, drawing him closer, and letting their souls touch.

This woman. His wife. She was everything he'd ever needed and wanted. If only he could find a way to keep her. Forever.

As if sensing his silent plea, she broke away and took a rapid step back, her cheeks flaming and her eyes glassy. "We can't—"

"I love you."

Her gaze shot up to his. And this time the glassiness spilled over, and tears cascaded down her cheeks. "You were trapped into being with me. Now you can be free to find the woman of your choosing."

"I love *you*, darlin'. And I don't want to lose you." He didn't care that his voice contained a note of desperation.

"Oh, Dylan." She shook her head. "I can't stay with you. You might forfeit your position as sheriff, and you won't be able to get reelected."

"I don't care." He'd give up everything for her, even his own life.

"Maybe you can say that now. But what about in a year when you wish you could be sheriff again?"

He shrugged. "Don't matter—"

"But God's gifted you. You care deeply about people. You know how to defuse difficulties. And you can also be really tough when you need to be."

"I'll figure out ways to do all that even without a badge."

"But your family. I've made a mess of things with your family."

"They can see how much I love you, how important you are to me. That's why they came and helped me get you free."

She watched his face as though trying to see the truth before shaking her head again. "Already I've stained your reputation. We must part ways now before I ruin you altogether."

"No!" The word came out harshly, filled with all the frustration of the past couple of days.

Her eyes rounded.

"No." He gentled his tone, but he sensed he was losing the battle, that she'd made up her mind to separate from him. He frantically searched the landscape, the sky, the distant horizon, as if somehow he could find the answer to their predicament. He lowered his head and blew out a tense breath. The only way he'd convince her to stay was by proving she was innocent of her crime. And to do that, he needed time.

She waited, watching him.

Was this gonna turn into another instance when someone left him? Maybe in the past such leaving would've drained him drier than dirt in a drought. But he wouldn't let it this time. And even if it did parch him, he wouldn't go seeking refreshment in the wrong places. He'd learned his lesson that nothin' but the good Lord himself could satisfy his thirst.

"Will you promise me one thing?"

"Maybe."

"Will you stay here in Colorado and live with Wyatt and wait for me to return?"

Her brow creased with uncertainty above her tear-filled eyes.

"When I get back, if you still want to leave me, I promise I'll let you go."

She held his gaze for a long moment, as if testing the sincerity of his words. Finally, she nodded. "Okay."

He hadn't won her yet. But at least he'd bought himself more time.

CHAPTER 30

Within the tight confines of the saddle, Catherine rested against the strong curve of Dylan's body, the sway of the horse giving her an excuse to be in his arms and revel in his nearness, likely for the last time.

Jericho had ridden off in the direction of town, promising to send word to Trudy to bring Austin out to Wyatt's ranch along with her carpetbag and satchel. Brody rode ahead of Dylan and her a fair pace, as if sensing their need to be alone.

She told Dylan all that had happened, and he shared the terror he'd lived through once he realized she was gone. She argued with him again that she didn't want to disgrace him, but she realized she was likely too late. She'd probably ruined his public image the same way she had her father's.

In light of the ruination, she marveled all the more that Dylan had declared his love. Although she was tempted to say the words in return, she didn't want to encourage him any more than she already had.

For now, during their last hours together, it was enough to feel his solid chest behind her, his thick arms boxing her in, and his hand on her hip. Her skin flushed all over whenever his thumb grazed the sensitive place just above her waistband. Her chest seized whenever he bent closer and his warm breath tickled her temple and ear. Her stomach flipped whenever he gently combed at her flowing hair.

Even with how much she relished the closeness and being reunited with him, she couldn't keep her eyes open after the past twenty-four hours of captivity and the lack of sleep from two deliveries in such short succession. When the horse came to a halt, startling her awake, she tried to sit up, only to find they'd arrived at Wyatt's ranch. She was still mounted in front of Dylan, secure in his embrace, but his family surrounded them, throwing out a dozen questions about all that had transpired.

Instead of answering, Dylan dismounted, then lifted her down. He didn't let her feet touch the ground before he was scooping her up and stalking into the house, carrying her like an infant cradled against him.

He called instructions to Greta and Astrid, and they clomped up the stairway ahead of him, rushing around, changing sheets, and preparing a bed. When the bed was ready, Dylan started to lay her down.

She had enough wherewithal to cling to his neck. "I'm a mess, Dylan. I can't get into bed like this."

One look at the dried blood and other muck on her skirt, and Dylan called over his shoulder. "Astrid, bring me a nightgown."

Astrid paused. With her light brown hair pulled up into an elegant knot and her silver-blue eyes, she resembled Greta, but she was more petite and delicate looking. Catherine had learned Astrid was Greta's stepsister and had lived with Wyatt and Greta ever since moving to Colorado. She was eighteen and apparently had caught the interest of quite a few of the single men in the area.

Catherine could see why. Not only was she pretty, but she was elegant and graceful and kind.

As Dylan stood holding her in the middle of an upstairs bedroom, the slanted roof pushed his face near hers. "You alright, darlin'?"

"Mm-hmm . . ." She couldn't keep her eyes open, the need for sleep overwhelming her.

A moment later, Astrid's light step returned. "Is this alright?"

Dylan took something from her. "Perfect. Thank you. Close the door on the way out."

Close the door? Catherine's eyes snapped open.

Dylan lowered her to the edge of the bed, knelt beside her, then began to unlace her shoes. "Dylan, you don't need to help me."

"I want to." His head was bent as he rapidly removed first one ankle boot, then the other. She had a deep longing to feel his hair in her fingers, and before she could stop herself, she toppled his hat.

She lifted her hand to comb his hair, but a yawn trembled through her. As she swayed, he swiftly slipped open the buttons up the front of her blouse.

"Dylan, no." She tried to bat his hand away, suddenly flushing at the realization that he intended to undress her. "I can do this myself."

Dylan kept going, his fingers undoing each button with

ease until he was pushing the blouse off her shoulders and sliding it down her arms.

"You really shouldn't." She needed to stand up and put some distance between them, but she was too tired.

He stopped, held her arms firmly, and looked her in the eyes. "Listen, darlin'. Someday I'm planning to enjoy taking your clothes off, but this ain't the day. Today I just want to tuck you in bed so you can get the sleep you need."

She was being a prude. Even so, she was used to the cover of darkness shielding her from his gaze whenever she undressed. "At least close your eyes while you finish."

He leaned back, and his grin kicked up on one side. "Close my eyes?"

"Yes."

He chuckled and was already tugging the nightdress over her head and down her chemise. "Alright, I'll close my eyes."

She felt entirely foolish. She pushed her arms into the sleeves of the clean garment and then toppled back onto the bed. Her head hit the pillow, and her eyes closed with exhaustion. As he tugged her skirt down from beneath the nightdress, she knew she'd never met a more honorable man than Dylan McQuaid.

He'd never once taken advantage of their hasty marriage of convenience, and he still wasn't. She loved him deeply and desperately for that and so much more. His past mistakes didn't matter. All that counted was the man he was now. And she wanted to tell him. But before she could form the words, the world and all its cares fell away as sleep claimed her.

As wakefulness pulsed through Catherine, a warm bundle snuggled against her. Austin.

Her heart swelled with relief, and she wrapped her arms around him. Someone at some point had delivered the baby to her side. She couldn't be more grateful. She'd missed him so terribly that she wasn't sure how she'd ever survive a future without him in it.

"Hi, Mama's precious boy." She kissed his head and drew him close. Still asleep, his hand tightened around a fistful of her hair.

At the warmth of the bed and the silence of the room, she realized Austin had been tucked into bed with her for a while. She pried an eye open to gauge the time of day only to find that the room was dark except for a lone candle.

With the movement of a shadow, she glanced up to find Dylan standing at her bedside. He was fully dressed, wearing his hat, gloves, and even a light coat, as though he was readying to leave.

Careful not to disturb Austin, she pushed up on her elbow. "How long have I been asleep?"

"Since yesterday midday."

Through the dormer window the sky was just beginning to lighten. "It's dawn?"

"Yep."

Something in his tone set her on edge. "Is everything alright?"

"Hope it will be soon." He placed one of his gloved hands on Austin's head.

The clank of a stovepipe told her that someone else was already busy at the early hour. But it was an hour she rarely saw unless she was still awake after delivering a baby.

"Any word on Minnie's baby?" she whispered.

"Went back over last night, and the little fella is hanging in there."

"Maybe I can go over and check on them today?"

"Only if my brothers go with you."

Her heartbeat pattered to a halt. "You can't take me?"

He shifted, then pulled his hand away from Austin. "I'm riding out with Bliss."

She pushed up higher. "Now?"

"Yep."

Her throat clogged with all the things she wanted to tell him but hadn't been able to say yet. She started to sit higher, but he stopped her with gentle pressure against her shoulder.

"Go back to sleep, darlin'." His voice was filled with tenderness. "Didn't mean to wake you. Just wanted to see you and Austin one last time before leaving."

Hesitantly she lowered herself to the pillow. "I should go with you."

With a curt shake of his head, he stuffed his hand into his pocket. "You promised you'd stay here and live with Wyatt until I come back."

She vaguely remembered making the promise, but she'd been so tired, hadn't been thinking clearly. "I want to go."

He took another step toward the door. "I need you to trust me and Bliss this time, darlin'. Let us take care of the messy business."

"But what if Rocky trumps up charges against you too?"

He shrugged. "We're gonna give him everything we've got and do the best we can to expose him for the crook he is."

"My father will help."

"I'm aiming to contact him."

What would her parents think when they heard from her husband and learned she'd gotten married? Would they be excited for her?

But she wasn't intending to stay married. She planned to give Dylan his freedom. The resolve throttled through her, chasing away any hope for a happy future.

"Promise me again that you'll be here when I get home." His soft command filtered through her inner tirade.

Why did he want her to wait? Why did he want her at all? The insecurities mounted faster than a late-afternoon thunderstorm.

He opened the door but paused, clearly waiting to hear her promise one more time.

She nodded. "I promise." It was the least she could do for this kind man. She could stay and take care of Austin while he was gone defending her reputation. Then once he returned, she'd make him understand he was better off without her. Wasn't he?

With a final long look her way, Dylan stepped out and closed the door behind him. His boots tapped rapidly down the stairs. A moment later, the front door scraped open and then closed with a faint thud.

A quiet urgency stole through her. She pushed up again, this time heedless of waking Austin. Her attention shifted to the side table, the candle there illuminating a jar filled with an array of flowers. And a mug with steam rising from the top. She breathed in the scent of wildflowers and coffee, but her breath caught on a sudden sob.

She cupped her hand over her mouth, the sob followed by more that were rapidly swelling. This man. He loved her. He truly loved her. For who she was. And instead of accepting that love, she kept pushing him away, allowing her old insecurities to make her believe he would reject her someday just like other men had.

Trembling, she stood, her nightgown falling down around her, the same nightgown he'd so tenderly put on her yesterday when she'd been too exhausted to move.

She couldn't let him leave without telling him how much she cared about him in return.

Austin croaked out a cry, as though to complain of her absence. She swept him up and then hurried out of the room and down the stairs, her bare feet pattering against the cold floorboards.

At her appearance, Astrid, who was setting plates around the table, paused. Her eyes rounded. "Is something wrong?"

Catherine swiped at the tears still trickling down her cheeks, but she didn't stop to answer and instead crossed to the door, threw it open, and stepped outside. The chill of the morning greeted her, and she pulled Austin closer to keep him warm.

She gazed over the ranch yard, praying she'd see Dylan readying his horse or giving last instructions to Wyatt. But the light radiating from the open barn door revealed only the chickens strutting around and a dog sniffing in the dirt.

In the distance to the north, faint dawn light revealed the outlines of two horses and riders galloping hard. Dylan and Jericho. They were too far away to hear her if she called out.

Her chest squeezed with pain that radiated up into her throat. Maybe this was for the best after all. She was tired and emotional. Once she had the chance to put her situation in perspective, she'd realize the truth—that setting Dylan free was for the best.

CHAPTER

31

Catherine reined in before the freshly painted Healing Springs Inn and glanced at Brody in surprise. "Someone needs my help here?"

"Yep." Brody was already hopping down from his mount.

"I didn't think the inn was open yet."

"It's not."

"But a guest is here anyway?"

"Yep."

She gave up questioning him, knowing by now Brody didn't say any more than he had to, and pestering him wouldn't work. She'd already tried pestering him for news of Dylan that had apparently arrived earlier in the day, and he said she'd have to wait and hadn't budged.

Already the past three weeks of waiting had been a form of torture like none she'd ever experienced. She guessed Brody's news was that Dylan and Jericho had finally arrived in Chicago, which was likely if they'd taken a train straight there.

Three weeks was already too long, and she couldn't imagine having to go many months more without seeing Dylan. She was beginning to think she simply needed to go to Chicago, wished she'd pushed to stay together all along.

As much as she didn't want to admit the truth, it was becoming clearer with each passing day that she couldn't live without him. Even though her head warned her that she had to let him go, her heart warned her she needed him and her life wouldn't be complete apart from him.

In the meantime, she was trying—although usually failing—to keep from thinking about him every waking and sleeping moment.

She swept her gaze over the inn. The building looked more like a mansion with its sprawling side wings branching out from the Greek Revival center hall, with four grand columns that formed upper and lower balconies hemmed in by elegant cast-iron fences painted white.

Astrid had brought Catherine over for a tour the previous week, excited about the impending opening, which would be just as soon as they finished furnishing the ten guest rooms. Wyatt and his crew had completed the exterior the previous summer, and they'd spent the winter and spring working on the interior. They were waiting on the last of the furniture and supplies to be delivered now that the June warmth and sunshine were melting the snow in the higher elevations and making the passes more navigable for the larger supply teamsters.

The project had been an enormous undertaking, spurred in large part by Greta's vision of having a place where people suffering from consumption could come to find healing at the hot springs located just a short distance from the inn.

Astrid had also taken Catherine to the spring and the bath-house next to it, with changing rooms, towels, and lounge chairs for the residents to use. The spring itself wasn't enormous, the size of a pond, and it was shallow and lined with slick, smooth stones. But it was beautiful and serene amidst the wilderness backdrop of the foothills. And the water itself was clear and hot and steamy.

Astrid had shared how she'd experienced her own healing at the hot springs when she'd been just a little girl. While the petite young woman still suffered from shortness of breath from time to time, she'd survived the dreaded disease that had brought Greta and her to the West. And now Astrid was interested in becoming a nurse so she could help others. She'd been full of questions for Catherine, an eager pupil and ready to learn all she could.

While Catherine had been living with Wyatt and his family, her new friendship with Astrid had been the most unexpected blessing. The young woman was a delight, and though Catherine didn't want to lose her new friend, she'd begun to encourage Astrid to consider taking a nursing course. Catherine had heard of a six-month training program at a hospital in Chicago developed by one of the first female physicians, and she'd suggested that perhaps Astrid could live with her family during her training.

"Ready?" Brody stood beside Catherine's horse and held a hand up to her.

She took the offer, grateful Brody and Wyatt and Flynn had been so willing to accompany her on the few visits she'd made to patients. The visits were an imposition and took time away from their work, but they never complained. She'd followed up with Minnie twice, and both mama and baby were surviving. Minnie was making plans to move to Denver to be closer to Frank while he awaited sentencing along with the other rustlers.

The area ranchers had been able to locate most of their missing cattle up in Tarryall. They'd worked to divide the livestock among the rightful owners, and from what she'd heard from Wyatt over dinner, they hadn't lost a single steer since.

Wyatt claimed that the ranchers were full of praise for Dylan and his ability to bring an end to the rustling without causing any loss of life. But with the spread of the news regarding the wanted poster, nobody knew what to believe about her.

She prayed hard that the stain she'd caused Dylan's reputation would eventually fade. But her old insecurities about being a disappointment and causing disgrace were like weeds in a garden needing to be plucked from time to time. They might spring back, but she was working at replanting them with the truth that she was perfect the way God had created her.

As her feet touched the ground, she squared off with the inn. It was marvelous, truly a beautiful getaway tucked away in the high country. Once word of it spread, it would surely draw more visitors than it could hold.

Brody hitched their horses. Then he led her up the front steps and across the porch and swung the door open, motioning her through. She entered the spacious foyer with its tile floor and wide spiral staircase. With a few pieces of furniture along with rugs, the interior would eventually contain an elegance that would rival the outside.

Brody remained on the front porch and cocked his head in the direction of the big new house Greta and Wyatt and their children would soon occupy. It sat a short distance from the inn and only needed a few finishing touches before it, too, would be ready. "I'll be over at the house. Told Wyatt I'd help lay flooring."

Catherine clutched at her birth satchel and tried not to show her surprise. The brothers hadn't left her alone once since Dylan had ridden away. They'd hovered around her, even when she was at the main house.

When he began to spin away, she panicked and reached after him. "Where is the patient?" He had brought her here for a patient, hadn't he?

Brody stopped and almost smiled—at least she thought she saw the beginning quirk of his lips. "Upstairs."

Then without further instructions, Brody bounded down the steps and strode across the yard in the direction of the new house.

Catherine watched him for a few more seconds, waiting for him to tell her to be careful or to come get him when she was finished or something. But he didn't turn around, almost as if he'd forgotten all about the danger she was in.

With trepidation, she closed the door. The silence of the empty mansion was broken by the hammering and sawing outside nearby. She stood frozen in place, staring around, waiting for someone to come out and greet her, but it was eerily quiet. She'd expected at least a few people to be here working on the last details that needed to be tended, but the place seemed deserted.

Except for her patient. Perhaps the McQuaids had given a room to a relative or friend, someone who wouldn't care that the inn wasn't entirely ready.

Slowly she crossed the foyer and mounted the steps. As she arrived at the landing, she reluctantly released the railing and started down the hallway with bedroom doors on either side.

All of them were closed except one, one on the end, which was open a crack.

As she reached it, she paused, then knocked lightly. "Hello. I'm the midwife, Mrs. McQuaid. May I come in?"

The slight pressure from her knock pushed the door wider. Did she dare enter?

She poked her head inside to see that the room was completely furnished with an enormous four-poster bed draped with a beautiful satin duvet of pale pink. The tapestries in the window matched as did a luxurious rug in the center of the room. It was as elegant as she'd imagined the rooms would be with patterned rose-gold wallpaper above white wainscoting. And several candles were lit around the room, giving it a soft, romantic glow.

Strangely, the floor was also strewn with flower petals, and the colorful display seemed to form a trail.

A trail? She was imagining things. Even so, she stepped carefully into the room and followed the flower petals as they led her to an enormous bouquet gracing the center of a mahogany pedestal table with chairs on either side.

She bent to breathe in the glorious wildflowers, similar to arrangements Dylan had picked for her, but stopped short at the sight of a ribbon tied around the vase with a ring dangling from it.

She fingered the silver band, and her breath snagged. The seed pearl daisy at the center belonged to only one ring. The one Dylan had given her on their wedding day.

At the click of the door behind her, she spun to find the man of her dreams leaning casually against the closed door, wearing a dark suit, his arms and ankles crossed.

"Hi there, darlin'. Did you miss me?" His green-blue eyes

had never been brighter, and even with the scruff on his jaw and chin, his face had never been more handsome. His lips turned up in a lazy smile, as if he had all the time in the world to stand there and watch her.

Her heart started racing with a wild joy. She wanted to run across the room and throw herself in his arms. But she forced herself to remain calm and composed. "I'm here to see a patient."

"Yep. That's me."

"And exactly why do you need a midwife?" She meant her question to be teasing, but it came out breathless with expectation.

"I need her to be my wife. Forever."

She wanted nothing more than to put his ring back on and never take it off again. As hard as her journey had been, she was learning to accept herself just as she was. Maybe it was time to believe Dylan could accept her too.

The problem was that as much as she wanted to be with Dylan, she still couldn't reconcile with the possibility of bringing Austin and him harm and danger. Could she live with that? Could he?

"Dylan." She clutched at the table behind her to keep her hands from trembling. "I want to be your wife forever, but I love you too much to subject you to my problems."

At her declaration, he tipped up his hat, pushed away from the door, and started toward her. "And what if I told you that you don't have any problems?"

Something in his eyes made her heart quaver. "You'd be lying. Wouldn't you?"

"Nope." He kept coming and stopped only when he was a foot away.

"What happened to the problems?" And why was he here instead of in Chicago?

As if seeing the questions sparking in her eyes, his lips curled into the playful smile she loved. "Rocky's accusations against you have been dropped."

"What?" The quavering inside spread to her limbs.

"Turns out he murdered another fella and, this time, couldn't hide all the evidence. Eyewitnesses testified against him, including two bodyguards who claimed they saw Rocky kill Stretch. Your father's investigator had already gathered evidence from the women who live in the brothel, and they all testified to your innocence. The judge was left with no choice but to dismiss your case."

Oh, heaven help her. Could it be true? Her fingers tightened on the edge of the table. "So you didn't go to Chicago?"

"Nope. Me and Bliss got as far as Missouri when your father sent us the news of Rocky's arrest."

The news was too good to be true. Much too good. And yet the light in Dylan's eyes confirmed everything.

"Then it's over?" Her voice wavered.

"It's all over, darlin'."

A sob escaped, but she cupped her hand over her mouth. In the next instant, Dylan was gathering her into an embrace. She wasn't able to resist, didn't want to. She fell against him and buried her face into his shirt and vest, letting go of all the worry and frustration and fear she'd lived with the past months.

He held her gently and stroked her back as she cried. When her tears subsided, she drew in a shuddering breath and then released one of pure contentment.

Snuggling against his chest, she wrapped her arms around his waist.

He leaned his chin on top of her head and drew her tighter. "Meant what I said before I left. That I love you and don't want to lose you."

The words washed over her, words she'd waited to hear again, words she wanted to hear for the rest of her life.

"Did you mean what you said about us?" he asked more tentatively. "About how you love me and want to be my wife forever?"

She nodded, unable to play coy. That wasn't who she was, and she was okay with it. "The morning you left, I ran out after you."

His hand on her back stilled. "You did?"

"I realized it then and wanted to tell you. But you were already too far away."

"Probably a good thing you couldn't say it."

"Why?"

"I reckon I wouldn't have been able to tear myself away."

She smiled, loving his flattery.

He reached behind her and fumbled with the flowers. Then he lowered himself to one knee in front of her, took off his hat, and held up the ring. "Never should've let you take this off, darlin'. I'm putting it back on right where it belongs and hoping I'll never give you another reason to give it back." Gently he slid it on her finger, then kissed her hand just as tenderly.

She stared at the beautiful ring once again gracing her finger. "It's there to stay . . . if you'll have me."

He stood, his lips tilting upward as he drew her into his embrace once more. "Oh, I'll have you, darlin'. No doubt about that."

Her pulse pumped with the thrill of anticipation. He was back. He wanted her. And he never planned to leave her. This was everything she'd hoped for and more.

Of course, they would still have obstacles to overcome. Even if she'd been cleared of charges, they'd have to put in time and effort to repair the community's trust. But she intended to help Dylan, especially in winning the election in August. She would leverage all she knew about politics and campaigning but without compromising their genuineness.

His lips grazed her ear. "Tell me again now."

"Tell you what?"

"How you feel about me." His voice was low, demanding.

She pulled back enough to see his face. His eyelids were half-shuttered but couldn't hide the desire flaming to life in his eyes. "I don't think I'll tell you anything, Mr. McQuaid."

His fingers slid up to the base of her neck, and the gentle caress of the bare skin beneath her neatly coiled knot stirred the longings in her. "Tell me." He drew his finger around, circling her ear, then tracing a path down her jaw.

"I'd rather show you." At the sultriness in her voice, she could feel the heat move into her cheeks.

His grin spread, and in the next instant, he lifted her, giving her no choice but to wrap her arms around his neck and her legs around his torso.

"Dylan McQuaid." She laughed breathlessly. "What are you doing?"

"Giving you the perfect angle for showing me." His lips were so close, she could already feel the softness brushing hers.

She pressed in and meshed her lips with his, along with

her life and love. As she let her love pour out into the kiss, she silently raised a prayer of thanksgiving that she'd been given another opportunity to show this man how much she loved him and that she'd get to keep on doing so for the rest of her life.

CHAPTER

32

Dylan placed the hot cup of coffee on the bedside table and then perched on the edge of the bed. The light coming in through the cabin window was bright with the passing of the morning, and the softness of it brushed Catherine's sleeping face, highlighting the natural beauty that only seemed to grow with each passing day.

Even now her lips seemed fuller, her cheeks rosier, and her skin softer. And he wanted nothing more than to spend the morning in bed with her, holding and kissing her. Except that he'd spent the whole night doing that very thing and had dragged himself out from the covers a little bit ago. If he got back in, he'd have another battle to leave her side.

"Good thing you're a sound sleeper, little fella." He peeked into the wicker cradle he'd purchased the first day after they'd come home from their private honeymoon at Healing Springs Inn. He'd decided, right then and there, he was claiming the spot in bed next to Catherine. No one and nothing would keep him from it any longer.

Austin was growing by leaps and bounds and needed his own bed anyway. Someday, when the boy was old enough, Dylan planned to share with him the truth about his real mother, Kit Olson. Maybe he'd even let the boy have the journal his mother had written. At first, he hadn't wanted to read it when Catherine had shown it to him. But finally he'd made himself open it to the pages that talked about him. Only then had he realized his past burdens were buried in the deep, so the reading hadn't undone him. Yep, Kit's story had made him sad and filled him with regrets, but he'd taken it again to the Lord, who'd promised to bear his burdens for him.

Of course, Catherine's kisses after the reading had helped soothe him. Her kisses always helped him, no matter the occasion.

The covers were tousled, Juniper curled in the midst, and the empty spot beside Catherine beckoned again. Shucks. After two months of living as man and wife, he'd thought climbing out of bed would get easier. He'd never expected it'd be so blasted hard every morning.

Any other day, he'd have given way to the need to lie down again next to her and kiss her senseless. But today was the big day—the day after the local election. The ballots had been tallied, and the results would be read at the courthouse at noon. He'd know in an hour whether he still had the job of sheriff or whether the people had decided to send him on his way.

He drew a finger across Catherine's lips. "Hey there, darlin'. Got you some coffee."

She stirred, stretching her legs and then her arms, drawing his attention to her beautiful body.

The heat inside sparked up hotter than grease in a griddle. He jumped up and paced away from her, stuffing his hands in his pockets so he didn't reach for her. "Thought you'd want to be ready to go hear the election results."

At that, she sat up, her hair tumbling about her in delicious abandon. "I forgot. I'm getting up right away."

She swung her slender legs over the edge of the bed, tugging her nightgown down, still endearingly modest, which only made him crave her all the more. As she picked up the mug of coffee, she gave him a beautiful, sleepy smile. "I love you, Mr. McQuaid."

"You're just saying it so I'll keep bringing you coffee in bed."

She started to take a sip but then stopped. Her eyes widened. She practically dropped the coffee on the bedside table and then scrambled for the washbasin instead. In the next instant, she was retching into the dish.

He froze. What in tarnation was wrong? Catherine was one of the healthiest and strongest women he knew. She was always taking care of others, working at all hours and under all conditions without any thought of herself. Had she overdone it?

With a shake of his head, he rushed to her side and pulled back her hair, her thin body trembling. As she set the ceramic basin aside, she wiped a hand across her eyes. "I'm not sure what came over me."

"Maybe you oughta stay home and rest." He gently brushed her hair aside. She didn't feel feverish. Even so, he wanted her to remain abed. "I'll go get Trudy and have her come take a look at you."

"No, Dylan. I'm fine. Really—" She cupped her hand

over her mouth and reached for the basin again. When she finished, this time she didn't resist as he settled her against the pillows.

He didn't wait for her permission and jogged down the street to the Gundersons' house, banged on the door, and explained the situation to Trudy. With sweat streaking his face under the hot August sun, Dylan waited for Trudy to gather herself and then rushed with her back to the cabin.

As Trudy bustled inside and took control with her usual efficiency, Dylan stood in the doorway, uncertain what to do but unwilling to go anywhere until he knew what was wrong with Catherine. Even with the crowd swelling in the dusty street in front of the courthouse as the top of the hour grew nearer, he didn't want to go.

He caught a glimpse of Wyatt and his family along with Flynn and Brody with their wives and children. Bliss and Ivy were there, too, and even Judd. They'd all come out to support him. Whether he won or lost, they were there for him. They always had been. It'd just taken him time and maturity to see it.

"Uffda. You go on with you now," Trudy called from the bedside. "You can't miss the announcement. Dontcha know you've got half the town out there waiting."

"I can't leave Catherine like this."

"I'll be fine, Dylan." Catherine's voice was weak and strained. "In fact, I'll meet you out there."

"Oh no, you won't. You're staying put right here." Trudy's big voice boomed through the cabin. And somehow her presence and bossiness put Dylan at ease. The dear motherly woman would figure out what was wrong and would fix it.

"Now go on, Dylan," Trudy called.

"Please, Dylan," came Catherine's echoing plea.

He didn't have much choice. He needed to be present and face the results like a man. Harlan Hatfield would be there too.

Dylan could admit, losing would be mighty hard after he and Catherine had campaigned all around Park County. She'd known just what to do to form a rally, the signs to post, the people to personally invite, and the important things for him to talk about.

The biggest surprise for them both was the support they'd received from some of Catherine's patients. The Rossis in particular had rallied votes among the mining community, singing Catherine's praises from the mountaintops. Trudy had motivated the Ladies Guild to organize a social to allow him to answer questions and mingle with people.

He could also rest in the knowledge that he'd done everything he could to prove to the people in South Park that he was up for the job. He wasn't perfect, never would be. He reckoned there might even be times when he'd still fail. But through it all, he wasn't letting go of the people who were there to encourage and help him stay strong.

With a final polish to his silver star, he headed out to Main Street. It was impassable with the people who had come to Fairplay for the election results. Even some of the ranchers were there to show their support. An air of excitement, even festivity, filled the air.

Harlan Hatfield was milling about among his supporters, and his wife and passel of kids had come down from Como to be there with him.

Dylan made a point of shaking hands with near-to everyone,

even old Mrs. Fletcher, who'd insisted that she wanted to give him the money to build a house after the election.

Through it all, his sights kept straying to the cabin until Ivy socked him in the arm. "Can't go without your wife for even a few minutes?" From where she stood in the crook of Jericho's arm, holding her baby, she'd never looked happier.

His brothers and their families congregated around Ivy and teased him good-naturedly too. Normally he'd have taken the teasing and given it right back. But he could only shake his head. "She woke up sick, throwing up. And it's got me worried."

"Wouldn't be surprised if she's pregnant." Ivy's loud comment brought another round of teasing. This time as they bantered, a low hum began to wind through Dylan. What if Catherine was pregnant?

Before he could contemplate the prospect further, the mayor stepped out of the courthouse with Stu by his side.

The crowd quieted. And all eyes focused on Mr. Steele, who was as impeccably dressed as always in his dark suit and a stiff bowler. He began to say a few words about the importance of the law and the need for Fairplay to continue to be known as a law-abiding town, but Dylan could hardly focus on the speech.

A hand slipped into his, and he looked down to see Catherine standing beside him, properly dressed, her hair fixed, and looking as pretty as always, almost as if she'd never been sick.

"You alright, darlin'?" he whispered. What happened to Trudy making Catherine stay in bed? He had half a mind to pick up his wife, throw her over his shoulder, and dump her right back in bed.

She pressed a finger to her lips and peered intently at Mr. Steele. Her mouth almost seemed to twitch with the need to smile, but she didn't shift her focus.

A quick look at the cabin showed Trudy standing in the doorway holding Austin and grinning like a woman straight out of a Ladies Guild meeting.

"And the results of the sheriff election stand as follows." Mr. Steele was unfolding a piece of paper, and Dylan shifted his attention back to the matter at hand. "Mr. McQuaid received 150 votes, and Mr. Hatfield received 78."

As the crowd erupted into cheers, Dylan crossed quickly toward Hatfield, holding out his hand. Hatfield's expression was guarded as he accepted Dylan's hand.

"Thank you," Dylan said, even as well-wishers crowded around, jostling him.

"What for?" Hatfield's brows shot up.

"You were a worthy opponent and challenged me to be a better sheriff and a man of honor."

Hatfield gave a curt nod. "You've done the hard work of proving yourself capable of the position. I can walk away knowing that the county is in good hands."

Dylan held the man's gaze a moment longer. Hatfield would have made a good sheriff too. Even so, Dylan was happy the position was his, that he'd earned it. He knew his pa would have been proud of him for the man he was becoming. Maybe he and Ma were looking down from the pearly gates and smiling at this family of theirs, a not-so-perfect family, but one that never gave up on each other.

He accepted congratulations and well-wishes as he made his way back to Catherine.

She didn't wait for him to stop before wrapping her arms

around his neck. "Oh, Dylan. You did it. I'm so proud of you."

He drew her close in return, needing her support more than anyone else's. At the same time, he started to scoop her up. "I'm taking you back to bed."

She pushed against him, smiling with instant sunshine. "I'm fine, Dylan. I'm not sick, at least not with anything that won't go away in about eight months."

"I was right!" Ivy shouted above the commotion. "The midwife is gonna have a baby of her own!"

The crowd raised another cheer, and hands slapped Dylan's back as he tried to take in the news that Catherine was with child.

He glanced down at her still-flat stomach. "Are you sure?"

"Once Trudy mentioned the possibility, I knew that's what it was right away."

He studied her face a moment longer, seeing her delight in every changing fleck of her eyes. "So we're having a babe?"

"Yes, Dylan. We're having a baby."

He released a loud whoop and swept her up. She laughed, but he was quick to set her back down gently.

With Greta at his side, Wyatt clamped his arm. "Mighty proud of you, Dylan." Wyatt's youngest boy rode upon his shoulders and clapped his hands and cheered, although the kid probably had no idea what all the commotion was about.

Brody was wrangling his runaway son and shot Dylan a quick nod as though to say he agreed with Wyatt before chasing after the little fella, who headed straight for his ma where she was tending to a lame horse down the street.

Bliss socked him hard. "Glad you won the election. Guess God was preparing you for this position all along during those years in Chicago. It's amazing when He begins to fit all the shattered pieces back together and makes something better than we could have imagined."

"You got that right." It was amazing. Dylan had never expected that Catherine's and his experiences in Chicago would amount to anything. But God had used everything—including the brokenness—to bring about good.

Flynn, with one arm around Linnea, extended his other for a handshake. "You're a real good pa, Dylan. Just like ours."

A lump formed in Dylan's throat as he shook Flynn's hand. He cleared it and then spoke. "You stepped in and did a good job of being my pa when I needed it. Thank you."

Flynn's lips twitched into a grin. "Ain't gonna lie that I had half a mind to string you up a time or two."

Dylan grinned. "More like a few hundred times."

"Ain't that the truth." Ivy punched him as hard as Bliss had but wore a smile on her beautiful face. Then she gave Catherine a one-armed hug, and in the process, Catherine reached down to kiss baby Lily, named after Jericho's mother.

Ivy beamed at Catherine, then tossed Dylan a teasing scowl. "Don't go thinking you won. Just cause you're having a second babe before me."

Dylan chuckled and could only lift his gaze heavenward with a silent prayer of gratitude. Just when he'd thought he'd used up his last chance, the Almighty surprised him with another opportunity to do things right.

He picked up Catherine again and did the thing he loved doing best. He kissed her long and hard, counting himself a man blessed beyond anything he deserved.

Jody Hedlund is the bestselling author of over forty historicals for both adults and teens and is the winner of numerous awards including the Christy, Carol, and Christian Book Award. Mother of five, she lives in central Michigan with her husband and busy family. Visit her at jodyhedlund.com.

Sign Up for Jody's Newsletter

Keep up to date with Jody's news on book releases and events by signing up for her email list at jodyhedlund.com.

More from Jody Hedlund

Ivy McQuaid has been saving up for a home of her own with the winnings from the cowhand competitions she sneaks into—but everything changes when a man from her past returns. Undercover Pinkerton agent Jericho Bliss is on the hunt for a war criminal, but when Ivy becomes involved in his dangerous life, his worst fears come true.

Falling for the Cowgirl
COLORADO COWBOYS #4